Changes

in

Degrees

Changes in Degrees
Second Edition
Copyright © 2015 KC Riley-Gyer

Please note the author is Australian. Therefore, all spelling, grammar and punctuation will be Australian based.

This is a work of fiction. While based in a real location, any reference to anything real is a coincidence. All brand names belong to their maker.

National Library of Australia Cataloguing-in-Publication entry

Author: Riley-Gyer, KC, author.
Title: Changes in Degrees / KC Riley-Gyer.
Edition: 2nd edition.
ISBN: 9780992467746 (paperback)
Series: Riley-Gyer, KC Unnaturals of Brisbane; 2.
Subjects: Shapeshifting, vampires--Fiction. Fantasy fiction.
Dewey Number: A823.4

Published with the assistance of www.inhousepublishing.com.au

Changes in Degrees

KC Riley-Gyer

Also by KC Riley-Gyer

The Unnaturals of Brisbane Series

Acknowledgements

This story was inspired by two things: my hanging out at a particular pond that no longer exists and a dream that wouldn't leave me alone. I wrote this as a thank you to my fishie friends for their wonderful stories they had shared. Thank you for inspiring me and encouraging me to publish.

I would also like to thank my Picky Readers' ladies for letting me waffle on and for their proof reading. You are wonderful <3

As always, a special thank you goes to my oldest friend Doug for his time and patience every time I turned to him with a problem or question. Without you, I think my stories would be too much of a mess to publish.

Prologue

With the battle for leadership of Brisbane over this time round, people were in the process of leaving. Orenda, Chyanna and Max were surrounded by Varrik, Enola, Charlotte, Anoki, Itztecpatl, Sarah, Kaelan and others. All quietly chatting when Darius and Sonja joined the crowd.

"Well, Enola and I are off. Call me when you need me Orenda." Varrik stated as he wrapped an arm around Enola's waist.

"I will my friend. Be well both of you." Orenda responded.

Enola and Varrik next said farewell to Darius and Sonja then left. Orenda was telling Itztecpatl he didn't have to come back until the following evening. After a quick goodbye, Itztecpatl, Kaelan and Sarah exited into the night as well.

15 years earlier...

Chapter 1

"Funny thing about changes happening in one's life is you never know if it's going to be good or bad until it happens. Can't say, at the age of 23, that I've had any good changes lately, not that there's much I can do about it. Once given, the changes can't be returned like an unwanted gift, there will always be losses and/or revelations accompanying those changes. All one can do is the best with what one is dealt with." – Sarah.

"Changes... One may not have a choice in receiving them, but they can be anything one makes of them and this particular one was certainly interesting. It may not have started out that way during those first few moments, and I may have fought against it, but it certainly became interesting." – Kaelan.

~*~

It was a sunny and brisk winter's day and it was a perfect day to play now that he and his men were on leave. While the kiosk was playing some music which barely registered to him, he was leaning against the Jeep waiting for the rest of his players to turn up. He surveyed the area, sizing up the various people who came to play: the wannabes – more danger to themselves than to anyone else, the possible threats who obviously knew enough to hit only their intended targets and not everything else in sight, and the kids wanting to have fun. However, pretty much all of them ignorable. Until...

He first saw her at the paintball range as she hobbled from the ladies rest room and everything else around him was momentarily forgotten. He watched her walk towards him, her head down with the occasional glance up as if to make sure she was on track to her destination.

A slightly overweight young woman, standing 156cm tall, in her mid to late teens – early twenties maybe – leant heavily on her darkly painted metal adjustable walking stick. Then she slowly veered to her right towards the picnic tables. She was dressed in a navy blue simple heavy cotton dress with little purple and red flowers and black open toed slip on shoes.

'Her feet must be freezing.' The trivial thought caught him by surprise. Deciding to ignore the thought, he continued his inspection of her.

Her dull dark brown hair was tied back away from her face with a thin layer acting as a wispy fringe partially covering her forehead. Even though her hair was tied back he could see it was long, past her shoulder blades. Despite its length there didn't seem to be much of it, as in not thick. The one thing which saved her hair from being bland, in his opinion, was the faint red highlights that shimmered occasionally in the sunlight as she walked.

Regardless of her weight and dull looking hair, her face was cute in a plain sort of way even though it was etched with pain at that point in time. She wore no makeup as if, maybe, she didn't care about how people perceived her and, strangely for him, it added a level of attractiveness to her. Until that moment, he hadn't realised that could attract his attention.

Letting his eyes travel slowly down her body, he noted her left hand clenched, emphasising the pain he was seeing in her face. Although he could see she was over-weight, the dress fitted her well and showed off the potential for a reasonable figure. Then, he continued down her legs to her feet.

'There's the problem. She's obviously been in an accident of some sort, maybe recently. Her feet don't sit flat anymore.' He thought.

However, while she was wearing shoes, he realised one would have to really look at her feet to notice the problem with them. He noted the weight seemed to be on her heels and on the outer side edges of her feet, and that they turned in slightly. A few of the toes on her right foot were partially clawed and it looked to be permanent.

'With some nerve damage perhaps, in some way.' He speculated.

He continued watching. Observing the way she walked with the walking stick, suggested her left ankle was worse than her right. Her right leg carried most of her weight as she walked even though she tried adjusting her weight distribution every now and then. Her knee bending and foot lifting were exaggerated as she walked. Her feet barely moved in relation to her legs compared to the average person.

'It would seem she has lost some flexion, mobility, to her ankles.'

In checking her over, he realised she was no threat. She was out of condition – the effort of walking from the ladies to her destination left her sweating despite being winter. Disabled and definitely feminine in her ways, she looked like she didn't know how to fight back. The young woman was a victim, not a predator.

With that assessment he had every intention of dismissing her from mind and sight, but...

Watching her, she joined five other people at one of the tables nearby. He had just started to look away when their eyes locked briefly. Her hand paused in mid motion of taking her drink to her lips. Her lips, minutely parted, were a little pale but looked rather nice with a noticeable cupid's bow on her upper lip. Now she was close enough he could see them better. Then he noticed the flush creeping across her cheeks.

The six of them were sitting at a table near the kiosk, just an open shed serving basic food and drink with a few picnic tables and bench seats, when she saw him and held her breath. She couldn't stop staring at him.

As far as she was concerned the clear cool June winter's day had just become a little warmer for her. As if it was planned, to her way of thinking, out of the speakers of the kiosk played the song *'Breathless'* by The Corrs, and that was the effect he had on her when she caught sight of him.

Judging his height against the white Jeep Grand Cherokee at his back, which he was leaning against, she guessed he was over 185cm tall, give or take a centimetre or more. Unfortunately, judging height and distance weren't her strong points. His skin seemed like it could be naturally fair, but appeared to be lightly tanned. His sandy brown hair, with gingery highlights, was short cropped with it slightly longer over the forehead, but not too long as to get into his eyes.

His face... How to describe it? Describing faces was something she wasn't good at.

He had a typical Caucasian face. It was perfectly proportionate; along with the rest of his body. She shook her head as it was the best way she could describe him. Although, his nose appeared straight like it hadn't been broken and his ears weren't too large or too small and didn't stick out at all. However, he was far enough away she couldn't see his eyes, but they seemed pale in colour. Nor could she see his lips or complexion – as to if it was flawless or not – properly.

All she knew for sure was... nothing was glaringly obvious and that she liked what she could see very much.

However, his clothing – not so new black jeans that fitted rather snugly around his lower torso, black and grey polo shirt which fitted firmly across his chest and black hiking boots – fitted nicely so she could work out that his physique was well proportioned and well built, but not too much in the muscle department.

Just right, by her reckoning, with his shoulders broader than his hips. He also had an ever so slightly defined waist which would never be mistaken as feminine.

In a chance moment he glanced at her, their eyes met, and it took all her control not to look away as she had a tendency to do if she noted others looking at her. However, his eyes didn't stay on her for long but she felt herself blush slightly anyway.

In that brief moment, she'd been noticed and dismissed all in that one fleeting glance. While she didn't blame him for dismissing her, it hurt nonetheless.

Deliberately, he didn't hold her gaze however, as he continued to gaze around the paintball range.

'Does her reaction mean she's interested or at least likes what she sees?' He didn't know and at that point he didn't care. While momentarily a curiosity, he wasn't interested in her in any way. Or so he'd thought.

In the past eight and a half years, her husband of two years had been the only man to have ever shown any interest in her. However, she was more overweight than she would have liked and short – only 156cm tall. She also had thin fine dull mousey brown hair that only looked shiny for the first two to four hours after having been washed.

She also had greyish blue eyes, a mouth that looked like it was always frowning or angry even when she wasn't, pale skin and very plain looks. None of which, except her eyes, she thought of as appealing.

One would think she would be used to being dismissed by the opposite sex. She sighed and chastised herself for such thoughts. She couldn't believe she was thinking such things about a stranger when thoughts of her now deceased husband still made her cry.

Josie touched her arm lightly.

"Sarah, are you alright?" She asked softly.

Josie was 20 years old and taller and much slimmer than

Sarah. Her tanned skin caused her short stylised bottle blonde hair and pale grey eyes to look that much lighter and brighter. While she did have a sense of humour, Josie was quick to anger and slow to calm down. She was also quick to dump friends if she felt they had slighted her in any way. Sarah had seen that in action once...

'Sooo not pretty.'

Sarah had met her and Mark, Josie's partner, via her husband roughly a year before the accident.

Sarah gave her a sad nod, trying not to cry.

'Another of my faults... I'm too emotional. I cry in cartoons for fudge sake.' She thought critically.

"Are your ankles hurting you?" Mark asked gently.

Mark started going out with Josie just before Sarah had met them. At 23 he was too busy having fun doing anything that wasn't work related. As a result, he was so fit it was sickening. With his olive complexion, wavy brown hair and blue eyes, he thought he was God's gift to women. However, he doted on Josie practically 24/7, he was just that caring. Although, it was Josie who ruled the roost.

"When are they not?" She responded with a tired chuckle.

.o.O.o.

Sarah and her husband had been in a traffic accident eighteen months earlier, on a beautiful summer's day in January. He had died and she was left with damaged ankles and a proverbial crushed heart when they had told her he hadn't survived. She was still in hospital when she had started the ball rolling in suing the cretin responsible.

Since all she had was her husband, no other family, to care for her she had to go to a nursing home for the following six months for day to day care and physio-, and hydro-, therapy until she was able to look after herself without too many problems.

Seven months following the accident, after selling everything she owned (as well as all of her husband's belongings) to pay all the bills, she was left with nothing to remember him by. Except for the permanent disability of mostly non-functional ankles as a replacement for him being taken away from her.

She can, however, still walk, even if it is with the aid of a walking stick. Although, she can hobble (albeit badly) on flat level surfaces without the walking stick. For safety sake, she'd decided that would be in the home only.

She and her husband were married when Sarah was twenty. They had a wonderful time together as he showed her places she had never been to or heard of when they travelled. They'd had so much in common with their hobbies, likes and dislikes they'd become friends before becoming lovers when she was nineteen.

Little did she know two years later she would be left with nothing. No him and no mementos of their time together, other than her memories.

.o.O.o.

Despite having classified her as a victim and therefore of no consequence, he found himself glancing at her again. She appeared to be lost in thought and those thoughts seemed to be making her sad and, for some reason, seeing her sad upset him on a level within himself he didn't understand. Right at that moment he wasn't willing to delve deeper into whatever the reasons may be. Instead, he frowned at himself for his reactions to that mere slip of a girl he didn't know after all.

When her friends spoke to her, even her smile seemed sad and tired. Then the rest of his men arrived and, thankfully, his attention was taken away from her. He gave himself a mental shake as he pushed himself away from the Jeep to greet them and started discussing game strategies.

'Always a guarantee for keeping my mind away from things I don't want to note or think about.' In the back of his mind he thought that was rather shallow of himself. However, he had a life he was content in and didn't see the need, or have the space or time, for anything outside of that. She definitely fell outside of it; in his opinion.

He turned side on to talk to his mates and, as she tilted her head slightly to the left, she got to see the profile of his backside briefly before he leant against the Jeep again.

'Very nice indeed. What?! So I like a nicely defined butt. No harm in looking.' She thought to herself with a little internal smile.

Another touch on her arm brought her back to the present. "You sure you're okay? Shall we take you home now?" Mark asked, concern creasing his lovely face. With Mark and Josie making a fuss, the others turned their attention towards her as well.

She became embarrassed at the attention and smiled, "I'm

okay, just tired. This is, after all, the first game of paintball I have ever played, and the most exercise I have had since the accident outside of physio- and hydro- therapy."

When they'd finished their game Sarah had changed out of the motorbike boots she'd bought (for extra support around the ankles. The only ones she could find that hadn't cost her from the neck down), and the pants and shirt, into a simple cotton dark blue dress with purple and red flowers over it and black slip-on open-toed shoes.

Even though it was her very first paintball game, it was her third time to the range. The first two times she'd spent practicing shooting with her left hand, since she was right handed and the right hand was occupied with the walking stick. While she only ever got off one shot at any time, when she held the gun one handed, she did better than she'd thought during the four hours of practice she had up in total, and thought she would give the game a go this time.

Almost an hour after arriving, they had exited the gaming field. Sarah had 'killed' two of them and had been shot three times herself with none of them being a fatal shot. Despite the layers she had been wearing, all had hurt in varying degrees. At least one, on her arm, left a red circular welt.

However, she was really happy about her first game. Her friends were calling it beginners luck and had spent the next few minutes teasing her until food had arrived. But, when she saw him, the game had been all but forgotten.

"Hey Boss, are we going to look at doing this sort of thing on a regular basis? A fun way of keeping in shape?" Zac, a man as tall but broader than him, asked with a grin as the Boss leant back against the Jeep. He and Zac had met in the army and they had left at the same time when they joined their current line of work.

"Yeah, it would be great tension relief as well." Tyrrell said, a big smile spreading across his face. While shorter than the boss, his build was a little leaner.

'Met Tyrrell when he was first assigned to my team. Now that we've done a few jobs together, and seems to be good, I'll keep requesting him.' The Boss gazed at the two men and gave a slight smile.

"We'll see how it goes over the next few weeks before committing ourselves to this." Then he regarded Zac then Tyrrell with amusement, "Like you pair don't get enough chances at tension relief in our line of work, let alone keeping in shape. Maybe you two need to think of something else as a tension reliever."

The guys, including Zac and Tyrrell, laughed.

Hearing the laughter, Sarah glanced back at the man near the Jeep. He was talking with the guys around him. It resembled a strategy planning for their paintball game with, maybe, some jokes and teasing. She watched him as he took note of all the people in the parking lot, the kiosk and eating area, as well as those who were coming and going from the four paintball ranges.

With his casual gazing around he seemed to notice everything and she realised, in that moment, that he was a predator of some sort.

'Ex-military at least, assassin maybe, freelance hit man perhaps, but a professional all the same.' She mused. 'He had to have seen me walking – hobbling more to the point – from the ladies back to my friends, which could be why he'd dismissed me. I wasn't classified as a possible threat I guess.' She thought sadly.

Perversely, it also made her smile in amusement. It was all assumptions on her part, but since she figured she would never meet him in person she was free to imagine whatever she wanted. She certainly had no problems of thinking him as being a professional predator of some sort and still be attracted to him.

"Hmmm... What does that really say about me? Anyway, mourning or not, he's still yummy eye candy." She decided.

He and his men started discussing their game plan while waiting for their opponents to arrive. However, during his continual surveillance of the range, his eyes kept sliding back to her and he noted a smile on her face as she glanced at him. He didn't know how but for some reason he knew it had nothing to do with whatever her friends were saying. Strangely, and annoyingly, he was curious as to what caused her to smile while she gazed at him. Then her little group got up and left.

He frowned at himself because he felt relieved she was leaving and he didn't understand why it should matter. Turning back to the men, they kitted up to start their game once their opponents had arrived.

In the end, the whole session – which lasted only half an hour – frustrated the hell out of him because he ended up having to work a little harder that day in an effort to get her from his mind but the game just wasn't long enough to be that successful in keeping her out.

After the six of them finished their drinks and food, they left with the arrangement to come back next week. All seriously considered doing paintballing on a weekly basis if all enjoyed it. Sarah thought it might be a good way for her to start losing some weight, hopefully. They said goodbye to each other and went off in different directions. Mark, Josie and Sarah headed home. She was staying with Mark and Josie until her accident payout came through.

When the three arrived home, Sarah informed them she was going to get cleaned up. It was just simple courtesy as Mark and Josie had an en suite attached to their bedroom. She walked into the bathroom and gazed wistfully at the bath. She missed being able to have a bath, but she couldn't lower or raise herself into and out of the tub any more; at least not without help.

She never realised how much manoeuvrability was dependent on the ankles until she'd lost most of it in both of them. She couldn't even step up on tiptoes anymore and she never realised how much she used that manoeuvre to reach things just out of reach of her fingertips.

Sighing, she turned towards the shower. Having a shower just wasn't the same as having a nice long soak in the bath; it didn't stop her mind from thinking. Her thoughts went back to the two men she had been thinking of for the past hour or so...

Thinking of her dead husband brought tears to her eyes, while thinking of the man from the range caused her to fantasise and blush.

Sarah and her husband had known each other less than a month when they'd become engaged and a month after that they were married at the 'Births, Deaths and Marriages' Registry Office between Brisbane City and Fortitude Valley. It was a very simple ceremony for the two of them. The only time they were ever apart was when he worked. She'd been between jobs so had been happy to play housewife and he let her.

He enjoyed her being there when he came home from work and it pleased him when she got up with him and helped him get ready for work. When he wasn't at work, they were together, the whole time. Even after two years of constant companionship the pair of them were still so deeply in love and still constantly together whenever he wasn't at work.

Now, eighteen months after his death and her eyes fall upon tall, fair and stunning with pale eyes who could very well be a hit man or some such thing and her insides were acting like a schoolgirl with a high school crush. She had watched him.

He spoke with a minimum of words; short and to the point. While she couldn't hear his voice, she did get to see him give a slight smile to something one of his friends had said. It was barely a movement of lips, but it certainly made his lips look rather nice. Not that they looked bad when he wasn't smiling.

Sarah wondered what they would be like to kiss.

'Far out space cookies! But I hate it when I blush just because of my thoughts.'

She shook herself as she realised she'd been standing there with the shower running, mooning over a stranger she'd just seen and not met. She chastised herself for being so silly and unfaithful to her husband over a man she would never meet in person. Then she finished her shower and turned it off.

Drying and dressing herself, she went into her room and collapsed on the bed and just stared up at the ceiling as tears flowed. While she was sure the tears were because she missed her husband, she wasn't so sure they weren't for never being able to get close to the mysterious (supposed) hit man either.

Chapter 2

Three days after being at the paintball range, Sarah received a phone call from the solicitors. They informed her she was being offered $500 000 as a payout and the other side was unwilling to go higher. She told them to accept the offer, which was better than she thought she would be getting.

Besides, she knew if she fought for more, the likelihood she would get less in a court of law was rather high. Especially with court fees to fork out.

They told her she should be receiving the check within weeks. She was glad of that particular news. While they were under no obligation to do so, it had only been due to her severe circumstances they had rushed the proceedings so she would get the payout in half the time. It normally takes three years before victims receive their payouts.

After hanging up the phone, she thought about what she would do with the money. Most small houses, or even apartments for that matter, were that much or more to buy if she wanted to live in a decent area. Naturally, she wanted to. She wanted to feel safe if she was going to be living on her own.

During the past twelve months she'd been saving up to do a nail technician course. She only had another month of saving to go to be able to start the first part. Now, she realised, she could pay for all three parts in one go. Beautifying people's nails had always been a dream of hers. Now it looked like the dream was about to come true.

'Just a shame the price was so much higher than anticipated.' The thought floated up out of the depths of her mind. The weight in her heart seemed heavier than usual just then.

Then she shook herself. She didn't want to dwell, but it was hard not to. She hated self-pity, especially in herself, but couldn't seem to help it these days.

*

Like most people, he did the usual during his time off: made sure his expenses were paid – even if they were set for automatic payment, bought food, made sure his home was in good repair and general relaxing when he wasn't running around.

However, maintenance was an ongoing thing whenever he had down time because he barely spent time home to spread out the chores. In reality, he thought it was a good thing because he didn't do idle too well.

He didn't know how long this round of time off was going to last but while not called in he would enjoy it while it held out. It had been months since he'd had personal time and thankfully they had a significant lull this time round for him to have some playtime. The game last Saturday had been good and they would be having another game come Saturday again.

Despite all that, he logged into his laptop to see what jobs were up for grabs.

'Who knows? Maybe I'll find something really appealing and fun. Never been one to knock back a chance for a bit of fun. No matter what kind it is.' However, while he wasn't requested he was going to enjoy the down time by playing paintball on Saturdays.

*

Saturday had arrived again and they were at the paintball range again, and, yet again, the day was clear. A tad cool but fine with a slight breeze. With that breeze, Sarah wasn't looking forward to changing into the dress but it was all she'd brought with her. 'Oh well.'

The six of them were walking out of the range laughing at the fun they'd just had. She glanced towards their usual table to see if it was vacant when she caught sight of something large and white out of the corner of her eye. Turning her head towards it she saw what looked like the same white Jeep from last week.

He arrived at the range early, before the rest of his men like he usually did, just so he could survey the people coming and going from the paintball range. Regardless of it being a breezy day, he knew they wouldn't feel it once the game started. They would enjoy the breeze afterwards as he and his men tended to play hard and fast if that was the style of play they had agreed to at the beginning of the round.

The drive to the range was enjoyable regardless of the idiot drivers on the road. He'd just parked the Jeep, got out and was walking around to the passenger side to wait for the others to arrive when an interesting sight caused him to stop in mid step.

She was slowly, and tiredly, limping out of one of the ranges laughing with the rest of her friends...

As she looked, the man from last week walked around from the driver's side and paused when he saw her. There was no expression on his face other than a slight and very brief rising of his eyebrows, and that pause in mid stride, when he stared at her. His eyes travelled down to the gun in her left hand, across to the cane in her right and back up to her face.

...with a mask and paintball gun in her left hand. His eyes slid over to her right and there was the walking stick. She had on what looked like motorbike boots, maybe, and they seemed to help with her walking.

'Makes sense if they're the right sort but I can think of better boots for the job.' Only then did it just occur to him that he hadn't thought about her all week.

'I have to admit she looks rather attractive all open and relaxed like that.'

Then their eyes met.

Her smile froze and her eyes had widened slightly when they locked with his.

'It seems I may have underestimated her. Not often I let that happen.'

For her, the eye contact was like a shock zapping through her from head to toe.

'What's Mister Pale Eyes thinking while he's staring me like that?' She wondered. She was the first to break eye contact as she responded to something Tony had said to her.

Tony, a friend of Mark's, had the shape of a tree trunk... straight up and down. No chest, no waist, no hips and no butt definitions of any kind. What he lacked in body shape he made up in having a sense of humour. Tony constantly teased everyone around him and acted the clown. With his bushy, curly carrot coloured hair, it made the image of him as a clown all the more believable.

Then she excused herself and went to the ladies to change. Josie followed her so she could take Sarah's stuff to the car. All the while she kept thinking about Mister Pale Eyes reaction and what it could have meant.

When she came out and headed over to the table where her friends were sitting, she noticed Mister Pale Eyes watching her. In fact, his eyes never deviated from her at all. It might have been flattering if it wasn't for the fact his stare was totally non-sexual, but full of a curiosity, at what she guessed was, based on her having walked out of the range with a paintball gun in her hand.

'Well, that does explain why I never saw her carrying anything when she came out of the ladies if she played last week.'

She was wearing a dress similar to the one she had worn last week, except this one was a purple dress with orange and yellow flowers. She also wore what appeared to be the same shoes and her hair was in the same style as last week as well.

Yes, her injuries were real, of that he had no doubt whatsoever. While it is true the majority who have obvious physical disabilities usually don't play such physical games like paintball, it is not always the case. It would seem she fitted into the latter which he found very interesting indeed. He watched her join her friends and decided it might be interesting to go up against her to see how good she was.

'If I didn't know any better I would say he was thinking I might be fair game on the range. Geez I hope he didn't. Heh, such fanciful thoughts I seem to be having lately where he's concerned.' She gave herself a little shake and tried to ignore him.

Sarah quietly re-joined her friends, barely participating in the conversations. She just sat there eating a meat pie, drinking cola and gave the occasional smile at the appropriate moments.

Every now and then she would glance at Mister Pale Eyes only to catch him watching her. Her hormones had transformed into a flittering mass of swirling butterflies in her stomach and she couldn't stop glancing at him or calm them down.

'Who do I go to, to complain about not having been provided with a butterfly net?'

He found it amusing seeing her continually glancing at him. She seemed sort of embarrassed and nervous.

'Hmm... how perceptive is she, I wonder?'

When they had finished their food, Marci grabbed Tony and said they were leaving.

Marci was as dark as Tony, her lover, was fair. She was

Aboriginal. With brown skin, brown hair and brown eyes, she was about Sarah's build, but taller, so the weight looked better on her than on Sarah as far as Sarah was concerned. Tony called her his little chocolate dessert. Marci loved him so much it was rather embarrassing to watch them together at times.

Sarah nodded at Mark and Josie to inform them she was ready as well. To herself...

'I'm willing to admit I'm running... sorry, hobbling... away from Mister Pale Eyes and his scrutiny of me.' She sighed heavily as she slowly followed along behind her friends.

Her being attracted to him, despite her assumptions about him, were doing her no favours. Particularly since it was obvious he didn't think of, or see, her the same way.

Watching her leave...

'Think I'm going to make a point of arriving a little earlier again next week. Earlier than I normally do to see if I can catch a glimpse of her in action.. Yes, that sounds like an exceptionally good idea.'

He let his mind imagine the possibilities of going up against her while he waited for the guys to turn up. Never had he gone against someone like her before. He thought it would be interesting.

'Always good when a new way to have fun could be found.'

When the guys arrived, it took his mind off his fantasies. But not off thoughts of her. Then they kitted up and headed onto the range.

'Which is kind of funny really. One would think we would get tired of shooting at things considering what we do for a living, and yet here we are, shooting at each other in fun.' He shook his head at the irony of it.

*

Another week gone, another Saturday had arrived and off to the paintball range again. It was the fifth week in a row that the winter days were fine and clear, even if they were a little crispy cold and a little breezier than usual, but then what does one expect in the beginning of July.

When they arrived, Sarah searched for the white Jeep. She couldn't help herself, but it wasn't there and she didn't know whether to be happy about it or not.

After another relaxing week off and no calls for jobs, thoughts of seeing her in action were never far from the front of his mind. Once more he arrived before the rest of his team and, scouring the car park, saw what he was looking for.

'Good. She's here.'

He found which field of the four ranges they were in and tried to see if he could spot her; to observe what she was like, how she moved.

While he had caught a few of her friends in action – amateurs that they were, he didn't see her at all. She was either in one of the buildings or on the other side of them. So, he went back to the Jeep and leant against it to wait for her to come out.

'The time isn't right yet to approach her, but soon, soon.' As his thoughts from the past week entered his mind he had to admit to himself he had a difficult time containing his excitement.

The Jeep, however, was in the parking lot with him leaning against it watching them... her, as the six of them walked out of the range. Their eyes locked as he noted her automatic glance in his direction. She paused momentarily as she tried to ignore Mister Pale Eyes then did her usual of changing into a dress.

However, she found it difficult and as she walked back towards her friends, he continued watching her. It didn't help her any that she couldn't stop glancing at him no matter how much she tried.

From the moment he saw her he watched her the entire time. Again, her limping was slow and obvious, and she appeared tired. Despite the pain and exhaustion it caused her it seemed she didn't let it interfere with her participating. Those hidden little aspects of her drew him to her and kept him speculating as to what she would be like with a gun in her hand.

As she walked back to her friends her eyes travelled from the ground to him, to her friends to him, to the ground again and back to him. It was like she wanted to look at him but didn't, yet couldn't stop herself from doing so anyway.

'I wonder what my face reveals. Normally I keep it blank when dealing with the general population as they tend to be rather tedious at the best of times. But this woman, this girl, intrigues me and I want to see how good she is. However, I seem to be scaring her a bit. Not sure. While her emotions are there for all to see, she seems to be trying to tone them down whenever she glances at me.'

"Umm… guys? You don't mind if we leave fairly straight away do you?" She asked them quietly.

"Not feeling well Sarah?" Joey, Marci's brother asked. She didn't know him so well, but he was an athletic, taller version of Marci. He treated her nicely, but in such a way that said he wasn't really interested in her. Much to Marci's disappointment, the matchmaking romantic that she was.

Sarah told a simple lie and said no with a tired smile.

'Truth be told… Mister Pale Eyes is having such a powerful effect on me. Hormones are traitorous things, even if one is in mourning. In addition, his watching me that way is scaring me a little.' She thought to herself.

They left.

He was surprised to see her not sit down, then a few moments later the rest stood up and they all left. Staring at her feet as she walked passed. She didn't have any problems keeping her eyes averted at all that time.

'Well, there is always next week. Oh yeah.'

This time he couldn't dismiss her from his thoughts.

Chapter 3

The day was brisk and bright, and Scott, Zac and the Boss were already at the range when they received a call to let them know their team mates and opponents had been called away on a number of jobs and couldn't make it to the game. The three men were just debating what to do when she turned up. He had been encouraging the debate, by being non-committal, in the hopes she would arrive soon.

Sarah was both fearful and excited and neither feeling had anything to do with the upcoming game. When Mark, Josie and Sarah turned up, the Jeep was already there. Mister Pale Eyes and two of his pals were huddled together.

'Probably planning for their game I suppose.'

As they walked over to the picnic tables, Mark's mobile rang and after a moment he told Josie and Sarah that the others wouldn't be coming today.

"Geez! They could have let us know before we left home. That way we wouldn't have wasted the time coming here." Josie said explosively. She seemed a tad ticked off, not that Sarah blamed her really, as travelling time was forty-five minutes to the range and forty-five minutes back home.

'Even if I don't think coming here's a total waste of time if I get to see him, no matter how much the intensity of his scrutiny might frighten me at times.' Sarah pondered.

He listened to them and knew now was the right time.

'Perfect timing.'

"I think we may be having our game after all guys." He smiled slightly as he looked at her and noticed her watching him. She had invaded his thoughts all week and now that the time had arrived, he wasn't going to pass it up.

Suddenly she went still as she noticed Mister Pale Eyes, with his arms crossed over his chest, push away from the Jeep and letting them drop to his sides as he walked towards them.

The way he pushed away from the Jeep, a sort of flick with back and rear end to stand upright, was one of those totally male actions and she thought it was so damned sexy that her breath caught in her throat. Seeing him walk towards her was a mixed blessing. A dream-come-true for meeting him, but a potential nightmare for his possible reason for coming over.

With a quick flicker of her eyes, she noted the other two men were just a step or two behind him. His walk screamed military, and leader, at her.

Stopping the smile from growing with great effort, he walked towards her and watched her bite her bottom lip in what looked like nervousness.

'Damn! At 156cm tall, she's so tiny.' He thought as he neared and seemed to loom over her. He noted her cease all movement, pale blue eyes going wide, as she watched him walk towards her.

'She looks like a baby rabbit caught in the sights of a Brahminy Kite.'

'I'm sure I look like a moth caught in a flame. I'm just grateful I'm not blushing. At least... I think I'm not.' She thought as she tried to keep herself calm as part of her fantasy was coming true.

"Hi, we couldn't help overhearing you. The rest of our guys aren't coming either. Would you be interested in going up against us?" He asked, looking at her when he said the last part.

'Yep, that's the possible nightmare reason I was expecting.' She thought glumly.

He sounded well educated, his voice mid-range and smooth. Very city boy bred. It's the sort of voice she could sit and listen to for hours and hours, but she also got the impression that he didn't really speak much. Then she started noticing how much her neck was bent backwards just so she could see his face.

'Oh my goodness but he is soooo tall. I don't think I come up to his shoulders.'

Sarah, Mark and Josie barely made up any two of them put together. The three of them looked at each other and with just expressions, they'd decided yes. She looked up at Mister Pale Eyes and had to force her voice to work as she said in a soft tone that gave a slight squeak on the first word.

"Sure, why not."

'Shee-oot, how embarrassing.' Now she knew she was blushing.

Her voice was a little deeper than he was expecting and he felt his lips twitch in amusement.

'Definitely a tiny rabbit caught. Maybe she isn't going to be that hard a target after all. I'm almost disappointed already.'

"I'm Kaelan and these two are Scott and Zac." Mister Pale Eyes – now up close Sarah could see that they were a pale hazel, almost a pale green with little flecks of brown and a slightly darker green through them – Kaelan said as he thumbed at Scott and Zac respectively.

None of the three men offered their hands to shake, so neither did Sarah and her friends.

Scott appeared to be roughly 178cm, about the same height as her husband. He had blonde hair in a military buzz cut, more American style than Australian. He was only slightly broader in the shoulders than Kaelan and his skin more tanned. In fact, he was slightly broader all over. His blue eyes were a little darker than hers, but looked so much colder and made her shiver a little when he looked at her.

Zac was slightly shorter than Kaelan, but much broader than Scott. He looked like a small mountain, with dark brown hair, brown eyes, dark complexioned skin... not Aboriginal, at least not fully. The facial features didn't seem right for being Aboriginal or for any of the other dark skinned races, but that didn't mean he wasn't; it just meant that Sarah didn't have a clue. As he scratched his jaw line, she noted that his hands were as big as her face. He was scary just by size alone.

"Hi, Mark, Josie and I'm Sarah." She said pointing to Mark and Josie respectively.

Up close he could see her cupid's bow wasn't perfect. The right side was slightly lower than the left while the right side was slightly narrower. He wondered if they were as soft to the touch as they looked. He gave himself a mental shake for noticing such an insignificant little detail. However...

'Sarah. Her name is Sarah. Hmm... yeah, I think she could look like a Sarah. It suits her.'

"Are you sure you want to team against us? You guys look professional and we're so not that. We're not going to be much of a challenge for you three." She asked nervously, looking at Kaelan with a slight frown.

'I think I did well to ask that without sounding like a breathy teen with a high school crush or sounding too shy for my voice to squeak in a whisper as it has a tendency to do.' Sarah congratulated herself.

'No squeak this time but still a little nervous sounding. Don't know why. It's not like she knows what we do for a living. Or does she since she mentioned us being professionals?'

"I'm sure we'll manage." He said with a slight smile, but it didn't reach his eyes. Kaelan's eyes stayed neutral, almost cold. She never thought hazel eyes could look cold, but his managed to.

"Besides, we'll be a challenge for you." Now, his eyes looked anticipatory, and that scared her a little.

"Yeah, I'm sure you will." She responded softly then looked at her friends. They just gave slight shrugs then the six of them entered the range after paying for fees and gathering their equipment.

The range was a combination of a mini derelict building or two, giant sized tyres that Sarah could hide in – with her standing upright with a bit of room to spare – that were either standing upright, laying down, half buried or made into earth-packed walls, as well as bushes and trees.

Kaelan and his team gave her and the other two the head start. She had a suspicion that he would be hunting her. She didn't know why she'd thought that but she couldn't shake it once she had.

Kaelan decided to leave the other two to Scott and Zac. They didn't interest him. If anyone asked him to describe them, all he could say was the guy was fit and she was blonde. Nothing more because he wasn't interested in them. And, for him, that was highly unusual. He was usually a stickler for details, it was necessary in his line of work.

It was because Sarah was his target for the day. He and his men let the three of them go off into the field first and waited for about five minutes. During that time…

"Sarah's mine. You two can take the other two, but if you see her, don't shoot her." He ordered as he watched the two men. They stared at him with surprise.

"I want to see how good she is since she seems to participate in the games." He finished.

"Do you really think she'll be that good?" Zac asked quietly with a frown.

"I don't know, but she has permanently injured feet yet she plays paintball and I'm curious." Kaelan stated just as quietly.

"You're the boss." Scott commented in such a way that he thought Kaelan was wasting his time.

He let Scott's comment ride this time since he has known the man for as long as he has known Zac. In fact, the three met in the army when they were assigned to the same team.

After five minutes the three of them parted ways. Kaelan made his way towards the one building in that particular range.

'It's the logical choice for her to hide in since she's such a slow mover.'

Once against the wall, he carefully crept along to the first opening, a window. Cautiously, he peeked through the window but the room was empty. The building did have a roof but was sporadically marked with holes and therefore made the shadows in the corners darker than usual. Depending where the sun was, of course.

Due to her limited mobility, Sarah searched for spots that would give her cover, but still allowed her to see and shoot. This time round she found a nice spot at the corner of the building that was covered by a large shrub that she was able to hide behind. It was taller than she was and the bottom of it was so low to the ground that it was difficult to see her feet from the other side, let alone the rest of her.

'Hmm... good spot, must remember it for next time.' Gazing around occasionally, she watched a few ants, a small spider or two, beetles and other bugs trundling along the branches.

'As long as they all stay away from me then they'll live another day.' She thought with a slight shudder with regards to the ants and spiders.

Even though Sarah was just standing there waiting for her first 'victim' to creep past, her feet were hurting. She hated the fact she only had a standing time of between five to ten minutes these days before her feet and ankles started aching. Standing in the one spot without moving made the pain worse and build up faster. She was about to shift her position to try ease some of the increasing pain when she heard a soft scrape of a boot against the corner of the building.

He moved on to the next opening, a doorway. Looking in, that room was also empty. After entering, he carefully checked out the whole building, but it was completely empty.

'Where is she?' Kaelan frowned in consternation.

Her heart rate increased as hands with gun came into view and she knew it wasn't Mark or Josie. Then arms, then the beginnings of a broad chest came into view. Finally, the rest of Zac crept forward. So close, her heart hammered in her chest so hard that she thought he would hear it. Then, luck favoured her... He turned towards her, but made no move, as if he hadn't seen her. Their eyes certainly hadn't locked.

Wasting no time, Sarah shot him through the branches, in the vicinity of his chest and then hobbled in the opposite direction as fast as she could. She knew she couldn't stay there because he would either come after her or, if he was 'killed', more than likely tell one of his mates that someone was there.

Despite his consternation, Kaelan's curiosity, and excitement, built.

'She's not as easy as I thought she would be.'

Out of the corner of his eye he saw movement to the left so he went back the way he'd come and worked his way to the other side of the building. When he got there, no one was in sight. With each section of searching for her, his excitement grew. So, he started scouring the rest of the area carefully.

'She has to be here. She can't have gone too far too soon.'

Sarah found another large bush to hide behind. This time she had a tree at her back. She'd just gotten between them when someone else came into the little clearing. She tried to slow her breathing down in the hopes she wouldn't be heard, but she was so excited and nervous all at the same time that it was difficult to get herself under control.

Kaelan thought he heard the sound of a foot shifting, but couldn't discern where it originated from. Entering a small bare dirt clearing very slowly he silently, and vigilantly searched it.

This time, to shoot whoever it was, Sarah would have to wait until he was all the way around to her right then step out of her shelter to get the shot, because the bush was too thick on the left. Whoever it was finally moved to a spot where she could see him through part of the bush, and it was Kaelan. Sweat trickled down her face, sides and back.

'I swear my pounding heart is going to give me away.' She thought apprehensively.

Kaelan confirmed her suspicions of him. He moved very slowly and very quietly. What she could see of him he was looking everywhere as he crept forward. She was so intent on watching his movements that he was suddenly in the spot she needed him to be in and she moved quickly to make the shot.

He was just passing a large tall bush, with a tree behind it, when he heard a noise. Spinning around, she fired at him less than a second after he had pulled the trigger.

He must have heard or sensed her because he had spun around faster than she thought he would and fired at her just as she pulled the trigger at him.

'Unbelievable! She's ambushed me!' Was all he had time to think of.

Sarah only got the one shot off while his second shot got her in the upper arm just below the shoulder. They were so close his first shot hit her in the side, a flesh wound so to speak – and felt like it too, that the force of the impact caused her to lose her balance and she landed hard on her rump.

His gun and eyes travelled with her falling, but she fell at an angle and that was how his second shot hit her just below the shoulder. She started to look up at him waiting for the third – death – shot that he was now open to take. However, when she gazed up at him, she was greeted with a look of utter disbelief and surprise. Then, he peered down at his chest and her eyes followed.

Sarah had 'killed' him.

He was about to fire a third shot when he caught a splotch of lavender on his chest in his peripheral vision as his sight targeted her. 'I don't believe it!'

He was so surprised he ripped off his mask and couldn't hide his expression as he gaped at her then down at his chest.

'She's killed me!'

'I can't believe it! I got him!' There was a large lavender splotch right where his heart was. She wasn't elated though. Not yet anyway.

'Him being a professional, and taken out by mere slip of a girl who can't even walk properly... a civilian even... I mean... I'm expecting a sore loser here.'

Instead, after regaining some composure, he gazed at her intensely this time.

'That was an amazing shot. She's good, really good. Both in her ambushing and her shooting. To hit me like that while falling is incredible. I definitely want to try a longer game with her.' He held his hand out to help her stand.

"Well shot." He stated calmly.

'Oh, nice grip… Warm and gentle, firm and soft… but not feminine soft, just not heavily calloused. Well fudge!' She cursed silently as her hormones started a riot; yet again. 'Traitorous little buggers!' By the feel of her face, she thought she was blushing. 'Thank goodness for the full face mask.'

With her booted foot against his to stabilise her rising, she surprised him with a reasonable grip even though her skin was soft and a little cold to the touch, but then it was winter after all and she didn't have gloves on. Then he couldn't help but notice her hand in his.

'Such a tiny hand and it fits so well in mine.' Then he gave himself a mental shake at such irrelevant thoughts as he let go of her hand.

"Th-th-thank you." Sarah stammered around her thundering heartbeat as he picked up her gun and walking stick, which had flown out of her hands when she fell, and handed them to her.

'Oh yeah, definitely over 185cm tall.' She finally removed her mask when she thought she was safe to do so.

Masks in hand, they walked back to the kiosk area in silence, his pace matching hers, which must have been painfully slow for him.

'Blast, but I don't even come up to his shoulder. I know I'm small, but that truly is ridiculous. I hate being short. I'm so going to get a crick in my neck if I have to look up at him all the time. Maybe him sitting, or laying, down would work.' She shook her head slightly at her silly thoughts and concentrated on just moving forward and nothing else or, at least, she tried to.

Almost painfully, he matched his pace to hers as they walked back to the kiosk and their waiting friends.

'Damn, but she is so slow with her small steps. I have this urge to just pick her up and carry her to the table. Don't think she would appreciate it though.'

He gazed down at her and was surprised to see she didn't even come up to his armpit let alone his shoulder.

'I know she's tiny but I hadn't realised by how much. Wonder what she's thinking though? Whatever it is it doesn't look happy by that little shake of her head. Her thoughts can't be game based that's for sure.'

However, she wasn't sharing her thoughts as they walked. While he's not big on idle chatting or talking in general, it was a silent walk back to the kiosk area.

As the two of them approached the others, he silently groaned at the surprised expressions on Scott's and Zac's faces and watched their eyes flick from him to Sarah and back again. He knew he would have to explain it to them later. He mentally sighed. Mark and Josie didn't say a word, but had huge grins on their faces.

Then he glanced at Sarah staring at her feet and he frowned slightly. He didn't understand why but she didn't seem happy even though she should have been. In fact, she should have been elated.

"I'm just going to get changed." Sarah mumbled to no one in particular and hobbled off. She was still rather stunned at her luck.

Kaelan sat on the corner of the table next to Scott and Zac, on the other side from her two friends.

Mark looked at Josie and asked quietly "The usual?"

She nodded then followed after Sarah while he headed to the kiosk. A few minutes later he came back with food for the three of them. Scott walked off to buy the three of them drinks and came back with a fruit juice for Kaelan.

Josie caught up to her so she could put Sarah's gear in the car while she finished changing. On the way to the ladies Josie babbled about what luck it was to have shot Kaelan. Sarah nodded but didn't say a word.

When she got back to the picnic table, Sarah sat down in front of the waiting meat pie and cola – which, to Kaelan, looked like she didn't want – when Mark started retelling what happened to them after entering the range. While Kaelan did hear what Mark was saying, he watched Sarah take some painkillers, then eat.

'Interesting. Despite the pain it causes her, she still plays.' Unintentionally she had impressed him then he frowned at himself as to why anything about her should matter at all.

"Well, Josie and I decided we would pair up to ambush whoever came into view and it was Scott. But while we shot him Zac took out the both of us." Mark said with a smile that turned into a grimace, and then chuckled.

His retelling of their part of the game was basically how Kaelan had expected it to go down.

'I figured the only way they could take any of us down was if they teamed up against any one of us.' After a pause of what seemed to be an awkward silence Kaelan received a surprise when Sarah spoke up.

"Well, sometime after that, I guess, I managed to shoot Zac. I must admit though, I hadn't taken notice if it was a fatal shot or not. Since he didn't come after me, I guess it was." Sarah said softly and glanced at Zac then away again. The shot was lung that was so close to the heart, which qualified.

Kaelan also looked at Zac at that point and let a slight smile show. 'I'm surprised I'd missed it when I first looked at him after coming out of the range.'

Zac had the grace to appear a little uncomfortable.

'So, I'm not the only one. I can't believe I'd underestimated her so badly. I mean, she's 'killed' two of us after all!'

She continued in the same quiet and embarrassed tone.

"After I shot him I changed my location and waited for the next guy to come into sight." She didn't look at Kaelan at all. She couldn't.

Kaelan watched her. She was staring at her hands, her meat pie still untouched. It confused him as to why she wasn't elated. He certainly would have been in her position.

After a slight pause…

"I'd just hidden myself when Kaelan came into sight. I had to wait till he was in the right spot before I could shoot." She took a sip of her drink and almost choked on it in her nervousness.

It was the first time she had said his name and he liked the way she said it. He had never experienced such a feeling before just because some female said his name. Then he mentally sighed again at such a stupid thought, along with all the other earlier pointless observations, as he resumed listening to her retelling.

Then he noted her hand shook slightly. 'Nervous? Why is she nervous?'

"When he was there I stepped out and we shot each other. He

got two shots off and I only got the one because his first had knocked me to the ground. I could only sit there while waiting for his third shot." For some silly reason Sarah was self-conscious about the whole thing.

He didn't understand why but she genuinely seemed embarrassed. That in itself was annoying to him. 'Why should it matter how she feels about it? Unless it's an act to hide her true capabilities?' He just didn't know enough at that point in time to work out if that thought was true or not.

"I guess I just got lucky." She finished softly and rather lamely. With the three professionals there, she just wanted to fall into a deep hole where they couldn't see her. She knew it was silly to feel that way, but she couldn't help it.

'If it had been our other friends we would have been laughing and whooping it up big time. However, it's Kaelan and my hormones have a thing going for him. So embarrassing. So confusing.' She just stared at her hands until...

"Maybe we were just over confident with ourselves." Kaelan offered in that quiet tone of his. He blinked.

'I can't believe I just said that. Why did I even say that?! I know I hadn't acted over confident during the game.'

Sarah's head snapped up with a look of disbelief plain on her face. She didn't believe that and looking at him, he didn't either. Not really. A quick glance at Scott and Zac showed her they were just as surprised at his comment and didn't believe him either. She thought she'd just got a lucky shot.

'Somehow, I think Kaelan may be thinking I'm better than I'm claiming. I'm not... Honest.'

'Oh, she's good. Definitely need to have another game.'

He gazed at her again when Sarah stood up, so she could get herself another drink, when a severe wave of dizziness hit her. She tried to grab the table to steady herself but missed. Her fingers clutching at empty space. Blinked at the faces above her, she found herself on the ground on her back with the world spinning and her innards churning and she wasn't quite sure how she got there.

'Uhhhh... I seem to be missing a second or two.'

"Sarah?" Mark called as he knelt down beside her, his voice so full of concern it almost made her cry. She just blinked instead.

"Are you alright?" Kaelan asked in the same tone and at the same time Mark had spoken as he knelt on her other side. He cursed himself for being too slow, but the fall was unexpected.

She blinked again. Something didn't look quite right but Kaelan couldn't work out what it was.

"Well, that's different." Sarah mumbled as she slowly looked from Mark to Kaelan, but had to close her eyes as just that action made the spinning worse and she was sure she was going to be sick.

Kaelan, though, didn't think she was really seeing either of them.

However, she had to open her eyes again almost immediately as the sensations worsened, but it wasn't really that much help without something to stare at. Sarah didn't know if it was deliberate or not, but she suddenly locked her eyes onto Kaelan's and just stared while she waited for everything to stop spinning and trying to tip her over.

'Yeah, very lovely eyes.' The thought flitted through her mind as he started to frown at her.

'This young woman confuses me... So shy she practically jumps at shadows let alone at a stranger should they pay attention to her, takes out two of us despite her disability then just stares at me for no apparent reason which also contradicts her shyness.'

"Help me to get her up." Mark said to Kaelan as they grabbed her hands.

"No!" Sarah managed to squeeze out past the nauseous sensations in her stomach, still staring at Kaelan. As an effect of the dizziness she still wasn't breathing properly. Because the dizzy spell was so bad, it was taking longer than usual to settle.

'Something's definitely wrong.' Kaelan thought. With her staring at him the way she was he couldn't help but see her eyes. They were more than a simple greyish blue as there were also light grey streaks and tan-ish splotches around the pupils. They would almost look like storm clouds if it wasn't for those splotches. Something about them bothered him though, but he couldn't work out what it was.

"Not yet please." She pleaded through clenched teeth. 'Geez, I hate this churning feeling in the gut.'

If she closed her eyes or moved them about it felt as if the world, or herself, was doing a sideways sliding spin as if she was... falling? Not quite the right word, but she couldn't think of any other that would fit... falling into an abyss, or some such thing. While her innards were doing their own turny/twisty churn that if she had a weaker stomach then she would be very sick.

By focusing her eyes on a single spot, and not move from that spot, it helped ease the dizziness sooner than if she didn't do it.

Sort of acting like an anchor to keep her from spinning off into goodness knows what. For that reason she was grateful it was daylight as darkness made it harder to lock the eyes onto a stable point. The sensations were still unpleasant to say the least.

He frowned at her staring at him, gripping his hand like a lifeline, but it was hard to explain right then as to why she was. 'Mind you, he could be frowning because I'm sure my eyes are looking spastic with their weird flicking, side-sliding, movements in time with the spinning motion.' She wasn't sure if they were or not, since she couldn't see her own eyes, but that was the way they certainly felt as she tried to stay focused.

Unfortunately, they were gathering a crowd around them, all wanting a gawk at the young woman on the ground. The rest of their little group were keeping the crowd back as best as possible.

'Shame it's illegal to shoot them.' Kaelan mused as he noted the crowd with his peripheral vision, not willing to break eye contact with her just in case it impeded her recovery. However, he couldn't stop frowning with confusion and concern with her continually staring at him, blinking as little as possible.

It was like she was having a difficult time focusing, her eyes kept... drifting ever so slightly and she seemed to have to drag them back. Something one wouldn't notice unless they were looking closely at her eyes the way he was right at that moment.

'A dizzy spell perhaps?' That thought caused him to remember the last one he'd had after major blood loss. 'Now that was a bitch to go through.' At that moment it was the only thing he could think of.

Management came over to see if they needed an ambulance,

but, without moving her eyes, she said, "No, it's nothing serious." Sarah paused slightly as she fought the closing of her eyes. "I just need a little bit more time and then I'll be alright." Her voice still rather strained from the effects. They asked if she was sure and she said yes.

Roughly five minutes after she hit the ground dizziness and symptoms had finally eased sufficiently enough to risk moving.

"Slowly, and gently, help me up please?" She asked softly as she carefully looked at Mark then Kaelan.

"Are you sure you are alright?" Josie asked her.

"Yeah, just a dizzy spell. Admittedly the worst one I've ever had, but it seems to be gone now. I just had to lay there and focus on a single point to help ease it, that's all." Sarah responded while moving carefully so as not to start the dizzy spell again. She glanced at Kaelan, while Josie and Mark dusted the back of her, and then helped her to sit down.

He was right. His tension eased as she explained why she was staring. 'Some dizzy spell; but it sounds like she's suffered them before. She should really get them checked out.' However, it wasn't his place to say anything about it to her. Instead, he handed her walking stick to her for the second time that day.

"Thank you." She said so softly that it was almost a whisper.

Now that the situation was over she was embarrassed at having used him as a focal point and she couldn't look at him again. At the same time, however, she couldn't stop glancing at him either. Around him, confusion reigned supreme within her and she didn't know what to do about it.

'It doesn't help that I'm too damned shy to say something about what I think of him out loud. Oh well, not like that's anything new to me.' She thought glumly.

She turned to Mark and asked him if he could get her some water since she was still feeling a little nauseous from the dizzy spell.

After all that, Sarah and her friends finished their food in an awkward silence – at least awkward for her, politely thanked the three men for the game and made their way back to the car to head home. She was so ready to just lie down and pass out, she was that tired.

"Zac, did you see her before she shot you?" Kaelan asked quietly as he watched her limping towards their car slowly. 'Almost carefully as if she's still feeling the effects of the dizziness. Or maybe she's just tired or her ankles are hurting her.' Then he wondered why it mattered. With a sigh he shook his head in frustration at the thoughts that girl was awakening within him.

"No, I didn't see her until she started moving away after she shot me." Zac answered in the same tone of voice.

"You two interested in having a rematch with those three?" Kaelan asked the two men as he continued to watch her as she got into the car in such a manner that was extremely lady-like but was more than likely just due to her ankles, he surmised.

"Yeah." They chorused quietly.

Just as she started to close the door, a hand gripped it. She looked up to see Kaelan bending down to look at them... her.

She appeared tired as she gazed up at him then gave him that little wide-eyed baby bunny look again. Seeing her with that expression was growing on him. He liked it and it amused him.

"Would you guys be interested in a re-match same time next week?" Kaelan asked in that lovely voice of his.

'Think Liam Neeson but not quite as deep.' Sarah thought as she looked at Mark and Josie. They indicated yes so she said, "Sure, see you next week."

Kaelan nodded, let go of the door and walked back to his Jeep eager for next Saturday to arrive as they drove off.

'Hmmm... not a bad view of him walking away either.' She sighed and turned back to the front.

Chapter 4

Two days later Sarah received a letter. It was her accident payout check. She went to her bank the next day and deposited it then made an appointment with a financial advisor for the best way to deal with it.

'I so don't want to spend it all at once and then be left with nothing.'

Thankfully, she didn't have to worry about any outstanding expenses as they'd all been paid off the previous year, so all she was left with was the weekly expenses that everyone has.

She decided she didn't have enough money to buy a decent house or apartment so renting would be the way to go if she still wanted some money left over to do other things with. However, she still needed advice on the best way to deal with the money. Gratefully, the advisor was able to see her there and then.

While the advisor made suggestions, Sarah latched onto the idea of saving half and spending the other half to set herself up comfortably. The advisor helped her work it all out. In the end they divided the amount into non-equal thirds. Half of the total to become a nest egg for later in life, half of what was left for bills and other inescapable expenses, while the other half of the left over for Sarah to spend on herself however she saw fit.

They set up the necessary accounts, she signed the various paper works, the bank set up the automatic deposits for once the check had cleared and she went home.

Sarah sighed. She never realised how hard any of it was until right then. When her husband was alive it never seemed that hard. They had done everything together and, maybe, that just made everything seemed so much easier to deal with.

She started thinking about what she was going to do for transportation. She couldn't drive any more. Weeks ago, Josie had suggested a scooter because the gear changing and acceleration were done by hand instead of feet. Having thought about it, Sarah figured yeah, sounded good.

First, she had started researching about learning to ride a scooter and discovered – within Queensland – only those with an existing car license can learn to ride a scooter. While it was no problem for her, since she had her license and it was still active, she thought it was a stupid rule.

'Why did they even change that rule? Surely there are people out there who don't have a license because they can't drive a car, or maybe never want to drive a car, but would like a scooter instead?' She shook her head at such a ridiculous ruling.

A few days later she started taking lessons.

Then she started looking in catalogues and realised she would end up buying two scooters. First one being smaller in power to start out on, then the second one being bigger once she became comfortable enough with riding the smaller one. She logged into an online auction website, looked at second-hand scooters for her first one, and chose something that would look nice. A Yamaha Cygnus 125 at 116 kilos sounded good. There was a mid to deep blue one for $900 with one month registration remaining, a matching top box on the back and totally roadworthy.

As for upgrading to a bigger model…

'I'll buy brand new I think.'

She loved the look of the Yamaha T-Max 500 in a deep red that could do highway speeds. It sounded fun. Besides, from the front, it almost looked like a motorbike. 'Oh yeah, I'm hooked.' She thought as a smile of joy slowly grew.

So, reviewing her plans…

'Finish moving into my bland one bedroom apartment, do my nail technology course and continue to learn to ride a scooter. Nervous as heck, but yeah… all do-able.' Sarah couldn't help smiling. Her life was slowly, but surely, starting to get back on track.

~*~

After a quiet week of trying to keep busy with now non-existent chores, so he wouldn't notice how slowly time seemed to be crawling, Saturday had finally arrived. While the day was rather cool and fine Kaelan had no interest in what the day was like. He had pulled in at the range, with Scott and Zac having arrived moments later. They parked then stood beside his Jeep while they waited for Sarah and her friends.

The three men didn't have to wait long. Whether he wanted to or not, Kaelan couldn't help noticing her. Like last week she was already dressed in the gear she would wear to play the game… a new green checked flannel long sleeved shirt – which looked like to have a couple of layers of other items underneath, new heavy duty dark blue jeans and her black motorbike boots. While sensible clothing, she actually looked rather cute dressed liked that. However, her friends were dressed for fashion instead of practicality.

'Idiots.' He thought dismissively.

He also observed how she reacted the moment she saw him. Kaelan knew her reactions had nothing to do with Scott and Zac because her eyes sought only him and never deviated to anywhere else other than to the ground and back again.

'So nervous like a damned baby bunny.' He thought and didn't understand why. The only thought he could come up with was possibly because she'd picked up on them being professionals. It did make him wonder, yet again, as to how perceptive she truly was.

Once she and her friends had joined the three men they all paid their fees, bought the paintballs, kitted up and headed into the range.

Forty-five minutes later, the six of them were sitting at the kiosk tables. For the second time in a row, Sarah had successfully 'killed' Kaelan. He was her only hit for the day. Scott took out Mark while Josie took out Scott and Josie and Zac took each other out.

'That sounds so funny, like something out of a comedy.' She thought as she stared at her drink listening to them.

As for Kaelan and her, however, they both got off one shot each after he found her in one of the buildings.

'Damn, but she's good at ambushing!' His shot was supposed

to hit her in the chest, but she had timed her move at the right moment. So, he ended up hitting her in the upper left arm, just above the elbow instead. Annoyingly, her movement at that moment gave her a better angle to shoot from.

When she fired, she had hit him in the heart. Her reactions were exactly the same as last time.

'I just don't understand her. She's good, but seems to be acting the shy novice who gets lucky. It has to be an act. There's no other explanation for it. Damn, I just want to give her a real gun to see the real her.'

After helping her off the ground again and handing her walking stick and gun back to her, the two of them slowly headed back to the kiosk area where the others waited for them.

Surprisingly, no one said a word about the paint on his chest even though he knew Scott and Zac would rib him about it later. At least, not in front of the Sarah and her friends.

Sarah and her friends parted ways with Kaelan and his with the arrangement to play again next week. While she'd agreed to another re-match, she had the feeling her luck was going to run out, and soon.

One thing she had noticed was that Kaelan didn't talk much.

'The strong silent type huh? Did that mean he was a man of action? I could live with that. Hmmm... something to think about.' She privately smiled to herself over such a thought. Even though she knew those thoughts would never become real, she indulged in the fantasies anyway.

Despite having all agreed to play again the following week, Kaelan decided there and then that he and his men would not be turning up. He decided to end the situation before it got out of hand.

'I'll think of some excuse to give the guys. The desire to give her a real gun is heady and almost overpowering.' He thought as he watched her walk to the car.

However, it wasn't just that. He also wanted to protect her, care for her. He had never felt that way about any other woman and it confused, as well as annoyed him.

After Sarah and her friends drove off, a message came through to Kaelan's mobile phone. They had a job. He read the details and came to the conclusion they would be away at the time of the next match. Glancing at Scott and Zac with their mobiles in their hands, he realised they'd received the same message. So, they headed off in separate directions agreeing to meet up at the rendezvous point in an hour and a half.

After arriving home, he did a quick search for Sarah's details. He had noted her surname on her Proof of Age ID card at the range. It wasn't until he had seen her ID had it occurred to him that of course she couldn't drive. However, looking further, he saw she still had a valid driver's licence.

While the info didn't say anything about any professional training in regards to guns and the like, that didn't really mean a thing. It just meant they either didn't know or it was blacked out. Although, he couldn't find any electronic blocks attached to her file... if such information had been blacked out. If he was to believe the 'no security blocks' then she has had no training and had been extremely lucky with all three shots.

'I suppose she could have been but... somehow, I just don't believe she was that lucky.'

Her info stated she was twenty-three but, to him, she appeared younger, like under twenty and a senior at high school. She was also married but her husband was now deceased. He never imagined she would have been married at her young age. Not only that but he hadn't seen a ring on her finger so he had assumed she wasn't.

Strangely, it pleased him some other man had been attracted to her because it didn't look like guys were giving her a second look these days.

Then, berating himself, he didn't understand why she, of all the women who had crossed his path over the years, has elicited such thoughts and responses from him. He was a work-aholic and he knew it. Too much down time allowed him to think of things he didn't want to.

Then he resumed reading her information. After reading a bit more about her, he found her mobile number and had started to dial it when he paused.

'No, I won't.' He frowned to himself. So, he cancelled the dialling and closed her info without reading any more or saving any of it.

"It will be better this way, safer for her as men like me don't make good lovers because we tend to die at a young age. Although, I seem to be doing well so far." He muttered with a frown then thought, 'Not only that, but our loved ones could be used as hostages against us.'

Shocked that the words 'lovers' and 'loved ones' had entered his thoughts, he shook his head in confusion and disgust then shoved away from his laptop. Going through the house, he locked up and packed the gear he needed for the job. Anything, to get his thoughts away from her and the thoughts she elicited within him then headed out to the rendezvous point.

Chapter 5

Sarah's weekdays were now taken up with learning to ride a scooter. In another two weeks she would be starting the nail technology course. Both will be time consuming because she'll study and practice every single day. She already does so with her scooter lessons but wanted to make sure she passed both of them first time round. Besides, it wasn't like she had anything better to do with her time.

She'd managed to buy the Yamaha Cygnus 125, so she now had her own transportation. She also bought a new helmet, gloves...,

"Kid sized because ladies small was still too big, that was embarrassing." She muttered softly to herself.

...motorbike leather jacket and matching leather pants. Having been in one accident, she wasn't going to risk herself a second time.

She was dreading the coming Saturday because she thought her success at the range irked Kaelan.

'I don't think he'll be so gentle in dealing with me this time. The gloves, as they say, will be coming off, I think.' While she did dread the encounter on the range, she was also looking forward to it. Kaelan's the strong silent type.

'Not by choice originally, I think, but by necessity due to his line of work, I'm guessing. Having watched him move, I think my first assumptions about him were correct; definitely ex-military and definitely a professional killer of some sort. Just don't know for sure about the assassin or freelance hitter part. Could be a bounty hunter I suppose. If you know what to look for you can always pick out a military, or ex-military, person.'

'Their walk, for example, is a give-away. Their training is also a give-away. The more serious about their military career they are, the more obvious it is. Even when they're at home relaxing, one will still see their career choice to some degree because it becomes a way of life for them. With Kaelan, I'm thinking sniper. Definitely not just an ordinary army man, as he seems to be more controlled than the average soldier.' She mused.

'How do I know this? My Great-grandfather, my Grandfather, my deceased husband and various men on his side of the family were all in the military. Well, far out space cookies... Just thinking upon that, anyone would think I have a thing for military men.' The thought made her smile.

'Now, as for bounty hunters, could Kaelan be one?' That she didn't know.

Bounty hunting wasn't exactly a big thing in Australia, ever. The law here discouraged it with a passion. Although, there had been the exception or two over the many decades (one of which was help in capturing Ned Kelly and his gang).

Now, bounty hunting is a growing business in Australia, but with strict laws attached from what she'd heard. However, she didn't really follow it so she wouldn't truly know. Although, over the past few years, the words 'bounty hunter' was cropping up more and more.

'Ah well, I guess I'm never going to find out. I think it is just going to be me and my fanciful ideas about Kaelan. If I didn't have a gun in my hand, I don't think he would give me a second consideration at all.' She thought glumly.

~*~

The following Saturday Mark, Josie and Sarah waited at the range for an hour. Kaelan, Scott and Zac didn't show up at all. Josie started grumbling about them being inconsiderate.

"Well they don't have any of our numbers and we don't have theirs." Sarah pointed out.

'Although, I have a suspicion that Kaelan would be able to find that information out without any problems at all.' She kept that thought to herself though. Sarah didn't know why she'd thought that about Kaelan, but she did and couldn't shake it once it had crept in.

She couldn't help but be disappointed that he wasn't there. Her reaction surprised her since the two of them were barely acquaintances, let alone friends.

'I so need to get a grip on myself.'

The three of them left.

*

Somewhere in the middle of one of Queensland's State Forests north west of Brisbane, it sounded as if a war was being fought.

With a start, Kaelan realised it was Saturday, but late afternoon. The week had been bloody, brutal and gruelling, and he had sort of lost track of time until that moment. In the middle of a one-on-one, he hadn't understood why the realisation should hit him right then at all.

Now that he knew, he wondered about her and what she would be thinking and feeling when she realised he wouldn't be there. He started to feel somewhat guilty about not having called her last week. The feeling didn't last long, however, when it was replaced with the pain of a knife slicing a little too deeply into his upper arm.

'That's what I get for thinking about her instead of keeping my mind on the job.' He thought and took his annoyance out on the man who had sliced him.

"She's not even in my life and yet she'll be the death of me I'm sure." He muttered angrily under his breath.

Right at that moment he realised how far Sarah had wormed her way past his defences. He didn't understand how she had managed to do so and take up residence within him, but she had. It shocked him to a stand-still.

As for the one who had wounded him, Kaelan was rather vicious in his dispatching of the man and looked down at the remains in surprise. He hadn't realised he was so thorough in taking the rogue out. He shrugged and continued with the battle as he moved on to his next target.

However, Kaelan decided he needed to talk to someone about her and only one person came to mind. Once decided, he then turned his mind back to the task at hand as he could do without more injuries because of her. Unfortunately, he wouldn't have the chance to talk to his friend until a year and a half after he was injured that day.

As the days, weeks and months passed, Kaelan had thrown himself into his job. Any down time and he was looking for solo work. Anything, to keep her out of his thoughts. Day and night he kept himself on the go until, eventually, he was forced to take time off. Out of the whole situation and time passing, all he could claim was some new scars to the growing collection.

*

That was the last time any of any of them played paintball together. Tony, Marci and Joey had found other things to do during the times Sarah, Mark and Josie played against Kaelan, Zac and Scott.

Now Mark and Josie had gone their own way as well, so it was also the last time any of them hung out together. Sarah wasn't included any more after she had to turn down one invite due to working late. As mentioned earlier, Josie was quick to dump people over any perceived slight.

With the last of her so-called close friends having drifted away, she was left to her own company from that point on. The following Saturday Sarah went back to the paintball range by herself. She was grateful they had a small shooting range attached to the complex so she had an excuse to be there by herself.

'Honestly…? I'm here hoping to see Kaelan again.' She couldn't believe she was doing such a thing. 'I've never done anything like this before. I'm seriously going to have to lock those traitorous hormones away.'

She spent two hours practicing shooting left-handed as well as with her right. However, still no Kaelan. She did this routine for another three Saturdays in a row with Kaelan being a total no show. Not even any of his men.

She went back to her apartment and cried.

She cried because he was gone and she would never see him again. She cried for being so silly about a man she knew nothing about other than her own assumptions about him. She cried because she felt she was cheating on her husband even though he'd been gone forever before she'd ever met Kaelan. She cried, allowing herself to wallow in self-pity. She cried for being so pathetic.

She fell asleep crying.

Chapter 6

Living on her own for the first time since her husband's death was an enormous learning curve for Sarah. She hadn't lived by herself for long between leaving home and meeting him, and once they'd become a couple they had done everything together. Now, it all just seemed so difficult, but she persevered in her struggles despite her distinct lack of interest in anything since that last day at the paintball range.

During the past eleven months she successfully passed her scooter lessons and renewed her driver's licence, successfully completed her nail tech course and got a job working in a beauty salon. When she wasn't working she locked herself away in her apartment. There she read, watched TV and movies, did a variety of puzzles and got on the net.

Even on the net, she found it difficult to make friends and discovered even there she couldn't not be shy. Occasionally, she would just stare out the window not thinking of anything... or at least, tried not to. She didn't even go away for holidays, even when she was forced to take them by her boss.

When she did go out to shop and minor treats of cinema or eating out, no one came near her. If they walked past, they either cleared the way or bumped into her as if deliberately trying to knock her over. No one looked at her and smiled or said hi. Suffice to say she rarely went out and became more withdrawn. She didn't even have a pet of any kind. Only because she wasn't allowed one in the apartment by the owner.

The only bonus to such an existence like that was she barely spent any money. It just sat in her account earning interest and paying taxes on that interest.

'Yeah, not much of a life. Not much to live for.' She felt. 'I think it's called passive suicide. Very passive.' She sighed.

'Maybe I'll start my own nail business. Maybe.'

Chapter 7

It was the end of February and Sarah was still getting used to having recently turned 25, as well as having packed on more weight because she was no longer active like she used to be.

'My ankles are still the same, but then the doctors did say there would be nothing more they could do. My dizzy spells are the same as always... unpredictable. Other than that, I'm just peachy keen.' She thought miserably to herself.

She now owned her own nail bar, renting floor space in a hair salon, doing people's nails. Having saved for the past sixteen months, she certainly had the money to set it all up. The business has been active for the past two months and she seemed to be doing well.

She'd started setting the business up a few months ago. After a lot of paperwork, running around, setting up accounts and automated payments, and buying of equipment and supplies, it was the most active she'd been in ages.

Her social life hadn't changed however. She had a chatting friendship with those in the salon, but only when she was there. After work... No one was interested. No matter how polite, chatty and nice she was. It would seem she was just too quiet and dull for their liking. A guess on her part naturally.

Also, Sarah bought herself the Yamaha T-Max 500 in deep red as a birthday present to herself a couple of weeks ago.

'I so love it.' She thought to herself, almost bouncing on the spot with excitement as she checked it out yet again after riding it home.

In addition, a few months ago, her life took on another change she hadn't been planning on. 'But that's how it usually goes right?' It was due to a chance meeting one partially foggy evening last year...

Having her own nail bar in a corner of a hair salon, which was inside a large shopping centre, had its ups and downs. The up side was plenty of clients. The down side in that situation was that the shopping centre was open till 9:00pm and so was the hair salon.

That meant so was she, due to clients wanting their nails done, even at that late hour. Worse was, still being winter at that point, it was completely dark by 6:00pm if not earlier.

'Hell, even if it was summer it would still be dark by 7-7:30pm. So no matter what, come 9:00pm, it's definitely dark by the time I get to go home.'

That particular evening was foggy and she was limping home after an extremely busy day. She had had more walk-ins than usual for some reason. Combine that with the noise of the busy shopping centre, with its screaming kids, just made the whole day long and tedious.

Trudging through thick patches of fog, she had to pass an estate on her way. It had a narrow pass-way between two houses to allow people living in that area access to the main road without having to go the long way. Head down and swamped with exhaustion, she heard a noise then a whimper. Sarah stumbled to a stop and peered into the night to see what it was.

"...ya freak!" She heard from one of three guys who had a woman backed against a narrow trunk of a young tree. At least, Sarah thought it looked like a woman since she had breasts and was wearing a dress.

The whimpering, pleading, was coming from the cornered woman.

While the woman appeared to be an adult, the other three looked young, in their early to mid-teens. One of the boys shoved her. The other two laughed then one of those two punched her when the shove staggered her towards him.

Despite the fact there wasn't much Sarah could do, she started hobbling as quickly as she could towards them and started waving her walking stick like sword or club and started yelling at them.

"Hey you little shits! Leave her the hell alone or you'll get to know what it's like yourselves." Sarah was so pumped up she, didn't stop to think about what she was doing, even though she was scared witless they would turn against her as well that.

The three boys paused, stared at Sarah then ran off.

'Amazing! It worked. Hell, I didn't think I could be that intimidating; small, overweight and limping like I am.'

Then she turned towards the woman. She didn't have enough grasp on herself to hide her surprise when she saw the creature's features then watched them as they changed back into the woman she was. Finally reaching her, Sarah held out her hand.

The woman she had rescued happened to be a therian of some

kind. She couldn't make out any features or colours in the dark. Only a muzzle and some fur. Then the woman changed back into a woman. Being dark, combined with two huge trucks rumbling past at that point, Sarah couldn't see the change clearly and definitely couldn't hear.

"Come on, let's get out of here before they decide I'm not so scary after all. Where can I escort you to?" Sarah's voice came out breathless and shaky after a small pause. She was shakier from the encounter with the boys than from coming face to face with someone in therian form.

The slim dark haired young woman stared at Sarah's hand for a moment as they both shivered from a gust of wintery wind. Then she placed her hand in Sarah's – both of them shaking like a leaf from the encounter as well as winter – and Sarah helped her to her feet while trying not to lose her own balance.

"Th-th-thank you s-s-s-so m-much. I'm h-h-heading just up the r-road that w-way." The young woman – she appeared to be about the same age as Sarah – stammered, indicating the way Sarah had just come from.

Mentally, Sarah groaned at having to double back. Outwardly, she smiled and walked as fast as she could as she escorted the woman across Manly Road and into Hargreaves Road passed the shopping centre. Fifteen minutes later, due to Sarah's slow pace, the timid young woman was knocking on the door of a two storey pale brick house in a large yard that could fit two more houses in it.

The door opened and a tall slim attractive man with short dark straight hair and olive complexion glanced at the two women before settling his gaze upon the woman Sarah had saved.

"Hillie, what happened?" He exclaimed in a rush as he ushered the pair of them in. He had a slight accent but Sarah couldn't place it. However, she now knew the woman's name.

Unfortunately, by that point Sarah was so exhausted she didn't hear what the woman said. The adrenalin had worn off, combined with the long day and many hours since she had last eaten, Sarah no longer had the strength for anything else. Embarrassingly, as far as she was concerned, it must have been noticeable.

"Whoa there Miss. Here, sit down." His hands gently guided her to a seat and helped her to sit.

"Thank you." She murmured softly and slumped back into the seat with her eyes closed. 'A dangerous thing that. It leads to sleep before one's ready for it. I still have to get home.' However, a hand gripped hers and that contact forced her eyes open.

"No, thank you. It was so foolishly brave of you to save Hillie like that. The both of you are extremely lucky." His hands were so warm.

"Antonio, what are you doing to that poor woman? Can't you see she needs a cup of tea before anything else?"

With more effort that she would like to admit, Sarah glanced up to see a woman her age or a little older coming towards them. She was taller than Sarah, slimmer and much prettier than her as far as she was concerned. The woman's shoulder length hair was as dark as his with her complexion almost the same olive tone as his. Her slightly stronger accent hinted at Italian maybe and, with a name like Antonio, she guessed he was probably Italian as well.

"You see to Hillie's injuries and I'll tend to this young lady."

She bustled then turned her attention to Sarah. "I'm Maria and I apologise for my husband's lack of manners." She clucked softly as she handed Sarah a hot cup of tea with enough sugar and milk in it to make her taste buds happy.

"Thank you. I'm Sarah" She murmured tiredly and sipped the tea.

"Honey, what possessed you to step into the fray like that when you could have been hurt or worse?"

Regardless of being exhausted, Sarah suspected what Maria was referring to when she said 'or worse'. Hearing the boys call Hillie a 'freak', Sarah had guessed the woman was a therian before she had decided to help her.

"Apart from not really thinking about the situation at all, I just couldn't let them hurt her. It's wrong and against the law to discriminate. Even against therians." In spite of the cup of tea, she couldn't stop sounding tired.

Maria didn't say anything but Sarah thought she saw surprise flit briefly across the woman's face. "Well, drink up Dear and I'll get Antonio to drive you home."

'What a wonderful thought.' However...

"Oh no, he doesn't have to. I don't live too far away."

'When will I learn to keep my mouth shut?' She mentally sighed at herself.

"Nonsense. You can barely hold that cup of tea let alone be expected to walk to the door just there. Now, no arguing."

Sarah nodded her capitulation. Mutely, she was extremely grateful.

Maria left her side and spoke to Antonio. She didn't hear what they were saying to each other and, at that point in time, she didn't care. Once she had finished her cup of tea and Hillie had been spirited away to some other part of the building – which at first she thought was a home but the inside was more like a business – Antonio grabbed her hand and helped her to stand. While managing not to groan, she couldn't suppress the wince of pain. Thankfully, no one said anything.

After Maria hugged her goodbye, which surprised the hell out of Sarah, Antonio escorted her to his car and helped her in. A moment or two later they were on their way. While it was silent between them at first, it didn't stay that way for long.

"You're in a lot of pain there. Do you need a doctor?" He asked as he pulled up to a set of lights, indicating to turn right at her instruction.

"No thank you Antonio, there's nothing they can do anymore. Only pain killers and rest will help."

After a pause...

"Call me Tonio, Tony or Ant, Luv. It was nice of you to help Hillie. So few of the unaltereds would even consider it once they knew the victim was a therian or vamp."

"Okay Tony." She then sighed and stared out the window as he drove down Manly Road.

"That's the trouble with the human race. They scream blue murder when no one comes to help them yet it doesn't occur to them that if they helped others then maybe others will help them in return. I've never discriminated and I won't let them being a vamp or therian or some other nationality start me doing so now." She paused then glanced at Antonio.

It appeared that her response surprised him.

"What is that place? Since it's not a house like I'd first thought." Tired or not she was curious.

"That's the Queensland Therian League's... or QTL... help line and meeting venue."

"Help line?" She had her suspicions but had to ask.

"Yeah. During times of the new and full moons new therians can get themselves into trouble. Hell, any time really. So, we have a help line they can call where older, more controlled therians can be sent to them to save them from a nasty situation where they could end up executed for having accidentally killed an unaltered. We're always understaffed despite the amount of vamps and therians in Brisbane."

"Would you like another volunteer?" With a nervousness she always felt when asking questions, her voice came out so quiet she was sure he wouldn't have heard her. She needn't have worried.

His head quickly turned towards her, looking at her intently before turning his eyes back to the road. The last couple of minutes of the drive were done in silence. Slowly he pulled up outside her apartment building then turned to face her.

"Are you sure you want to volunteer?" His voice was a mix of curiosity and surprise.

"Of course I'm sure. Yes I am scared but I'm like that when I open my nail bar for clients every day." She sighed and glanced at her hands then looked back up at him.

"I'm a shy person Tony, and find it hard to mix in with people. So, that's my biggest concern strangely enough." She silently cursed herself as her voice dwindled to a barely audible murmur.

Antonio just stared at her for a long moment and she thought he was going to decline her offer. Then he reached into his back pocket, grabbed his wallet, pulled something from it and handed it to her. Looking at it, she realised it was a business card.

"Think about it, seriously, and if you're absolutely certain then call me when you have some free time."

"Thank you Tony, I will."

When she opened the car door, he rushed out and helped her out of the car and to her front door.

"Thank you." She said again.

"You're welcome Sarah and thank you once again."

With that, he was gone and she was inside. She took pain killers then went to bed.

*

When she woke up the next morning she searched the word therian and the following was what she found...

Therianthropy – from the Greek therion meaning wild animal or beast, and anthropos meaning human being. While the words therian and therianthropy were never commonly used words, after much discussion and finally a voting session it was decided to use those words to refer to all were-creatures as the word lycan refers only to wolves. Due to were-wolves being outnumbered by the rest of the were-creatures combined, they lost the vote. Therefore, in mid to late 1993, the words therian and therianthropy became a regular part of the spoken language around the world. However, all groups refuse to list themselves as shifters because they don't change into full animal form.

...She sat back and thought about what she had just read. While there was more information, she decided to read the rest of it later.

Thinking about it all, Sarah started rearranging her schedule so half of her evenings were clear and so were her days of the new and full moon. Once she was sure it would all work, she called Antonio to confirm being a volunteer and then let him know what dates she was available for.

On her first night there, Antonio and Maria welcomed her and introduced her around. Others on the help line were a mix of unaltereds and therians. However, unaltereds were few on the help line. As for vampires, if they were there then it was whenever she wasn't. About a third of the time she was the only unaltered. Eventually, she became the only constant unaltered there on a weekly basis.

When Sarah had met up with Hillie again she, yet again, expressed her gratitude and they became friends. Soon after that, she discovered Hillie was a were-fox. Through Hillie, Maria and Antonio she was introduced to the world of the Therians and that was how she ended up volunteering to answer phones for them. It freed other therians so they would be able to go out and help each other without worrying about no one being at the phones.

Sarah also did some more research about therians in general but especially those of Brisbane.

Apparently, for the past twelve years or more, the were-creatures of Brisbane had banded together to provide support to each other in times of need, as well as setting up a committee to deal with any form of politics that would arise.

The concept originated from the United States some twenty to twenty-five years ago. Some thought it might have started in Europe, but the majority of them were still fairly superstitious about therians back then. Sydney and Melbourne were the first to start up their branches of the organisation in Australia.

Brisbane already had a small unofficial group but set themselves up officially after Sydney and Melbourne had. Then the other states followed. Western Australia and Northern Territory were set up a little differently. As to how...? She didn't know. However, Queensland actually had three branches: Brisbane, Rockhampton and Cairns.

That was basically all she knew about the Therian League at that point in time. She would eventually learn more as one tended to do when involved in the subject. But for now, she let her life settle into its new routine.

The day was muggy and warm, the last day of summer, that's why she was sitting outside one of the seaside cafes in the Wynnum/Manly area. A breeze blew off the water as she watched yachts, seagulls and pelicans bob around on the grey-green water. She was grateful to that breeze or the day would have been unbearable.

She'd just managed to get a table when a man walked out of the cafe with his order, looking for a seat. He walked towards her.

"Hi, okay if I share your table?"

He had a typical boater's tan, skin peeling, alternating between sunburnt and tanned. His eyes were the same colour as hers, but his hair was sun bleached blonde... thick and wavy, touching his collar. He was of medium build and very fit looking. His hands were calloused and were obviously used to hard work.

"Help yourself, plenty of room." She said quietly then resumed eating her lunch and keeping her eyes down as her shyness kicked in.

"Thanks, I'm Abel." He said as he sat and offered his hand to shake.

She ducked her head to hide the smile at his words.

"What? What's so funny?" He frowned and slowly took back his hand.

"I'm sorry. I'm Sarah and just wondering if you were willing as well. Just my whacked sense of humour." She said softly and blushed as she offered her hand to him.

Abel laughed as he took her hand and shook it, "I'm only willing to my wife." He said with a wiggle of his eyebrows. They both laughed.

The two of them ate their lunches and chatted. Abel and his wife, Brandi, have been married for seven years now and enjoyed their weekends away north west of Brisbane, near Caboolture, on a huge piece of property they'd bought a couple of years ago.

"You and your husband should come over for dinner this weekend. Brandi would love to meet you."

Sarah looked down at her hands and played with the wedding ring she still wore. The only times she had taken it off was during the paintball games because she hadn't wanted to lose it.

"My husband died 3 years ago." She said softly.

"I'm sorry Sarah. I didn't mean to put my foot in it."

"It's okay Abel. You had no way of knowing."

"Well, the invite is still there if you would like to come." He offered gently.

She didn't bother thinking too hard about it as she really was in need of a social life.

"Sure. When and where?" She said with a small shy smile.

After noting the details…

"Well, I've got to get back to work." He rolled his eyes with a smile.

Sarah and Abel stood up, said farewell until Friday night and went their separate ways.

She turned to leave when she saw a white Jeep Grand Cherokee heading down the road towards her. She couldn't see the number plate well enough, but some of the characters seemed the same from what she remembered. She peered at the windows, but light glared off the windscreen so she couldn't see the driver and the windows were tinted.

The Jeep slowed, but continued forward. Thinking about it, it could have slowed due to nearing the pedestrian crossing but that thought wouldn't occur to her until much later that day.

"Kaelan?" She whispered, but the Jeep never stopped. Gripping her walking stick tightly and clenching her left hand into a fist, she chastised herself as she turned, her gaze following the Jeep down the Esplanade.

'Jeeps are common in Brisbane, especially white ones, so his wouldn't be the only one.' That thought didn't stop her chest from tightening up. 'I so thought I had gotten over him. It seems I'm wrong. After a year and a half, I am so wrong.'

The rest of the day was a downer at the reminder of Kaelan and the knowledge of the traitorous escapees she had for hormones were running riot and free once more and informing her they... she... still had a thing for him.

In Brisbane briefly to meet up with a friend from years ago, Kaelan couldn't have asked for a better looking day to be by the seaside. They had agreed to meet down near the Manly wading pool. He had decided to enjoy his short time off and arrived earlier than planned, to take advantage of the views before meeting up with his friend. It was one of the few places he didn't mind watching people as they tended to be a little more or less, depending on how one looked at it, interesting.

It was a weekday and there was still a reasonable amount of traffic on the streets as others with time off had the same idea of a seaside jaunt without leaving the capital city. Passing one of the many seaside cafes, Kaelan caught sight of two people standing up out of the corner of his eye. Normally he wouldn't have bothered, but something was familiar about one of them, so he slowed down to have a better look at them.

"Well, I'll be! It's her, but she's with another man." He muttered in surprise, followed by disappointment then annoyance at his reaction. He kept watching her as he passed slowly by. Kaelan noted the man leaving and as she turned around she paused as she noted his jeep.

'Wonder if she can see me? Somehow I don't think so. Huh! Seems like, after nineteen months, she still remembers me despite the new love life.' He watched her stare at the Jeep as he went past. He didn't stop.

Even though the man she was with was gone he didn't want to know about the new man in her life. However, if that man was the new love of her life then her reaction to seeing the Jeep confused him.

Kaelan tore his eyes from the side mirrors just as one particular scar gave a slight twinge of an ache. He sighed and continued on to meet up with his friend. Seeing her just emphasised his need to talk about the situation.

A few minutes later, he pulled up at a seaside parking bay, stopping next to a dark green Nissan Pajero and saw his friend was already there and was looking good. It seemed like his friend had the same idea about seeing the scenery. Kaelan smiled as he walked towards his friend

"Ed, you old dog, how the hell are you? Oh, and congrats on making Captain a few months back."

"Ha, late as always, but thanks. Doing great, but was surprised to receive a text from you though. How long has it been and how are you Kael?" Ed smiled as the two men thumped each other on the back.

"Too long, but not dead so doing well." Kaelan smiled but even he knew it didn't reach his eyes. It rarely did anymore.

"You may not be dead, but I can see you're not doing that well. What's wrong Kael?"

Just like that, Ed had Kaelan's ticket. But then, they did grow up together and was the only person to truly know him. Kaelan stared out at the water watching yachts, seagulls and pelicans bobbing as they moved with the ripples and waves. He had no idea on how to start.

"Kael?" Ed asked in a low voice. His concern could be heard.

"I'm lost Ed and I don't know what to do about it. She's gotten in so deep I didn't even see it happen, and now it looks like she has another man." The words just came tumbling out as Kaelan continued to stare out over the water.

'Smooth Kaelan, real smooth. Not the way I'd wanted to start this discussion.' Kaelan chastised himself harshly.

"Tell me about her." Despite being surprised at his friend's words, Ed kept his tone quiet.

Kaelan snorted, part in amusement and part in frustration. He looked down at his hands on the table then up at Ed.

"She's tiny, overweight, greyish blue eyes, mousey dark brown hair with natural red highlights in the sun, fair untanned complexion, damaged ankles and walks with a cane and a limp, highly emotional and like a... a... scared tiny baby bunny, and, yet, she's 'killed' me twice on a paintball range. I even got myself injured because I was thinking about her while on a job."

Ed started looking amused as his childhood friend told him about her then he stared in amazement at the reason for the injury.

"Oh man, are you doomed big time." Then he laughed. He couldn't help it. Never had Ed seen his friend in such a state where the opposite sex was concerned.

Kaelan frowned at him. 'What a cheek, the bugger!'

"How long have you known her?" Ed asked still grinning.

"I've seen her a total of five times when I bailed out on what would have been the sixth encounter with her. That was over a year and a half ago." Kaelan said still frowning at his friend.

'I hadn't heard anything funny in what I'd told him.' He mentally grumped.

"Oh yeah, you are totally doomed. Hook, line and sinker Boy." He said, still grinning.

Kaelan groaned and dropped his head on his arms.

"I so didn't want to hear that. Why her for fuck sake? Out of all the women I've been with over the years, only to have found them so damned tedious I'd wanted to kill them, why her?" He looked pleadingly up at Ed. Both men knew Kaelan wouldn't have killed the women even though they knew he could get away with it.

Ed sighed.

"I don't know Kael. There must be something about her which appeals to what's left of your heart you tried to bury years ago."

Ed gazed at Kaelan intently and Kaelan didn't know what Ed was expecting to see.

"Don't go there Ed. Please." Was the dead-pan warning.

"I take that to mean you still haven't talked about that night to anyone?" Getting no response of any kind, Ed exclaimed in frustration at his childhood friend.

"Damn it Kael! Fifteen years is a long time to never talk about it."

While there was no accusation in his tone, Kaelan could hear the beginnings of obvious concern. He just stared at Ed, his eyes going cold. It was not a subject Kaelan wanted to discuss. Ever!

"Don't Kael. Not at me. You and I are all we have left. You cut me out and you'll be lost forever and I'll never recover from the cause and the effect." Ed pleaded with him.

Kaelan sighed and let his head collapse onto his arms again.

'He's right. I know it even if I don't want to admit it, but none of it makes it any easier.' He raised his head again.

"I'm sorry Ed. She's knocked my world upside down and I don't know how to fix it because I don't know how she did it in the first place. To top it all off, I haven't seen her for a year and a half and she's still in my mind."

Ed gently gripped his friend's arm, "Tell me about her Kael. Start at the beginning."

So, Kaelan revisited his first encounter with her at the range, as well as the rest, in his re-telling of it to Ed.

Talking to Ed about her hadn't really helped him all that much as she still haunted his thoughts. Just not on the job any more. Ed's advice to go see her was one Kaelan just couldn't bring himself to do. Surprisingly, and confusingly, still no one had come close to killing him for real or otherwise; plenty of injuries though. That alone suggested to him she was a professional.

Again, pushing himself hard, he took as many jobs as he could before his body forced him to take time off. He didn't even let the weather interfere. In the efforts to keep her out of his thoughts he went from freezing to being baked alive. He didn't do any of it to see the country as he had already seen it a number of times long before he first saw her.

Even on his down times Kaelan kept himself busy around his second home, in Noosa Heads north of Brisbane, as he stayed away from Brisbane as much as he could. So much so his second home was back to immaculate condition after years of neglect.

Strangely, even by that point in time, it hadn't even occurred to him to have his contacts keep an eye on her because he spent his time trying to forget her.

Chapter 8

With Abel's address programmed into the GPS that was attached to her scooter, Sarah headed north west towards Caboolture. She suspected it would be a weekend stay so had extra clothes packed just in case, along with a large bottle of Bailey's Irish Cream. She would buy a 3ltr bottle of milk, cream and cola...

'For when I don't feel like drinking alcohol.'

...when she was closer to her destination. It was a beautiful March day, glorious to be riding.

Before she left home, however, Sarah had decided to take off her wedding ring and place it on her necklace. Until Abel had invited her and her husband to this weekend away she had never given thought to how she would feel at having to explain why her husband wouldn't be joining her. While she wasn't ashamed, far from it in fact, it was the emotional pain of vocalising her loss that spurred her into finally removing the ring from her finger.

'Thank goodness for the scooter!' She thought as she turned onto the property. They had one of the longest, windiest driveways she had ever been on.

'I can't walk to the letterbox without plenty of rest stops and a bag of food to munch on there and back to the house. Shee-oot, it was a day outing all by itself. Okay, okay, I'm just carrying on, but honestly, it does seem that long.'

After parking the scooter, she walked to the front door with helmet in hand. She left her clothes in the top box, but grabbed the drinks to see her through the night, then rang the doorbell. The butterflies were fluttering around inside her. Being outside her comfort zone had obviously set them off.

'Silly little critters. Me nervous? Hell yeah.'

A minute or two later the door opened and a woman a few inches taller than Sarah smiled, "Sarah? I'm Brandi. Come on in."

"Hi and yeah I'm Sarah." she shyly smiled.

Brandi was slim, tanned with shoulder length brown hair that had sun-bleached streaks framing a lovely set of sparkling dark hazel eyes that had flecks of brown and yellow through them. She was dressed in a simple sundress that was pre-dominantly white with little yellow flowers with bright green leaves all over it.

She looked at the bag in Sarah's hand and said, "While I like your sense of priorities, is that all you brought with you? No clothing?" She asked with a frown.

"I have clothing in the top box of my scooter." Sarah said quietly, thumbing back at the scooter.

"Oh, good girl." She smiled as she took the bag from Sarah with her left hand and looped her right through Sarah's left arm. "We'll send one of the boys out for it later." She said with a wicked smile as she made her way through the house. "Come this way Sarah. Hmmm... I do hope you have cooler clothing in that top box of yours instead of more of what you are currently wearing."

Sarah chuckled, "Yes I do, no fear. These leathers are only for protection while riding." While she was nervous she was surprised and pleased when Brandi didn't comment about her... disability. She hated the word but it was the right word. Obviously Abel had told Brandi all about her.

"Wonderful, well, this way to the kitchen and we'll put your drinks into the fridge." Brandi led the way.

The two women came across Abel, dressed in simple mid to dark grey knee-length shorts and a light teal green t-shirt, at the breakfast bar and he gave Sarah a hug.

"So glad you could make it Babe. Come on through. Want something to drink?"

Sarah couldn't believe how they were accepting her so openly, so quickly. No one had ever done that other than her husband and his dad when the man had been alive.

"Sure, I brought some Baileys, milk and cream to mix together and some cola for when I don't want any more alcohol." She replied softly. The butterflies still hadn't settled down.

"Oho, just love a woman who comes prepared. How do you want your Baileys?" Abel chuckled as he waggled a glass.

"Double shot of Baileys with a single shot of cream and topped up with milk please." Sarah had expected Abel to open her bottle of Baileys, but he went to the pantry, grabbed their own bottle, and made three drinks all the same.

"Just have to try it like this. Usually drink it straight." Abel said.

"Apart from being creamier, I usually have it this way so the Baileys last longer. It also allows me to drink longer and I don't fall to sleep so soon." She explained with a blush and chuckle.

Years ago, someone had criticised the way she drank her Baileys, calling it pathetic and some other choice words. She'd stopped hanging around with them.

'I just don't happen agree with trashing others choices of beverages just because I might not happen to like it.' She thought to herself.

"Ice or no ice Babe?" Abel asked.

"Ice please." She said with a smile plastered to her face. She had to keep it plastered for a little while longer. She just wasn't used to being treated this nicely by anyone so quickly.

Abel handed Sarah her drink after giving each glass a quick mixing and adding ice.

"Hey, not bad. Means we wouldn't go through the Baileys too quickly. Don't know about the longevity of the cream though."

The three of them laughed. Abel and Brandi then showed Sarah around the place.

It was huge with exposed beams. The exposed beams were all done in bloodwood (so she was told) – a deep pinkish red, with the rest of the walls and ceilings done in a smooth plaster finish in cream with a very faint pinkish hue to them. Four bedrooms, two offices, a sewing room, a hobbies room, an enormous room set up as a library with floor to ceiling bookcases chockers with books of varying sizes, thicknesses and colours.

Sarah's favourite room so far; the library. The kitchen was the largest she'd ever seen outside of a large restaurant and was all modern with a brushed metal finish. They also had a games room, lounge room (with a real wood burning fireplace), media room and their own personal gym room. Suffice to say the house was two storeys. All bedrooms and the sewing room were upstairs, everything else downstairs.

They next took her outside onto a back patio that had a large twelve-seater metal-trimmed glass table and a barbecue that had all the bells and whistles. The backyard was breathtaking. Australian native plants everywhere – not even any weeds, no foreign plants at all, surrounded three sides of an in-ground pool made to look like a natural large pond with a waterfall at the deep end.

No stairs at the shallow end, just grass then the pool sloping down into the water. As stated, it was all made to look like a natural lake-like pond. The shell of the pool had been painted a sandy colour with flecks of earthy reds and browns. A smaller matching spa pool was just off the side near the middle of the pool length on the side nearest the plant line.

Sarah was so in heaven.

"Oh my... This is so beautiful. If you can tolerate me you have a friend for life." chuckling as she said in awe.

Brandi dramatically grabbed at her heart and widened her eyes, "Loved only for our home. How... devastating." The effect was ruined by the smile that slowly spread across her face. It would seem that her personality was the opposite to Sarah's... bubbly, outgoing and open.

Abel just grinned, "Glad you like it Babe. We're quite pleased with it as well."

"Like it? I love it. It's a piece of paradise. Both outside and inside your home. I can't imagine it looking any other way. Your library is awesome as well." She stated breathlessly with her astonishment obvious.

Then the three of them sat down at the table on the patio and just chatted, slowly getting to know each other. They nibbled on crackers and cheese, fruit and drank whatever they felt like at the time. As Sarah looked around the yard and the screen of native plants around the pool area she saw a space between two callistemon viminalis – red flowering Weeping Bottlebrushes. She only knew what they were because she'd helped researched them not so long ago for one of the ladies at the hairdressers. 'Curious how I hadn't seen that gap earlier.'

"Where does that path between the two callistemons go?" She asked.

"Oh, that leads to a manicured garden and past it is natural bushland. We'll show you around that area tomorrow morning." Brandi said with a big smile.

"Sweet, I would love that."

Both Brandi and Abel worked for a big insurance company in Brisbane city itself, but didn't go into much detail about it, and were avid yachters. Whenever they could they went yachting where others would go to the movies or other outings. They had no children and were only just starting to plan for them. They did mention that the house and property were theirs free and clear.

Throughout the afternoon, the three of them chatted. It wasn't until the doorbell rang did Sarah notice how much time had passed. It was dark. She hadn't noticed that before and didn't remember anyone rising to turn the patio's lights on.

Abel went to answer the door as she peeked at her watch and noted that it was 8:00pm, over an hour after the sun had set. After a few minutes, Abel walked through the door with another man. Sarah silently groan to herself.

'Oh no… I smell a setup here.' She sighed. 'Oh well.' Then plastered a small smile on her face.

He was about the same height as Abel, not that Sarah knew how tall Abel was. All she knew was that Abel was taller than Brandi, who was taller than her, making the newcomer tall as well. His build was slim and if he had muscles, then they were hidden by his clothing. His skin was whiter than Sarah's, which was really saying something. She was pale by normal standards.

She'd never seen a man with such pale skin before. His hair was thick, black, wavy and short enough that it didn't touch his collar yet. As for his eyes, she's never seen a colour like them before. They were almost a brown, but seemed too yellow or maybe orange – 'or maybe they were swirls of the yellow or orange… I just can't make it out clearly enough' – with what looked like streaks of… red??

'Wow.'

"Sarah… Daniel. We'll let the two of you get acquainted while Brandi and I start dinner." Abel said with a smile as he and Brandi walked away.

Sarah held out her hand and said "Hi."

"Hi and call me Danny." He smiled.

When their hands touched, she was shocked to discover how cold it felt. Her mouth fell open slightly as she stared wide eyed up at him. Maybe her feared showed as Danny started to remove his hand and his expression went from smiling to neutral. She held his hand a little tighter.

"I'm sorry," She started, "but I've never seen, or met, a vampire before. It's just a surprise that's all." This time she let his hand go.

"Well, there is always a first time for everything." He had become cautious.

"Yes there is. Please sit." She said as she indicated at the chair next to her.

"You are not afraid?"

'Yep, I must have had a bit of fear showing.'

"Of course I am, but that doesn't mean I have to be rude and not treat you like a person. I may not be able to control a lot of my fears, but it doesn't mean I'm going to run screaming from the place." She responded softly.

"Thank you for your honesty. Why are you afraid? Is it just me, what I am or just vampires in general?"

"You're welcome." Sarah thought about his question before answering, "I guess I'm afraid because you, as in vampires, because you guys are the ultimate predators and we're your food source since synthetic blood hasn't been perfected yet. Vampires started as human once so you know how we behave and are able to hunt us in our own elements, unlike other predators.

"While the majority would never attack us just for food, it doesn't stop me from being afraid." She paused slightly, "Please don't take this the wrong way, but I'm scared of ants as well. Not just because they're small and numerous and get everywhere, but because they're capable of stripping the carcass of something so much larger than themselves. They too are predators. Size and intelligence has nothing to do with it." She felt herself blush at her speech and it took all her effort not to squirm in her seat.

"Well, that was highly refreshing..."

"Now you're teasing me." She wasn't good enough to keep the

hurt out of her voice as she stared at her hands in her lap. She was embarrassed enough as it was.

Danny gently took her hand in his and Sarah looked up at him.

"I am not teasing you. So many who meet me either hate me and want to destroy me or want to go to bed with me to boast to their friends they have been with one of us. It is refreshing to meet someone who is willing to try and treat us as if we are normal people."

Danny let go of her hand and sat back.

They chatted about anything and everything, and nothing in particular for the following forty-five minutes. Just the typically safe topics two people talk and ask about when they first meet, especially when one of them was shy.

Finally, Brandi and Abel came out with dinner and drinks. The four of them sat, ate (except Danny), drank and talked the night away. For the most part Sarah sat there listening to the three of them. Occasionally she would join in but the majority of her contributions were either smiles or chuckles. But the reality was, she just didn't know enough to be able to comment, actively join in on the conversations and she was too shy to ask questions.

Abel and Brandi went to bed sometime around 1:00am. Danny and Sarah stayed up quietly chatting with long companionable pauses as they watched the night pass. During those silent moments, they listened to the nightlife and watched bats, cats, possums and other creatures when they weren't gazing up at the stars. As dawn started creeping up from the east, Danny stood up.

"I am sorry, but I have to go inside, and hopefully get some sleep. Thank you for the lovely evening and for staying up with me. Although, you do look rather beat yourself." Danny said with a chuckle.

"My pleasure Danny. I..." She said with a smile and then let her voice and smile dwindle away to nothing. 'Just once I would like to not feel embarrassed about something, anything.'

"What, Sarah?" Danny asked softly.

"I know we've only just met but would it be okay if I watched you fall asleep?" Her voice faded away to barely a whisper by the end of such a personal and intimate question. She knew she was blushing so badly. However, she was curious. But, not only that, she sensed loneliness in him.

"I would like that. I spend so much of my time alone that it would be really nice to have someone else there as I fell asleep." Danny confirmed with a smile as he held his arm out to her. "Mind you, we do not have to sleep, but I am not my best right now, so I will more than likely end up sleeping."

She took Danny's arm with her left hand and, as they passed the kitchen, Sarah grabbed her walking stick. She caught the end of his look of surprise, but he didn't ask any questions and she didn't volunteer any answers.

The pair went upstairs to his bedroom and she helped him close the curtains covering two sets of windows. She could see why they put him in that particular room, the curtains were heavier and made the room dark when closed.

Danny started to undress and she hurriedly turned her back to him, feeling a flush creeping over her face. What she saw of his chest looked nice; subtly muscled. She heard him chuckle.

"It is safe to turn around now." He said with a smile.

She faced him with a sheepish grin, biting her bottom lip. He was under the covers, his chest bare, but she knew he was wearing pyjama pants because she had seen them on his bed. She walked over and sat on the edge of the bed.

"What's it like? Do you fall asleep like a normal person? Or is it like something else?" She asked in a whisper, afraid to ask any louder.

"It depends on our physical condition at the time. If we are uninjured or have not expended too much energy, then we do not have to sleep and we tend to drift off just like an average person. If we are injured or have expended too much energy, then, yes, we do need to sleep. When we have to, it is not like falling asleep. As the sun rises above the horizon, it feels like a great pressure on the chest. It does not hurt per se, but it is not a pleasant feeling either. Then nothing; until I awake. Length of sleep will depend on how injured, or how much energy we have expended." He responded softly. He took hold of her hand, gently at first, and they watched the light brightening behind the closed curtains.

He gripped her hand a little tighter and held for a little longer than was comfortable. She watched his face and saw a fleeting grimace, then his face went slack and his breath left his mouth in a soft whoosh. His hand loosened its grip on hers and she slipped her hand out of his. She sat there watching him while flexing her fingers.

She didn't know how many minutes had passed, but she finally saw his chest move with a single beat of his heart, then stillness to wait for the next beat. It was a bit of a fright the first time and she jumped a little, but she stayed to watch for one more beat before she crept out of his room. With her mind too tired for any real thought, Sarah was just closing his door when

Brandi, then Abel, walked out of their room.

"Morning." She said softly, leaning heavily on her walking stick. Now, she was so tired she could barely keep standing.

"Morning." They choroused softly at her.

"You look like you haven't slept yet Sweetie." Brandi frowned.

"Danny and I spent the night talking out on the patio until dawn and then I sat on the bed with him until he fell asleep."

"Then off to bed with you and we'll show you the garden when you get up." Abel said with his usual big smile.

Tired as she was, she was rather surprised they so willingly believed her. 'Have I been hanging around with the wrong sort of people all these years? Ugh! I'm just too tired to think through such things.' She watched them as they headed down stairs then she slowly and painfully made her way to her assigned room and collapsed into bed without undressing.

*

She awoke to a warm stuffy room. Turning her head, she watched as the clock changed to 12:00pm. Sarah groaned as she swung her legs over the side. Six hours of broken sleep, of tossing and turning. She tried to remember the last time she had unbroken sleep.

Sitting there for about five minutes thinking about it and she realised it had been well over thirteen years. Not including hospital time that is. She slumped where she sat.

'Sometimes I so hate my life.' Then she mentally abused herself for the self-pity and grabbed the walking stick, clothes from the top box that Abel must have brought in for her at some stage that morning and headed to the bathroom.

Forty-five minutes later, she was downstairs with a cup of tea in her hand and chatting with Brandi, while Abel was organising lunch. The day was clear and warm with white and light grey clouds racing across it. Every now and then a puff of fresh air wafted in, only to disappear again for a little while.

"So, what were you and Danny talking about that you didn't get to bed till just after dawn?" Abel asked as he came out with lunch.

"Oh, anything and everything. I... think... he was just glad of another person to treat him as a person. Seems like that doesn't happen often?" Sarah said, giving the last part a questioning lilt.

"Yeah, that's why he likes coming here. Some of our other friends don't quite treat him as normal and the poor man does try hard to act normal." Brandi responded.

"How did you pair meet him?"

"We were at a restaurant being our normal selves when Brandi saw him looking at us with a sort of wistful look on his face. She pointed him out to me so we beckoned him over and included him. We're shameless like that." Abel finished with a chuckle.

"Oh, I've noticed." Sarah said with a smile. "That's how I came to be here after all." A big grin spread across her face. And she truly was grateful to their openness. If they weren't then she wouldn't be there or with new friends, but locked away in her tiny apartment.

Brandi and Abel just laughed and nodded, unoffended at her words. Another fact she was grateful for because her tone could sometimes sound offensive without her meaning it to be.

After they finished eating, Abel and Brandi led her along the path – between the callistemons – to the sight beyond. The view it revealed was breath taking.

Sarah had never seen a manicured garden that consisted of nothing but Australian flowering natives. She had seen a mix of natives and non-natives, but nothing like the vista before her. While she recognised some of them by sight, she wouldn't know the name of the plants if someone had told her about them (except some of the bottle brushes, banksias and gum trees).

However, they were stunning in their colours of red, yellow, white, pink, pale icy greens, light greens, bright greens, dark greens, purple, cream, orange, blue, brown and black... A veritable rainbow, just a sea of colour in logged off sections. Think British display gardens, with nothing but Australian native plants.

On the right, with the house at their backs, was a huge mango tree with its branches sprawling outwards. No one had been trimming it to keep it under control, so it was extremely tall, wide and shady. Under it was a garden setting of table with six chairs, on a semi-circle of pavers, with a stretch of shade cloth between the setting and the branches. The shade cloth looked like it was acting as a protective barrier from falling leaves, dropping fruit and other stuff. Simply gorgeous.

"Oh... my... goodness... So amazing." Sarah breathed softly as she just stood there taking it all in. "This must have cost a fortune to do up." She commented as she gazed at Brandi and Abel.

"Certainly wasn't cheap, that's for sure." Abel said as they both chuckled.

Pointing to the path at the other end of the garden, "I take it the path continues into the surrounding bushland?" she asked.

"Yes, narrow trails criss-cross their way through the three and a half acres of land." Brandi responded.

"And you own it all?" she asked in a soft voice of wonderment.

"Yeah, we got so lucky on that as we hadn't realised the bushland acreage was part of the property at first." Abel said with a smile.

For the next few minutes, Sarah wandered amongst the flowerbeds just to look at them. 'If there's a heaven then I hope it has a home and property just like this one.' After she had finished drooling over the garden, the three of them made their way back to the back patio to sit and relax.

"What would you like to drink, Babe?" Abel asked.

"Something cold please." Sarah said.

"Soft drink, water, cordial, iced tea, milkshake?"

"Iced tea sounds great." She smiled.

"I'll have an iced tea as well please Darling." Brandi commented.

"Two iced teas coming up."

"What do you say we watch some movies while waiting for Danny to come down?" Brandi asked.

"Sounds good to me." Both Abel and Sarah said at the same time and they grinned at each other.

"Well, that's settled then." Said Brandi with a smile.

The three of them relocated into the lounge room. After much discussion they agreed to a disaster session. They watched one modern and two classics movies: 'Day After Tomorrow',

'Volcano' and 'Towering Inferno'.

During the end of 'Towering Inferno' Danny joined them. When it finished Abel turned to Sarah.

"Have you ever watched vampire movies with vampires around?"

She gazed at all three of them and shook her head.

"Well, you are in for a treat then. Danny, if you will do the honours of choosing what you would like to watch." Abel asked as Danny got up and went to the cabinet with the dvds in. "You see, Sarah, we have almost every vampire movie from all over the world and at least one night of the weekend is dedicated to watching some of them with Danny. It's great fun."

With Sarah still sitting on the lounge, Brandi and Abel went into the kitchen to organise dinner, and Danny put a movie into the player then sat on the floor beside her; his shoulder touching her leg. A few minutes later, Brandi came out with a bowl of popcorn and set it in front of Danny.

"Thanks Love." Danny said with a smile. Sarah just looked confused.

Brandi patted her shoulder as she went past. "You'll understand shortly Sweetie."

Once Abel and Brandi joined Sarah and Danny, Abel sat on the lounge with Brandi sitting on the floor between his legs. The play button was pressed.

And understand Sarah did. What a hilarious night. Danny cheered the good parts and booed, hissed and threw popcorn at the TV screen at the bad parts. Abel and Brandi joined him and Sarah just laughed at their antics. She laughed so much she had sprayed her drink all over the place.

'That certainly explains why there's no carpet in the lounge room.' She noted, she was the only one to have sprayed her drink.

After switching to water to drink and a few trips to the bathroom, it was almost dawn when all went to bed. Sarah stayed with Danny again until he fell asleep and then crawled into her own bed.

She got herself comfortable and smiled at the hilarity of the evening. She fell asleep wondering if vampires got together to do the same thing. 'Would hate to have to clean up after that one.'

*

She woke up with a start and a vague memory of a dream with fire, immense pain and two men she didn't know. She settled back into the bed and stared up at the ceiling.

'I know I have some really weird dreams at times, but that one was so weird that I can't even remember it properly.' She turned her head to look at the clock and saw that it was 4:00pm. 'Wow! First time I've slept straight through in years.'

She threw the covers back, sat on the edge of the bed and did some arm exercises to unstiffen them. After fifteen minutes of that, she got up, grabbed some stuff and headed to the bathroom.

"Good afternoon sleepyhead." Brandi greeted her with a grin when Sarah came downstairs and into the kitchen.

"Hmmm... Afternoon." She returned with a smile but in a less than enthused voice.

"Still tired?" Brandi asked as she got up and switched the jug on to make them both a cup of tea.

"Yeah, despite sleeping all the way through." She murmured, stifling a yawn. "Thanks." Sarah said as Brandi handed her one of the cups.

"Well, today is a relax day since all of us will head back tonight to our own homes for work tomorrow. Anything you're interested in doing?"

"If it is okay with you I wouldn't mind looking through your library."

Seeing the eager look in Sarah's eyes, Brandi laughed, "Sure, help yourself."

"Thanks. Okay to take my cuppa with me?"

"Of course." Brandi laughed her response.

Sarah grabbed her cup in her left hand and her walking stick in her right and eagerly, but slowly and carefully, hobbled off to their library. When she entered she turned on the lights and started looking around. She spent the last of the afternoon and early evening in there.

Leaning her stick near the entry, she wandered around. Grabbing a book that looked interesting she supported their spines, read bits and pieces if they weren't a novel and put it back on the shelf. She lost track of time as she lost herself amidst the towering rows of books.

It wasn't until a quiet voice from behind said hello in her ear did she come out of her reverie with a huge jump and a small squeal of fright. She was glad she'd placed the tea cup on the shelf beside her as she dropped the book she had in her hand and started to fall as she lost her balance.

Danny's hands were quick in catching Sarah around the waist

and keeping her upright. He chuckled.

"I am sorry. I did not mean to frighten you that much."

"Far out space cookies! Don't sneak up on me like that." She said, laughing breathlessly as she tried to get her heart back under control.

"Far out space cookies, huh? What a saying." He laughed.

"Sorry, just something my husband used to say." She said quietly as her grin softened to a smile.

Danny's grin faltered.

"I did not realised you were married." He sounded somewhat disappointed or as if she had deceived him. It would seem Brandi and Abel hadn't told him about that part of her.

Sarah didn't know how to respond to that hint of disappointment so she let it slide for the time being.

"He died three years ago." She quietly commented.

"I am sorry you lost him through death."

"It happens."

"But it still hurts does it not?" Danny gazed at her intensely.

"As any death does, and, whether we like it or not, life goes on." She responded.

She bent down, at the same time as Danny, to grab the book she'd dropped. Their fingers touched, with his over hers, and together they picked the book up. With a quick glance up at him she looked away and took her hand away, leaving him to put it back on the shelf. She didn't know how she was expected to react. Especially so soon after meeting him.

After a moment's silence, Danny and Sarah then walked out into the kitchen area to join Abel and Brandi, after grabbing her walking stick as they left the library.

"Ah, there she is." Abel greeted, "Enjoyed the library?"

"Oh yeah." She said with a smile. She was fully aware of how close Danny was standing next to her.

Abel smiled, "What would everyone like to drink?" looking at each in turn.

"Porphyry Sauternes." Brandi said.

"Red naturally." Said Danny. It was his polite way of saying blood. The first time Sarah had heard him say that, on Friday night, she was confused then surprised once she realised what he'd been referring to and thought it was a rather nice way of asking for the obvious without freaking others out.

"Milk please." While Sarah usually felt self-conscious when she asked for it, she keeps doing so in defiance. 'In all honesty there's nothing wrong with milk and don't think I'll ever grow out of liking it.'

"A sweet white for the Missus, a splash of red for the gentleman, a long tall glass of moo juice for the little lady and a spot of brandy for me." Abel said the last with a wiggle of his eyebrows. Brandi smiled and gave him a slap, Danny shook his head in amusement and Sarah just chuckled softly.

Once the four had hold of their drinks, Abel raised his glass and said in a more serious but quiet tone, "Here's to more weekends away with good friends."

They clinked glasses and chimed quietly, "To good friends."

They chatted for about an hour before all decided to leave. Brandi and Abel hugged Sarah and Danny shook her hand with his lingering on hers. She went to grab her top box, after changing into her riding gear, only for Danny to have picked it up and took it out for her. After the top box was re-attached all of them headed off to their respective homes.

In this case they headed back to Brisbane. It didn't escape her attention that Danny stayed behind her the whole time. However, her T-Max was more than capable of keeping up with them as they all stayed within the speed limits of the Bruce Highway.

During her trip back home Sarah couldn't help but think about how well she had been treated by them. She was the black sheep of her family and despite never having done anything truly wrong she was always punished in small ways that most people never saw. As a result, she had become shy and withdrawn and found it hard to talk with people. So, the acceptance she had received over the weekend was something she hadn't experienced for over three years. Before that, she'd never experienced it until she had met the man who had become her husband.

However, she had enjoyed herself and was glad she'd accepted the invite via such a chance meeting. Sarah felt like a weight had been lifted off her during the course of the weekend, so she was heading home happier than she had been for the last few years.

Chapter 9

The past seven months had been awesome. Sarah's nail business was flourishing with a steady set of clients and the occasional walk-in customers. She made a few friends at the Therian League centre, two of whom were Antonio and his wife Maria. They were definitely of Italian descent and both were were-leopards.

While she socialised with them and others at the centre, she was never invited anywhere near them during the time of the full moon. She had never even seen any of them – that included Hillie the were-fox – in their were-forms.

'While I don't count the night I rescued Hillie because I couldn't see her form that clearly, I have to admit, I'm not sure I want to. Still, I am curious.'

Also during that time she'd discovered she'd managed to lose a few kilos. While not as many as she would have liked at least it was a start. However, it would take two years at that rate before she would lose the rest.

'Oh well.' She sighed.

Furthermore, she'd been spending time and weekends with Abel, Brandi and Danny. The four of them had become good friends and they had plenty of 'vampire' movie nights which were so hilarious. Occasionally, if the movie was in a foreign language they would add their own dialogue in. Sarah would be laughing too hard to be able to participate.

It didn't go unnoticed by her that Danny seemed to go out of his way to be nice to her and get to know her. In return she got to know him.

He was born in London in 1859 and was embraced in 1892. Ten years later he moved to Australia. While Sydney was the first place he lived in, he said he has lived in all of the cities and some of the major towns, with his final residence being in Brisbane. With the vampires being out in the open, Danny said he no longer had to move around.

Sarah had asked Danny what he did for work, if he worked. He said he did, that he dealt with rare books; as in he hunted for, found and sold them if he didn't want to keep them for himself. She thought that was awesome; the book lover that she was. As a result she had been invited to his place to see his own massive collection. Suffice to say she lost herself amongst his books, much to his amusement, and she had been back to his place numerous times. Sometimes without Brandi and Abel.

His house was a large modern version of the traditional Queenslander with wrap-around verandahs on three sides and two storeys – that's the part that makes it modern as true traditionals were only single storey and raised about a metre or so off the ground; depending on the severity of the flooding the area might suffer. Sarah so loved Queenslander homes, especially the older, which were coming back into fashion, styles which have the verandah around all four sides. The three sided ones were okay, but she loved the four sided ones better.

His house, however, had been totally renovated on the inside.

The first thing he had done was to raise the house and improve the drainage outside. Then he had closed in the underneath with walls and gave it verandahs so it matched the upper floor.

The downstairs catered to a car garage and laundry, office, living room, downstairs bathroom, kitchen and entertaining area. The upstairs had a private lounge, library, four bedrooms and two bathrooms. It sort of looked like an English Victorian home with Queenslander accents to it.

However the house looked, she enjoyed her stays at his home. In fact, the coming weekend – the next day being Friday and the weekend leading into Halloween...

Sarah groaned at the thought of the wrongly dated event for the southern hemisphere.

...– Brandi, Able and Sarah were spending it at Danny's place. She smiled to herself at the thought of immersing herself in his books yet again.

She was still a little shy around Danny because she could see his interest in her growing into something more than just friendship. However...

Two and a half months after they first met, Sarah and Danny were alone. Sitting at opposite ends of the lounge in the sitting room of his house, curiosity got the better of her.

"Ummm... Danny? Can I ask you something personal?" She mentally cringed and thought, 'Oh no! One can't half tell I'm nervous. Not just by listening to me. Yeah right!'

"Ask Sarah, I do not mind." The moment she spoke his eyes stayed on her.

Blushing, her voice came out softer than she had intended.

"What's it like to feed from a person?"

He blinked; slowly. It was the only indication he gave that her question had surprised him.

"Well, apart from being a liquid diet, it is really no different to you sating your hunger. Only, there is no true pacifying of that hunger for us. We can lessen it to varying degrees but we can never obliterate it."

"It must be horrible to live like that." She murmured. She understood intense hunger, she suffered from it every now and then. However they eventually went away and she couldn't imagine always suffering like that.

"It can be but those of us who are law-abiding tolerate it. Sometimes I barely notice it. I am that used to it." He stated the last part rather offhandedly as if it was no big deal.

"I see."

"Why such a question Sarah?" His voice low and sounded so intimate.

She stared down at her hands and felt a blush creep up her face. Then she gazed up at him with a shrug.

"You are the first vampire I have ever been around... met even, and I was curious." She went back to staring at her hands again.

"But you volunteer at the QTL. Surely you met some there?"

Sarah shook her head.

"There never seems to be any there whenever I am."

"I see. Now let me ask you a question."

Looking at him again she nodded.

"Would you like to experience it? Me feeding from you." His

eyes were dark and intense as he watched her; his eyes never leaving hers.

Sarah's eyes widened in surprise. She was both curious and fearful and her heart started thudding hard and fast in response. Suddenly he frowned.

"Forget that I asked." He stood up. "Would you like something to eat?"

She could feel him withdrawing and went to grab his hand but missed and the tips of her fingers touch it instead. He went still.

"Yes I'm afraid, but I'm also curious." She blurted out in a rush as she gazed up at him.

His fingers wrapped around her hand and he gently pulled her up off the lounge.

"I treasure your honesty. I will not hurt you Sarah. I could never hurt you." He murmured down to her. It was the closest he'd come to revealing how he felt about her.

She nodded her understanding.

"May I drink from you please?" His voice erotic and almost a whisper.

Unable to get her voice to work, she just nodded. Barely a movement of her head. She knew by his colouring that he had fed earlier and figured, while nervous, she would be safe.

Gently and slowly he pulled her close to him so their bodies were just touching. With his lips parted, she gazed up into his face and saw his fangs grow before her wide eyes continued up to his eyes. It took a bit of effort on her part to drag her eyes from the tips of his fangs as they peeked from below his top lip but she managed.

His left hand slid leisurely around her waist and she couldn't help shivering a little because it tickled. His right hand glided up her arm, along her shoulder to the curve of her neck. Then, he tilted her head to the side and practically nuzzled her neck as he placed his face against it and inhaled.

"Mmmm, you smell so good." His coolish breath fanned across the bare skin of her throat.

Again she shivered from the tickling sensation his breath had caused. As his arms tightened a fraction, he kissed her neck firmly then she gasped at the quick sharp pain as his fangs pierced her soft flesh. Her hands clutched at his sides, fisting his shirt in them as he held her tightly against him.

The pain was gone as quickly as it had come. Now, all she could feel was his mouth working, sucking, at her neck. It was so reminiscent of when her husband gave her love bites. At first she felt him tense then move as if he was about to withdraw and she became a little disappointed it was ending so soon.

Then he relaxed and held her tighter and continued drinking from her. She couldn't help noticing his erection pressed against her lower abdomen and, in that moment, knew exactly how he felt about her.

Danny feeding from her neck like that felt so erotic that her dampening panties clearly stated what her body wanted. Even if her mind was still unsure. Even her heart started beating a little faster and her breathing quickened. Lost in the sensations, she didn't know how long he drank from her before his tongue slowly swirled over the spot he'd been drinking from.

Yet again she shivered and, with half closed eyes, she gazed up at him with a soft sigh of pleasure. Still he held her tightly.

"I can smell your desire Sarah. Let me show you what pleasures we can have together." His voice and gaze were so intense she had difficulty breathing.

Right there and then, she was all prepared to go to bed with him regardless of the indecision sitting in the back of her mind. Barely opening her mouth to say yes, he chose that moment to move back a fraction and lessen his hold on her. Then, a wave of dizziness and weakness swept over her, followed quickly by darkness.

Later that night, upon opening her eyes, she discovered him sitting on the bed beside her. He looked like a statue. An unreadable statue that she interpreted as him not pleased with the situation.

"How are you feeling?"

Pausing to take stock of herself...

"I'm okay. A little weak and dizzy but I feel fine otherwise." Only then did his monotone voice register to her. She stared at him and frowned.

In a sudden burst of motion she barely saw, the statue came alive as Danny stood abruptly and started pacing.

"My sincerest apologies Sarah. I honestly never meant to hurt you..." He paused and she could hear the anguish in his words.

"Danny? What do you mean? What's wrong? What happened?" She wasn't afraid and it never occurred to her that she should be. While blacking out wasn't common, weakness with dizziness was normal to her and she didn't understand why he should be so upset at her having a dizzy spell.

Just as quickly, he was sitting on the bed beside her. He gently held her hands in his. It was a rare moment where she could see the evidence of his old world up-bringing; his old world charm. She realised she liked it. A lot.

"You passed out. I never meant to drink so much. It was meant to be just a sip but you tasted so sweet..." He blurted out then paused.

For the first time she got to see something of the young man he had once been. In that moment she saw a man who was unsure of himself, who was upset that his gentlemanly ways had failed him in what he – herself included – considered an important moment.

Also, with his words, she finally understood the situation. The dizziness and weakness were due to blood loss, not one of her dizzy spells.

Still, she wasn't afraid as she knew she should be. Instead, she was flattered and was actually grateful for the lack of blood as it meant she wouldn't actually blush even though she felt like doing so.

Danny suddenly looked surprised and gently cupped her cheek.

"Faint as it is, why the blush, Sweet Sarah?" He murmured.

She blushed a little harder at his words. Another, but smaller, wave of dizziness washed over her as a result.

"I'm flattered you think I taste so good." She murmured back with a small smile, but then she had difficulty in making her voice go louder.

As if a weight had been lifted off him, he relaxed and appeared to be back to his usual self. He caressed her cheek.

"Despite this evening's fiasco, if you are willing to let me drink you again it will not be for another three months. I took too much from you and you need the time to replenish your loss." He informed her gently.

"I understand." She stated slowly. She realised she had a lot to think about.

"You need sleep and sunrise is not too far away. I will see you this evening my dear sweet Sarah." Then he leant down and placed a tender lingering kiss on her forehead as he caressed her cheek and left the room.

Later that day, when she woke up and went into the kitchen for some food, she discovered he had been so worried after she had passed out that he hadn't left her side. With that knowledge and their earlier talk she now knew how he truly felt about her.

Sarah, however, was still struggling. Now that time had passed, her shyness had kicked back in. Even so, she did let him drink from her again. However, before it could go beyond that, they were interrupted and he had to leave for about an hour. In the end she chickened out on taking the next step with him.

...And so, their 'relationship' stayed at that point. While she did think he was good looking and a lovely gentle person, she didn't know if she was really ready to enter into another relationship yet. However, after three and a half years since the death of her husband and never having seen Kaelan again, maybe it was time to move on.

'Can I love a vampire? Maybe. Will I allow myself to love Danny? I just don't know and I'm not sure what to do about it.'

During their time together, that thought was never far from her mind. As the weeks then months passed, Sarah was still as indecisive as she was during that first time with him.

*

It was Friday afternoon, a few days before the end of October, and she left work, went home to shower and change to get the smell of the hairdressers and nail products off her, then headed to Danny's place. She couldn't remember if it was going to be a weekend stay or not, so she packed extra clothes into the top box just in case.

Danny had fed from her again a month and a half ago and she was expecting him to feed from her again soon. Like maybe that very weekend. However, she still hadn't let their 'relationship' progress past that point and didn't know if she ever would. She was just too nervous and shy to take that next step. Maybe they would do so this weekend. The thought notched her nervousness up some more.

'If only he wasn't so much the gentleman and would take the initiative, the decision, out of my hands.' Sarah thought, knowing it was the coward's way out.

Mind back on the traffic around her, the going was slow because it was still peak hour traffic. It was raining so the roads were a little slippery, along with other drivers not paying much attention to those around them because they just wanted to get home as quickly as they could. She'd had three near misses on the way to Danny's and was so glad when she finally entered his driveway without a scratch on her.

Brandi and Abel turned up just minutes after she did. Sarah was on the front veranda peeling her gloves, helmet and glasses

– she had three types of glasses for on the scooter: clear, lightly tinted and a pair of sunnies. Which ones she wore depended on the brightness of the day. However, all were to keep bugs out of her eyes if the visor was opened even a little bit.

The three of them were greeting each other with smiles and hugs when the door opened. Toby, one of two human males who attended to Danny's day time chores and protected him, answered the door before any of them could ring the bell.

"Hi guys. Danny will be up and around in about hour, so come on in and make yourselves at home." Toby said with a smile.

Toby was a little taller than Danny and Abel, and was the obvious muscle, as in bodyguard. His hair and eyes were brown and had tanned skin that was naturally fair, but still darker than Sarah's, where the sun hadn't touched it. He also had that t-shirt tan. He was a nice guy, easy to get along with and had a quiet sense of humour. The first time she saw him he seemed familiar to her but she knew she hadn't seen him before.

"Hi Toby." The three of them chorused then laughed as they went inside. Sarah set her jacket on a hook just inside the door then set her glasses, gloves and helmet on a little table beside those hooks before entering the sitting room.

"Would you like anything to drink?" Toby asked.

"Water for me." Abel said.

"Fruit juice here." Chimed Brandi.

"And I'll have a glass of milk please." Sarah requested to smiles of amusement from the others. Apparently, there was more milk in Danny's house now than before she had met him.

Abel, Brandi and Sarah started talking about their week while they waited for Danny to arrive. It seemed all three had a decent week which made the start of their weekend good so far. They had just finished their drinks when Danny entered the room, looking immaculate as per usual.

They said hi to him and he greeted them, leaving Sarah to last. He always did, which left him standing next to her. He gazed at her.

"Amongst your clothing here, do you have anything to wear out?"

"Apart from what I left here last time and some smart casuals in my top box, no I don't." She said with a slight frown. "I didn't realise I would need anything fancy this weekend so I didn't think to bring anything along those lines." She stated softly. With low self-esteem it didn't take much for Sarah to feel foolish even though she knew she shouldn't have.

Sarah had been buying the occasional fancier going out clothing because Danny, Brandy and Abel tended to go out more than she ever had before meeting them. Therefore, she got into the habit of taking them with her whenever she was to spend the weekend with the three of them.

"Not to worry. Come with me." Danny said with a mischievous smile as he grabbed her hand. His hand was warm she noted. He had obviously just fed, which meant he more than likely wouldn't be feeding on her. She didn't know how to feel about that so she pushed it off to one side so she could deal with it later. Much later.

"Brandi, you might want to come up as well. I will be right back, Abel." He said with a big grin.

"I'll be here." Abel replied with a smile.

Brandi, Danny and Sarah went upstairs towards the room that

acted as Sarah's bedroom whenever she was there. She found out later Danny had the room painted and decorated in colours and a style she liked.

The new look started off with cream walls, ceiling and carpet. The sheets, curtains, rugs and bedspread were in varying shades of blue, the numerous pillows and throws were also in shades of blue, along with cream and silver. All with different patterns and designs, yet complimenting each other.

Also, there were lots of gauzy fabrics in different shades of creams, blues and silver everywhere. They were pinned from the centre of the ceiling which were then draped back towards the walls with the rest of the excess fabrics trailing down the walls. There was a curtained four poster queen sized bed, matching bed-side tables and an old styled mirrored dressing table with matching high backed chair.

All the furniture was a deep golden brown wood with art nouveau designs carved into them and fittings, while of a metal she didn't know, were also art nouveau in design. The whole effect was harem-like with a Middle Ages/Victorian touches in silk, velvet, jacquard and damask.

Danny stopped her in the middle of the room. "Now, close your eyes."

Smiling with a slight frown, Sarah did as she was told. A moment or two later she heard Brandi give a soft gasp. Sarah only heard it because Brandi was standing right next to her.

"Open your eyes."

She did, and did her own audible gasp.

On two fingers of his right hand hung a large thick wooden hanger. The hanger displayed a floor/ankle length dress that had bell sleeves to the wrist that had slits from shoulder to elbow then elbow to wrists in them. The neckline was a combination of a V and a slight half heart shape to it. The dress was cinched in slightly at the waist. His left hand held out one of the sleeves

He let go of the sleeve and placed his hand behind his back. Then he turned the dress around to show the back of it. She saw it was a plunging back that was wide and bare except for the lacings that criss-crossed from shoulder to lower back.

Sarah walked towards Danny to feel the dress. It was velvet in a... she didn't even know the name of the colour, but to describe it, it was a pinkish-purplish burgundy red.

"Oh, Danny. I love it." She whispered appreciatively.

With a flourish, he revealed his other hand. In it was a matching pair of low heeled, open toed slippers and satin shoulder evening bag. She realised they must have been on the dressing table behind him.

When she looked in the bag, there was a matching purse and a matching little mirror. She gazed up at Danny.

"They're gorgeous, I truly love them. Thank you." She said softly and suspected she was blushing as well.

Danny kissed Sarah gently on the forehead.

"You are welcome. Brandi will help you. I will see you down stairs." He said with a smile and left after he hung the dress on a clothes hook and placed the shoes and bag on the dressing table.

"Oh Sarah. These are stunning. I think he loves you, you know." Brandi said quietly with a gentle smile.

Sarah blushed and started stripping,

"Well, help me into this and let's see how it all looks." She said, neatly avoiding the subject of Danny's feelings for her. She thought she could love him.

'No, not just because he bought me this outfit or decorated my room to please me or all the other little things he's done for me, but because of him personally. To me, personality matters the most with a sense of humour. Looks and/or money are just bonuses should they happen to be included. Admittedly, he does have what matters and the bonuses.' She softly sighed and decided to deal with that situation later and concentrated on getting dressed.

The dress also had matching panties, but there was no bra to go with it. However, the two women soon discovered that the lacings at the back were positioned in such a way that it gathered the dress firmly under the breasts anyway. As it was, the bust area of the dress was double layered and that inner layer of fabric, combined with the lacing, acted like a bra.

Brandi helped with the lacing of the dress, styling Sarah's hair and with some of the make-up. Then her friend stood behind her as they looked at her in the mirror. Sarah hardly recognise herself.

'I look... elegant. I rarely look elegant.'

The dress fitted perfectly and, once again, he surprised her with his ability to choose clothing that fitted her well. The dress came down and out over her hips with a straight cut over the top of her thighs to flare out from mid-thighs to ankles. A really gorgeous looking gown.

"You look beautiful, Sweetie." Brandi whispered in her ear as she gave Sarah a hug from behind.

Looking in the mirror, Sarah could see the tears building and she gave an embarrassed little laugh. She grabbed her walking stick and frowned as it so didn't look good with the outfit. It was just a basic cheap wooden one. She sighed.

'There's nothing I can do about it unfortunately.'

"One moment, Sweetie..." Brandi said as she moved to the other side of the wardrobe. She reached inside, and when she came back out she had in her hand one of the most beautiful walking sticks Sarah had ever seen.

The stick looked to be made of some golden honey-coloured wood. The handgrip was carved into a crouching, crawling, snarling leopard that was creamy white with darker spots for fur, with blue eyes and a pink tongue and nose. The details were superb; from the white fangs and other teeth to the carved fur over the head, shoulders and front legs.

The fur stopped where Sarah's hand was to grip the handle. The cat was crouched on a platform carved to resemble the ground. As she looked down the shaft of the stick she could see tiny paw prints leading down the stick in a wavy line as if the leopard wound its way down the stick to prowl around when no one was looking.

The tears that had started to build as she had looked at herself in the mirror trickled down her cheeks. Brandi didn't say a word and just hugged Sarah. After a few minutes Sarah regained her composure and blotted her tears away without smudging her make-up; which was a first. Next she found a shawl made of lace that was a slightly darker colour than the dress and the two women made their way downstairs.

Brandi went into the sitting room first and cleared her throat, then beckoned to Sarah. Sarah couldn't help but look down at the floor as she walked into the room. When she didn't hear anything, she glanced up to see both Abel and Danny wearing similar expressions; stunned amazement. Sarah glanced at Brandi and saw the woman was grinning at them.

Danny came towards Sarah, "You look beautiful."

The way he looked at her made her blush. It was a stunned look. An incredulous look and something else she couldn't quite read.

'A hunger maybe?' She mused with uncertainty. 'Oh, I know he does hunger for me but there are still some of his expressions I'm not sure on how to read. Maybe he will feed from me after all.' A little shiver of excitement ran through her.

'Maybe tonight or sometime this weekend if nothing goes wrong.' And her nervousness shot up another notch.

"Thank you so much for the clothing and the leopard walking stick. They're all amazing." Her voice was just above a whisper and Sarah couldn't seem to get it to go louder.

'I so hate being embarrassed.'

"Actually, it is a jaguar, but that is okay. Not easy to tell the difference with a small partial carving like that." Danny informed with a smile. "It is all made of cherry heartwood." He added as a side note.

Abel came over to her.

"Wow, Babe! I mean, wow!" Then he laughed at what he said.

Sarah gave him a hug. Then she did a, very, slow turn so they could see it all.

"So, where are we going?" She asked breathlessly.

"It is a surprise." Danny said, then he turned to Abel and

Brandi, "Go and get dressed you two and we will then go."

Danny left with Brandi and Abel while Sarah went into the kitchen to grab a glass of water. Toby and Mick, the other human male who helped Toby to look after the day time running's of Danny's affairs, were there. She had a feeling of déjà vu the first time she saw Mick as well, but knew she hadn't seen him before either.

Mick was shorter than Toby, but much leaner so he gave the illusion that he was about the same height, unless they were standing side by side.

Mick had the typical surfer look. Scraggily sun bleached sandy blonde hair that was long at the neck but didn't reach the shoulders. He had muddy hazel eyes and a sun tanned complexion that was a little faded compared to his usual darkness, but the tan was getting darker as the weather grew warmer. He looked a typical scallywag.

However, Mick and Sarah didn't seem to get along as well as Toby and she did.

Sitting at the table, the two men gazed up at her as she entered.

"Wow, Sarah, you look amazing." Toby said with a wide eyed smile.

"Thank you Toby." She said with a blush and poured herself a glass of water.

"Hi Mick." She greeted softly. Regardless of how he has treated her, she still tried to be nice to him. Mainly because that's just the way she was – until someone was nasty to her, but also because he lived there in Danny's house.

"Hi." Mick said gruffly. She heard what sounded like one

kicking another under the table. She didn't turn around. "Yeah, you look good Sarah." Mick grudgingly said.

Then she turned to face the two men – she caught the end of Mick's scowl aimed at Toby, and with a small smile, she said, "Thank you Mick."

They could hear the others coming down the stairs, then their voices wondering where she was.

"Coming." She called out. "Night guys. See you later." She said in breathless eagerness to Mick and Toby. She started hobbling out towards the front door.

Peering down, she watched the careful placement of her feet. She didn't want to step on the bottom of her dress and trip and fall. She had just rounded the corner when she heard the sounds of varying gunshots happening at the same time and her head flicked up in shock.

Stopping in the doorway, she saw Danny with no head and slowly crumpling to the floor. Brandi was already on the floor with a hole in her chest. While Abel was falling with a growing rose of red in the middle of his back and two men in the front door with guns and other stuff she couldn't make out.

With those details just barely registering passed her horrified shock, she tried to shuffle backwards. Not one of her best abilities since the accident. Only, she ended up stumbling and falling backwards, having tripped on the back hem of the dress. Fear hadn't even grabbed hold of her yet.

However, as she fell backwards, she could hear Toby and Mick running towards her and heard two more gunshots. She felt pain in her left shoulder and her right thigh, then at the back of her head and things started to go grey around the edges. It had all happened so quickly, she didn't have a chance to utter a sound.

Suddenly, there was a smell of petrol and a loud 'woofing' sound. She felt heat then everything went black.

Chapter 10

After unlocking the door, he was greeted with the smell of a stale house. Kaelan wrinkled his nose in distaste as he stood there dripping water on the floor and letting fresh air flow in while he held the door open for a bit. The smell was not bad, but neither was it nice. Thankfully it was spring so now was a good time to air the house out. It had been two years since the last time he was in his house back in Brisbane and seven months ago when he had spoken with Ed out at Manly.

Regardless of how he felt about his reasons for staying away, it did sort of feel good to be back no matter how briefly. Although, the rain outside definitely smelled better. He sighed and hooked his foot around the door and nudged it shut. Dropping one of his bags to the floor so as to free a hand, he turned the hallway light on.

Ignoring the dropped bag for the moment and being drenched by the rain, he went into the kitchen to set up his laptop. Even though he had just gotten back into Brisbane, he wanted to check to see if there were any interesting jobs available. 'One down south might be nice for a change.'

Lifting his arm up high, he pulled the power cord towards himself so it had some room to move. However, in lifting his arm he was reminded that he was in dire need of a shower. Finishing setting up the laptop and turning it on, he then went had a shower.

Fifteen minutes later Kaelan had had his shower, a coffee and a sandwich made. He was sitting at the laptop, signed in and scrolling through the job listings with a towel wrapped around his hips when a notice popped up regarding a vampire hit.

However, the pop-up had not come from the job site, but from one of his watcher programs that kept an eye on other websites via meta tags and key words. Kaelan clicked the link and a new tab opened in his browser. Then, the most cheesiest looking site finished loading.

A picture of two dead-head wannabes flashed at the top with the bright yellow words 'Our Latest Hit' blinking in a vibrant blue chat bubble. He clicked it, waited for the fuchsia pink page with yellow text to load. Kaelan groaned at their bad taste, while highlighting the page so he could at least read the text without all that pink surrounding it.

He was just casually browsing through it when a name caught his eye. Frowning, he rushed back to the top and started reading it properly.

'They're lovers?' Kaelan thought to himself. 'Disappointing. I thought she had more class than that.' He thought, feeling more than a little disappointed then became annoyed with himself.

"Why the fuck does it even matter?!" He muttered.

Ignoring the way he felt, he kept reading. His eyes widened with growing dread as Kaelan read the information near the bottom. Sprinting out of his chair, knocking it over, he raced to the bedroom to get dressed, but didn't stop to pick the chair up.

In fact, it only registered because of the noise it had made as it hit the floor.

'Regardless of the fact that she's in love with a bloodsucker, I can't let them kill her. I won't be too distressed if I'm late in saving him but she doesn't deserve death for associating with the likes of him. Besides, the hunters are rogue and it's not a sanctioned hit.'

After dressing, he rushed back to the lounge room to grab his keys.

'Good thing I hadn't put my weapons away yet' He thought as he bolted to the front door. Kaelan slammed into it as his feet slid in the puddle he had dripped earlier on the polished floor. The door groaned slightly from the impact of his 193cm tall frame. Grabbing the bag he had left there, he ran for the car.

'Shit! Shit! Shit! Let me be in time.' The thought ran around in his head like a dog chasing its tail and wouldn't stop no matter what bone Kaelan threw at it. He had programmed the GPS while he raced through the suburbs, heading toward the north side. He tried not to think too much about the situation, or to speed too much since the last thing he needed was to be pulled over by the police.

Even with going via the Gateway Motorway and Bridge, he still had to continue north then deviate left onto the Southern Cross Way until he hit East-West Arterial Road. Turning west he cut through a number of suburbs south west to reach her location. Kingsford Smith Drive was just too busy. None of it helped matters any.

'Thank goodness those idiots supplied the vamp's address on their page.'

He was still roughly a street away when Kaelan saw dark greyish smoke starting to billow past the immediate horizon.

"NO!" He yelled, slamming a hand against the steering wheel. His heart hammered in his chest and he didn't like the feeling.

'The outcome can't be the same. It just can't!'

As he entered the street, a van passed him, almost rolling as it went around the corner at high speed.

'It has to be the idiots who announced their hit.'

Kaelan ignored them and raced towards the burning house when he saw two men emerging from the side carrying a woman between them. He almost ignored them until he saw one of the men had a walking stick in his hand.

Heading straight at them, he hit the brakes and slid to a stop beside them after he had swerved to the side slightly so he would miss them, and told them to get in as he reached to open the back door for them. Looking quickly, Kaelan confirmed his suspicions.

'It is Sarah they're carrying and she's bleeding. Badly!'

When he looked at her, Kaelan couldn't help thinking how stunning she looked in the dress she was wearing. His eyes travelled the expanse of exposed creamy pale soft looking flesh marred by the vibrancy of her blood against it. The sight caused his innards to clench tightly, painfully. He gave himself a mental shake to keep his thoughts on the job instead of her. Once the three of them were in he sped away.

"How did you know we weren't the bad guys?" Asked the sun bleached haired surfer looking guy. His voice sounded rather shaky, from the attack Kaelan guessed.

"You were carrying her when they wanted her dead. Is she the only survivor, other than you two?" Kaelan did not bother with the niceties. He was more interested in information at that point in time.

"Yes." The other one choked out. A moment's silence then... "Ah, man? You might want to step on it. She's bleeding, a lot, and her pulse is dropping."

With that, Kaelan slammed the brakes on again. 'Thank goodness for ABS.' The trivial thought popped into his mind as the vehicle stopped without sliding all over the place.

"Drag her out and lay her on the road." He ordered, getting out of the car.

The two men didn't move.

"NOW!" He barked the order as he ran to the back and grabbed out the first aid kit. Looking up and down the street, he noted it was deserted and that it wouldn't be long before dark would settle.

'Good.' He also noted it had stopped raining for the moment and hoped it would stay that way until he had her stabilised at least.

By the time Kaelan got to the other side, the two men had her on the road. He turned to the obvious muscle.

"Monitor her pulse." Then he started ripping her lovely dress at the left shoulder and the right thigh. As quickly as he could he bandaged both injuries.

The surfer guy was at her head. "She's stopped breathing."

Kaelan's own heart pounded painfully at that information but he didn't let it stop him.

"Shit!" He muttered as he started CPR. Without being told, the surfer guy breathed for her while Kaelan compressed her rib cage.

Everything was wet, grey and pain was everywhere. Shoulder, thigh and chest were hurting and the darkness was starting to swallow her again. Her head started to throb and she fleetingly considered letting the darkness ease everything. She had the momentary thought of how weird her body hurt but she couldn't feel anything else. Even sounds seemed muted.

"Her pulse is getting weaker." A male voice said sounding frantic.

However, she couldn't tell who had spoken. Other than the pain, it was like nothing wanted to work properly or cooperate with her. As a result, instead of briefly this time, she was now more than willing to let the darkness win since nothing mattered any more. Only, she couldn't remember why that was so.

"Don't you leave me, Sarah." Said a second, strained male voice.

Kaelan demanded of her through clenched teeth. He didn't want to think about her dead. Not like this. Strangely, in the back of his mind it occurred to him he had never said her name out loud to her until that moment. However, the realisation became buried under the need to stabilise her.

Even with the darkness dragging her down, she recognised that voice. Even if it was the first time he had ever said her name. That trivial fact registered to her briefly as she forced her eyes open with immense effort, and it was a fight to keep them open. They felt so weighted and kept closing.

Just for a split second she decided to fight the darkness because, for some strange reason she had to make sure she had heard who she thought she had heard. Her vision was blurry and darkening at the edges, but when she could see his face, his words angered her.

'How dare he?!' She raised her right hand up. It was clenched into a fist already, and hit him. Hard. Or, so she thought. Then the blackness won.

When she raised her right hand towards his face, Kaelan was too busy looking at her to take much notice of her hand. Until it hit him on the side of his jaw rather hard. Then her hand fell limply to the ground.

'Shit! But that hurt. I don't know if the hit to my jaw was deliberate or just a lack of coordination.' He thought as he started to rub his jaw.

Then she lost consciousness. To top it off, it started raining again.

"Great, just great!" Kaelan muttered to himself.

"Not breathing again."

So Kaelan started the CPR once more. Again her eyes fluttered, but not quite opening.

"Damn it, Sarah, fight!" He demanded but angrily this time.

Pain dragged her out of unconsciousness. By that point the pain in her chest hurt more than her shoulder and thigh. She didn't understand what he meant and, truthfully, she was beyond caring.

"Got a pulse, but dropping again." Said a voice that sounded panicked.

She still couldn't work out who had spoken. With a small sigh she gave up and let the darkness swallow her yet again.

When he heard her sigh, he thought she had died. With a rush he checked her pulse and was relieved to feel it even if it was weak. Then he checked the back of her left shoulder and was greeted with a faint outline of something which looked like it was ripping out of her skin. The red flesh and blood looked vivid and real.

He wiped his hand over it and was surprised to discover the whole thing appeared to be a tattoo. So, the bullet itself wasn't a go-through. Next, he checked her right thigh and found a pool of blood beneath her.

"Damn it! Roll her onto her left side now." He ordered as he ripped her pretty dress further so it wasn't in the way. He cut off the bandage he had applied since it was saturated. Placed new dressings on both the entry and exit wounds this time then re-bandaged her thigh. A minute or two after Kaelan had completed the bandage...

"Her pulse is... levelling out. Weak... but steadying." Muscles said, his relief obvious.

Kaelan sighed with relief.

"Get her back into the car." He instructed as he started to clean up the mess on the road.

After putting the kit in the rear of the Jeep and the rubbish in a bag, he grabbed a three litre bottle of water and poured it over the blood on the road to wash it away. He repeated the process with a second bottle of water. It was mostly successful as the blood had started clotting during the time the rain had stopped falling.

Looking up and down the street, he noted it was still deserted and was full dark. Then he got in the car and drove back home.

"Where are you going? We need to get her to a hospital." Muscles demanded.

Kaelan stared at him in the rear view mirror.

"I'm taking her back to my place where she'll be safe. If they find out she's still alive, they might try again."

"Because you said they wanted her dead?" The surfer guy asked.

It made Kaelan think a little better about him. The man was paying attention. "Yes."

"How do you know this?" Muscles asked with what sounded like accusation in his voice.

Kaelan was beginning to not like him. "The idiots who attacked the vamp's home have a web page informing their intentions, where and when, and listed the names of those who would be in the house at that time." He informed with as little inflection as possible.

"Names?"

"Daniel, Sarah, Abel, Brandi, Toby and Mick. Which two are you?" He knew neither of them were the vamp since it had still been daylight at the time they exited the house. Even if the sun was just starting to go below the horizon at the time.

Muscles spoke first. "I'm Toby, he's Mick. Who are you?"

"Kaelan, a... friend of Sarah's."

He was thankful that the rest of the drive proceeded in silence. 'The two rogue hunters may have been idiots, but they were idiots who had done their research well, if that list of names was anything to go by.' Kaelan frowned at that thought.

Stopping the car next to the front stairs, he dashed up them three at a time to open the front door and stood there while Toby carried her in. Kaelan led him to the first bedroom on the left, opened the door and stripped the bed.

"Hold her while I remake the bed." and he did so as quickly as possible. However, after turning the top covers down, he then placed a spare PVC shower curtain down over the base sheet to protect it and the bed from her blood.

Kaelan stood back to let Toby lay her down. He was covered in Sarah's blood. All three of them were actually. He beckoned for Toby to follow him, then to Mick.

"Toby, you can stay in this room. This is the bathroom and Mick, you can use that bedroom." Then he left them to their own devices while he gathered the items he needed to tend to her. He also grabbed a chair for himself to sit in.

Back in her room, Kaelan stared down at her with his arms full of stuff. He gently placed the items on the bed beside her and sorted them out. He placed the tank top and boxer briefs on the chair behind him.

'Hmm... Hope she fits into them. She'd put a little extra weight on since I last saw her.'

With a pair of scissors, he started cutting the dress and panties off, but no bra even though she was small enough...

'B cup I would think'

...to get away without one, and placed the clothing into a garbage bag. As his hands moved they brushed against her skin as he cut the fabric and he couldn't help noticing how soft and smooth it was. The brightness of the red of her blood just emphasised the creaminess of her complexion.

Slowly he gazed at her from head to toe and back again and

couldn't help but be surprised when he saw the second tattoo and then the piercings.

A smile slowly, leisurely, spread across his lips as he gently and unhurriedly wiped the blood away from her tattoo on the inner side of her right breast. What he saw was a fancy hummingbird in flight with feathers in a rainbow of pale red, green, blue and yellow. It also had a couple of extremely long tail feathers that curled under her left breast while its greyish-yellow beak pointed down at her right nipple from above.

Looking carefully at the bird, he realised there was something wrong with it that made him think it wasn't a hummingbird at all. Then he saw it. The beak was wrong. It was shorter and thicker and the markings weren't typical for a hummingbird. After another look, he finally recognised it was an Australian rainbow bee eater. He couldn't resist tracing the longest tail feather. With a groan of arousal, frustration and annoyance, he deliberately went back to cleaning her.

With a gentleness he had never shown a woman's body before – not that he had ever been rough or brutal, he continued cleaning the rest of the blood away with a small smile of surprised amusement over her piercings.

'Never knew she would be in to that sort of thing.' Except for them and the standard ear piercings, she had no others.

Yet again, she'd managed to surprise him. Kaelan had never been with a woman with piercings, other than their ears.

'Would be int...' He halted that thought before it could go any further as he shook his head, but it was already too late. The mind had already imagined.

'Damn it, but I'm going to need a cold shower once I've

finished here!' He thought with a groan

After cleaning the blood from the front of her, he gently rolled her onto her stomach – making sure her head was turned to the side – so he could clean the blood from her back. Taking a closer look at her left shoulder, he saw it was a second tattoo but of a panther done in white ink with its claws tearing through her skin to get out.

'What an interesting choice.' Once again, he was surprised to find her with such bodily decorations.

Personally, he wasn't into tattoos and piercings. The scars he had, while unwanted, were more than enough decoration on his body. However, Sarah's were minimal and rather tasteful and he found them attractive and intriguing, and wanted to know the stories/reasons behind them.

With another sigh he shoved his mind away from those particular thoughts and back to cleaning her and tending to her injuries. Once she and the shower curtain were cleaned, Kaelan rolled her onto her back then removed the shoulder bandage and proceeded to dig the bullet out.

'Shit, but it's a good thing she's unconscious right now because this is sure to have her screaming in agony.'

While still holding it with the tweezers, he placed the bullet into a plastic bag then put it on the bedside table for keeping. He knew his boss, at least, would ask for it. After cleaning the area again and redressed her shoulder, he then dealt with her thigh.

Checking her over thoroughly, he was thankful no bones were broken. At least that was one less thing to worry about. So, he inspected the exit wound of the go-through then checking the bullet in the little ziploc bag, he realised that both bullets were just standard ammunition like one would use on a general public gun range.

'She's damned lucky! It could have been a lot worse for her if the idiots had used ammunition like I use.' He inspected the wounds again and noted the entry wound at the front of her thigh was lower than the exit wound at the back.

'However, it seems like she'd been falling backwards and, therefore, at an angle at the time she was shot. Strange... why would she be falling backwards before being shot?' The evidence puzzled him but there was no disputing what he saw.

He redressed her thigh injury as well. After doing so, he carefully removed the shower curtain then dried her. Once dried, he gently dressed her in the tank top and boxer briefs so as not to aggravate her injuries. They were a firm fit but they did fit and, regardless of her size, she looked damned good in them.

He definitely liked what he saw if his body's reaction was anything to go by. Either that or it had just been a long time since he was last with a woman.

'Oh for fuck sake man! Don't diminish her like that. Be a man and admit, even if it's just to yourself, that just a lay isn't the reason for your hard on.'

Closing his eyes, he buried the thought and sighed yet again. He could see the situation with her was going to become a problem. How big or bad? He didn't yet know.

Positioning her carefully so she wouldn't be in too much pain when she awoke, he stared at her for a moment. Despite her weight she looked so small and pale. Regardless of her vitals being steady he wondered if she was going to survive the ordeal. If physically, what about mentally? With a shake of his head, he pulled the covers up to her shoulders and collected everything but the bullet and left the room.

Before he did anything else he had another quick shower to clean her blood off himself. He couldn't remember ever stripping so fast as he did right then. Closing his eyes and placing his hands on the tiled wall, he let the water rain down upon him.

'God! I hope I never go through that with her again. I truly don't like being covered in her blood like that.'

Despite his arousal earlier, the whole experience had left him feeling knotted and sick. He leant his head against the cold tile. His job was bloody under normal circumstances and had a tendency to have blood on him. Whether his or somebody else's was beside the point. It had never bothered him. She, however, appeared to be a different matter.

The shower was hot and longer than usual as he scrubbed himself clean and somewhat calmed down. Then he decided to ditch the clothes he had been wearing instead of trying to clean them. He didn't want the reminder. His memory was more than enough as far as he was concerned.

After the shower, Kaelan moved throughout the house opening doors and windows and turning on fans to air it out. He grabbed air fresheners and placed them in every room. Mick and Toby sat in the kitchen, still covered in Sarah's blood, watching him as he went around the place.

Once done, he went out to the Jeep and cleaned her blood from the entire interior. He followed it up by placing perfume styled bottles of air fresheners in the Jeep to help rid the vehicle of the smell of blood. Then he moved it towards the back of the house, stopping in front of the garage.

Once parked, he grabbed the weapons bag, personals bag and the rubbish, and put all away in their appropriate places. Cleaned her blood from and refilled the water bottles he had in the vehicle and cleaned any other spots of blood that he saw. Then headed back into the house with what was left in the personals bag and dumped it in his room. Kaelan glanced at the two men as he made his way back into the kitchen.

After filling the eight litre electric urn and switching it to boil, he then turned around and leant against the bench top. He eyed them a moment or two before speaking.

"While this is my house, feel free to move about the inside of it. The building next to the garage is out of bounds to all, even if you were my Grandmother. The small building on the right is a fully equipped home gym. The key hangs up by the door there so feel free to use it.

"You can use the pool as well but just make sure you clean it if needed and replace the cover when not in use. I don't have much in the way of food here as I've been away for two years and just got back a little over three hours ago. Would one or both of you be willing to do some grocery shopping if I gave you the money?"

'There, I can be polite if I want to. I just don't want to leave Sarah alone with either of them. I don't care if she knows them. I don't, and in my house that's what matters.' While he thought such thoughts, he had no intention of justifying himself.

"I'll go." Mick said. "Just give me a list of what you want."

Kaelan nodded, went through the cupboards, ditching anything out of date, and wrote a list.

"Grab whatever toiletries you both need as well. You might

also want to get yourself clothing if you can. The money here is for food for the four of us. If you have money, you can buy whatever else you want." Kaelan stated as he handed Mick the list and five hundred dollars.

"But, before you go, you'll need to clean up. I'll loan you some clothing, but they're going to be big on you Mick and tight on you Toby."

They both nodded. However, before things went any further...

"What happened to Sarah? Why was she falling backwards before being shot?" He watched them both like a hawk.

"How did..." Toby's surprise was evident but the pause wasn't long enough for Kaelan to say anything. Toby shook his head then continued.

"When we heard the gunshots we ran to the front door. We were in the kitchen originally. As we entered the hallway we... I... saw her trying to shuffle backwards to get away but the hem of her dress got caught under her heel and she started falling then she was shot twice." Toby responded. He sounded upset she had been hurt and for that reason alone Kaelan reserved his judgement about the man.

Kaelan nodded then retrieved and gave them the promised clothing, they showered then Mick left in the Jeep. In the end, Toby decided to go with Mick. Kaelan switched the urn low enough to keep hot, but not to be constantly boiling then went back to Sarah to watch over her.

Chapter 11

While sitting there watching over her, Kaelan was becoming worried about her. It had been over seven hours since the shooting and she was still unconscious. He checked her vitals but they were all fine, steady. Her wounds had stopped bleeding and were starting to clot over, and as a result her blood pressure was stable if still weak.

However, there was still no sign of her waking up. Then he became annoyed at himself for worrying, because his concern was deeper than it should have been. She still affected him, like she had when he had first met her, instead of it diminishing. That was the whole reason behind avoiding her during the past two years. Yet, it hadn't worked.

Regardless, Kaelan could not seem to just walk away from her. That too irritated him since he had been able to walk away from every other woman he had been with. But then, they had never affected him the way she did... does.

Deciding to distract himself earlier in the evening, before it became too late, he phoned his boss to let him know what had happened. Then, at his boss's instruction, Kaelan called the police on the number provided. The police told him they would send someone out some time the next morning.

When Mick and Toby had come back, the three men packed the groceries away and Kaelan showed them where everything was in the kitchen so they knew where to grab things to help themselves. He also showed them where the laundry was and told them their clothing was their responsibility or they could take turns doing the washing. Their choice. After that, he made dinner for the three of them then resumed watching over her.

*

The next morning at dawn, after so little sleep while watching over her, Kaelan made himself a coffee then checked his laptop. The website was still active, much to his relief, as it went a long way to setting him in a decent light with the police. Not that he needed it or cared but one less aggravation was one less worry at that point in time.

At 0800 hours, back in her room, there was a knock on the door. Shoving the bullet into the pocket of his jeans, he then opened the front door to two men in suits. Kaelan looked down at both of them.

"Mr... Kaelan Ridgeleigh?" The older of the two asked as he looked up at him with a hint of surprise.

Kaelan suspected the man wasn't expecting such a tall person. Kaelan had no problems in keeping himself from smiling even though he had found the visitor's reaction amusing.

"Yes, and you are?" Kaelan wasn't about to let anyone in unless he knew exactly who they were. While he already suspected who they were, he wasn't going to make it any easier for them.

The two men pulled out wallets and showed him their IDs. Kaelan took hold of each one and inspected them closely before handing them back to the two men. Their IDs were legit. He was looking at two plain clothes detectives.

"I'm Detective Harris and this is Detective Martin. We're here about the fire and deaths over in Wilston yesterday evening."

"Come in." Kaelan stood back and they walked in a few paces. Opening the door on his left, as he stepped into it, and indicated it to them.

"That's Mrs Sarah Brackenway, one of the victims. She was shot in the shoulder and thigh before I was able to get to her. While the men who did it were just fleeing the scene as I was arriving. No, I didn't see them but they were driving a brown van with emblems removed and the licence plate of GLT334. The other two survivors are the two men in the kitchen."

Kaelan ushered them out of the room and led them to the lounge room. Once there he handed Harris his photo ID and various licences.

"Go and start interviewing those two." Harris said to Martin as he took then looked at the licences before handing them back to Kaelan after making a note of each.

Martin nodded then headed to the kitchen.

Harris took out one of those micro tape recorders and set it on the coffee table after switching it on. He then sat back and settled himself into the chair as if it was going to be a long interview session.

"Let's start at the beginning. How did you know what was going to happen if you weren't a part of either group?" He asked.

Kaelan swivelled his laptop around to show the detective the cheesy website with the section stating the address, time and list of targets highlighted.

"I came home yesterday after being away for two years. I was checking to see what jobs were available when I discovered this site. I was reading through the details when I saw Sarah's name. Sarah and I met a couple of years ago and we became friends. The two men who own that website are rogue hunters and therefore, are not endorsed by the BHA... uh... Bounty Hunters Association." He clarified for the detective.

"Yes I had worked that out." Harris stated blandly then continued. "Well, if that's the case then they'll more than likely become the problem of the BHA. What did you do next after you saw Mrs Brackenway's name on the list?"

"I drove off to the address indicated. I had to program my GPS to find my way there. I was still a street or two away when I saw smoke rising. As I was turning into the street, the brown van was racing away. They almost rolled it as they rounded the corner, they were going that fast. That's why I think they're the rogues. Registered bounty hunters would have stayed until an official clean-up crew arrived. After entering the street, I saw the house was on fire and unsalvageable and thought I was too late. Until I saw two men carrying a figure out between them. As I got closer I saw they were carrying Sarah so I stopped beside them and told them to get in and I drove off with her injuries foremost in my mind."

"Please repeat the licence plate number for the record and why didn't you take Mrs Brackenway to the hospital?"

"The licence plate number of the brown van I saw racing away from the scene was GLT334. As for why I didn't take Sarah to the hospital was because she's on their list to kill and I didn't want to risk them finding her and killing her after I went to all that effort of saving her life. She's still in danger and I know I can protect her here far better than if she were anywhere else..." Kaelan stated plainly.

Then he was interrupted by a sound from his laptop. Looking at it, he was grateful for the foresight of having taken screen shots of the page earlier because it refreshed itself and the information was now different.

"Damn!" He muttered, picking up the laptop and started glancing through the new page.

"Mr Ridgeleigh, please put that down and get back to your recounting." Harris ordered sternly.

'He can be as stern as he likes but anything to do with this case is more important than the perceived blow to his authority.'

"Not meaning to be rude but they've just updated their page in regards to last night's hit and Sarah, Toby and Mick are still on their hit list. Unfortunately they know the three of them are still alive. Buuuuut..." He drew out the word as he quickly read what the idiots had to say. "...have no idea as where they are." While no outward sign was revealed, relief washed through him as he turned the laptop around to show the detective the new information.

After Harris finished reading it, Kaelan took screen shots of it as well. "I've just taken screen shots of the page and I have screen shots of the original page I saw yesterday afternoon. If you're interested I can email them to you when I email them to the BHA." Kaelan stated in an off-handed manner as if the situation was of no interest at all.

"That would be very helpful." Harris's tone was thick with

how unimpressed he appeared to be with Kaelan's attitude. Then he glared intently at Kaelan. "When you tended to Mrs Brackenway's injuries, were there bullets still in her and if so did you keep them?"

Digging into his jeans and pulling out a little plastic bag he handed it to the detective. "The one that hit her in the thigh went straight through and is somewhere amongst the ashes. That one there hit her in the shoulder and I haven't touched it with anything but tweezers before putting it in the bag." Kaelan stated bluntly, unfazed by the detective's attitude.

"Is there anything else regarding this situation you can tell me?"

Kaelan did a mental check to make sure all he knew had been told. "No, I've told you everything I know in regards to the event."

"The usual of: don't leave town and if you think of anything more then make sure you tell us Mr Ridgeleigh." Harris stood up and started to head to the kitchen, his impressions of Kaelan obvious.

"I'll be in Sarah's room if you need me for anything else." Kaelan stated then entered her room.

He was equally unimpressed with the detective, more in regards to his attitude than anything else, but he himself wasn't interested in influencing people and making friends. Her safety was all he cared about. However, she was still unconscious and his concern grew.

A short while later there was a soft knock on the door. Opening it, it revealed the two detectives standing side by side.

"We have statements from all three of you now. If we think of anything we'll contact you. If you think of anything then let us know immediately." Harris stated.

With just a nod, Kaelan showed them out then resumed watching over her.

For the past thirty-five hours he spent most of it sitting with her. She'd been unconscious the whole time and, due to the blood loss, he was worried she wasn't waking up. Unfortunately, he knew nothing about this side of a gun battle other than his own experiences and he was a fast healer. If she didn't wake up in a couple more hours, Kaelan decided he would call in a doctor.

Admittedly, he did get to sleep in his own bed for a few hours that first night, but not for very long. However, when he was with Sarah, Toby and Mick came in on separate occasions, asked about her and stayed with her whenever he needed to leave the room. Although, Mick's attitude was as if he didn't care about her and it made Kaelan wonder why.

'Why had the younger man bothered to save her and why does he stay if he couldn't care less?' Kaelan had no answers so he watched.

Chapter 12

'Well, I guess I'm not dead.'

Was the first thought she had as she became aware of her body. It hurt. She still had her eyes closed as she realised she was on her back. Opening her eyes she blinked up at a white ceiling.

'Where am I?' Her second thought because she didn't recognise the ceiling at all. She realised she wasn't in her home, nor Brandi and Abel's, not in a hospital and not at Danny's. While looking at the ceiling, she noted bright light ahead of her. Looking down towards her feet, she saw a window and it was daylight outside. She didn't know what time though.

Turning her head to the right, she closed her eyes and grimaced with pain from the left shoulder. She didn't understand why it hurt, she just knew it did. Slowly she opened her eyes. To her right was a curtained french doors. Gently she moved her head back so she was looking at the ceiling again and couldn't stop the groan from escaping her throat due to all the pain.

He had been dozing when a sound awoke him, causing him to become instantly alert. Looking at her, he saw she was finally awake and relief rushed through him. Concentrating on her, he didn't bother exploring why the relief regarding her was stronger than it was for his team mates whenever they suffered a similar situation.

She caught sight of movement from her peripheral vision on her left just as a weight settled beside her. Unfortunately for her, she turned too quickly and another groan of agony sounded as a sharp pain went through her left shoulder.

She'd closed her eyes when the pain had hit so she still hadn't seen who had sat on the bed. Slowly, she opened them and her mouth wasn't far behind when she saw him. A memory bobbed to the surface of hearing his voice telling her not to leave him and to fight.

So, she hadn't imagined him after all.

Watching her, he had a difficult time not to smile at her reaction. Somehow, he didn't think she would have appreciated his amusement right then.

"Kaelan." She'd managed to croak out around her surprise.

'Despite the extra weight, she hasn't changed.' He mused.

"Sarah." He acknowledged as blandly as he could because he had to break the bad news to her. Then he dragged his thoughts back to the business at hand instead of thinking how much he liked the sound of her name when he said it.

In saying that one word she knew he hadn't changed since the last time she'd spoken with him on the paintball range. Just as calm and composed and quiet-spoken as usual. He certainly didn't look any different. Just as good looking as ever as her heart started beating a little faster. That was extremely painful for some reason.

"What happened? Where am I? Why am I here and why am I hurting so much?" She blurted out, then blushed and hated it because it made the throbbing in her shoulder hurt more. She had to close her eyes and tried to breathe normally as she waited for the pain to ease. After she opened her eyes...

"What do you remember?" Kaelan asked non-committedly without a hint of any kind.

She frowned at him in thought then stared off down at her toes under the covers and thought.

"I... met with some friends..." She said slowly and thought some more. "We were... going to go out. I was the last one to... to get to the door..., when I heard gunshots..., then pain and fire." Her head rising too quickly to look at Kaelan, a throbbing agony pulsed through her shoulder. She had to close her eyes as she waited for it all to pass.

'Oh, that's going to hurt. Yep, there's the pain, oh... and nausea as well. Amazing how obvious they are as they flow across her face.' He thought sympathetically with a mental grimace.

He reached for her, placing his hand on her arm but knew there was nothing he could do to ease her pain. He then guessed, being last to the door and falling backwards the way she had, was the only thing that saved her from the same fate as her lover and friends.

She slowly opened her eyes and they glittered with moisture.

"Easy now, Sarah." His tone softening a fraction.

Tears started to stream down her face as she whispered, "They're dead aren't they?" She knew the answer even before he responded. 'Why hadn't I remembered when I was trying to work out where I was?' She had no answer.

"Yes. If the shots didn't kill then the fire certainly did. There's nothing left of the house." He knew there was nothing he could say that would sugar-coat it for her. His tone and expression were back to the way they were when she first saw him minutes ago.

She covered her face with her right hand and cried.

Kaelan just sat there, not that there was much he could do. He never was good around crying women. He never knew what he was supposed to do. Even though he knew what he wanted to do at that moment and that was to take her into his arms and cradle her. But not knowing how she would react was the other reason he didn't do so.

After a few moments, when her crying eased, "What happened to me?" She managed to get out in a sobbing voice.

"You were shot in the left shoulder and right thigh." Kaelan told her matter-of-factly. He was grateful her question changed the direction of his thoughts.

She guessed she should be grateful he wasn't sugar-coating any of it for her. Due to being blunt herself, she too preferred the truth. With the mention of her thigh, she tensed her right leg slightly and she could feel the pain spike through it.

'Well I guess she isn't any different to the men I work with when they're told about their injuries.' Mild amusement tainted his thoughts.

"Why does my chest hurt?" She asked as she managed to calm down some more even though she still had tears trailing down her cheeks.

"I had to do CPR on you a number of times." Watching her, he saw ghosts of memories pass quickly across her face.

She had a vague memory of someone saying her pulse was getting weaker, but that was all. She just nodded when she couldn't think of any kind of response. 'I mean what does one say to something like that?'

"Where am I?" She'd decided to be practical instead. An uncommon thing for her, but information she wanted to know anyway.

"My house." He stated, surprised at her calmness despite the tears still trickling down her face. She was taking all of the information better than he thought she would. He had to admit he had been expecting her to become hysterical since she does seem to be a rather highly emotional person. Still she managed to surprise him.

"Oh." She said. At that point, she didn't know what to think about being in his house. Especially when the need to go to the bathroom over-rode every other need and thought. She shoved the covers off herself and tried to sit up on the side of the bed, which was an agonising manoeuvre. She gritted her teeth and moved slowly with a soft grunt of pain sounding from her throat.

"What are you doing?" Kaelan asked slowly with a hint of warning in his voice. 'I have a suspicion being subtle doesn't always work with her.'

"I need to get up." She said through clenched teeth. She glanced down at herself and saw she wasn't wearing any of her own clothing.

"Uh... These aren't mine. Who changed my clothing, and why?" She asked as she turned to look at him but it was just a quick glance. Even after all this time she couldn't hold his gaze. Not if she didn't want to blush like a silly school girl.

"I did. Between the blood and the bullet holes, your clothes were ruined. I had to take everything off to clean you and then re-dress the wounds then you." Kaelan stated plainly and waited.

"I see." She responded softly, weakly.

While she was totally embarrassed at him ministering to her and seeing her naked with the extent of her overweight-ness, a large dose of relief seeped through her. Although she was worried about what he'd have seen having stripped and cleaned her, she was more worried about what he would say about what he had seen. After all, they weren't lovers, maybe not even friends and probably barely acquaintances, yet him tending to her to that extent was extremely personal.

To him, she sounded rather relieved. But not for long he surmised. Kaelan just couldn't resist what he said next.

"I must say I didn't think you were the piercing kind of girl. The tattoos were a surprise as well, but not as much as the piercings." He commented with a slight smile dancing upon his lips.

After a quick glance at him she closed her eyes and blushed profusely. 'That's the sort of comment I was worried about.'

"Things I had done years ago for my husband when he was alive." She blurted as her voice dwindled to a whisper. If she hadn't been so embarrassed she would have noted his smile more. She'd thought Kaelan had laughed, but was so embarrassed it barely registered.

And he did laugh, he couldn't help it. 'Damn but she's cute like that.'

Thinking about the panther made her ask, "Did the bullet pass out the back of the left shoulder?" She slowly grabbed her walking stick and noted it was the jaguar one Danny had given her.

"No, and are you always this stubborn?" He knew the frustration showed in his voice as well. 'Tough.'

With a few more tears falling, a sob escaped her as the stick reminded her of her friends. She forced herself to stand. The act of standing put a strain on both wounds and her chest and she groaned aloud with the effort. Feeling the bed move indicated that Kaelan had shifted position and she turned towards the foot of the bed. Glancing at him, she saw him frowning. He didn't look pleased with her being up and about. Not that there was anything she could do about it when nature called regardless of what one's physical condition was.

He moved so he could keep an eye on her. He couldn't keep the frown and displeasure off his face and knew she saw it when she peeked at him. 'The silly woman knows I don't like what she's doing but keeps doing it anyway.'

"Sometimes, yes." Muttering through clenched teeth due to the pain, she was relieved the panther was still whole.

'Now that I believe!' The thought muttered in his mind.

As she had hoped, the left shoulder started to ease with no pressure on it. The pain in her chest didn't ease at all as it hurt whenever she moved. The right thigh, however, hurt like hell and the pain was only intensifying. The reason being, even though she'd damaged both ankles, the left was worse than the right so most of her support went onto her right leg. Now, the right thigh hurt because of the weight she was placing on it.

He got off the bed and watched her. She was in so much pain he would have helped her if she would have let him. However, she wouldn't look at him or even ask. He moved to the foot of the bed and continued to watch her. She was exhausted by the time she reached him and it was just as painful to watch her move that slowly and carefully.

Strangely, despite being annoyed with her and her being in immense pain, she amazed him with her strength and determination. Especially for someone so emotional. He'd been expecting a woman with a lower pain threshold. 'I've seen men in my line of work scream more with less.'

She concentrated on trying to get to the bathroom. While she was determined not to make sounds of pain, she wasn't so sure what showed upon her face. By the time she reached him she was pooped and she still didn't know where the bathroom was.

"I so need a wheelchair if I'm going to make it in time." She muttered to herself as she stared at the floor.

"Make where in time?" He already guessed where she would be going, but he wanted to warn her not to do anything stupid. Even though he seemed to be too late on that point or maybe it wouldn't have mattered either way.

She hadn't realised Kaelan's hearing was so good. 'It figures.' She thought somewhat sourly, and quickly raised her head at his response. Unfortunately, the pair were so close together that, in tilting back to see his face, she lost her balance and started to fall backwards. Biting her bottom lip as pain exploded from her injuries when she initially tried to stop herself, she braced herself since there was nothing she could do to stop herself from falling.

As soon as he saw her starting to topple backwards, he grabbed at her and she ended up in his arms with him bent over her as if they were doing a dance dip. With his face so close to hers, she stared at him with eyes wide.

"You know you are too tall." She said breathlessly, then blushed for saying such a silly thing but that was what popped into her mind at the time.

In that instant, he knew it had been a mistake to bring her back to his place. 'Oh, not for her safety, but for my peace of mind.' He realised in that moment she had a permanent little spot inside him and he had no chance in hell of getting her out.

'Damn it all!' He thought as he tried to keep his face blank, but didn't think he had succeeded too well, and his voice came out a little deeper than he had intended, "You know you are too short."

With a look she found impossible to interpret, he said those words in a low voice she found incredibly sexy and it made her heart pound harder and faster. As much as she wanted him, she didn't know if the right time was now or not. However, her need for the bathroom pressed upon her the urgency to find it so she tried to stand upright again.

Holding her the way he was, he could feel her heart thundering harder than from just the fright she'd received due to the over balancing, but as to why it was he didn't know. She started struggling to stand up despite the pain it caused her.

'That's it! I've had enough and I don't care what she thinks of it!' He swept her into his arms as he stood upright.

"I'm too heavy, put me down before you hurt yourself." She whispered, eyes wide with surprise. She had a tendency to whisper when she became embarrassed.

"If you stop struggling, I can carry you to the bathroom with no problems." He practically growled at her. She was going to drive him mad. He could see it. If he had any sense he would take her to the hospital and leave her there. Then he mentally sighed with the memory of why he'd brought her back to his house in the first place.

'I seem to have made him angry with me and I don't understand why.' She blushed profusely and went still in his arms. His arms were strong, she could feel the muscles where they were pressed against her.

'If I wasn't so embarrassed I might enjoy this more.'

The thing was, she wasn't too heavy to carry at all. Either that or he was stronger than he'd thought. No matter, he was still surprised he could carry her without too much trouble and at how well she fitted into his arms.

As he carried her to the bathroom, she had gotten a brief view of lounge room and dining area. Despite his anger, Kaelan gently set her on her feet in the bathroom and walked out the door. A few minutes later she opened the door to see him standing there against the wall opposite.

Without a word he picked her up in his arms again and took her back to her room. "You are to stay in bed for another couple of days at least." He ordered and sounded like one used to having his orders followed without question or argument.

"I'm going to need to go to the bathroom during that time." She said gruffly as they entered her assigned room. 'He's treating me like a child and I don't like it.'

Mentally, he sighed yet again. Despite her petulance, he knew she was right. It would be less stressful for her if she had less distance to travel. Then a thought occurred to him. 'Why didn't I think of it sooner?'

All of a sudden, he turned on his heel and headed into the room opposite hers. It was another bedroom but with an en suite. When they entered the room she saw the en suite's open door on the left, behind a huge bed. The bed was longer than normal. She briefly noted that the additional wall between en suite and bed had been done to match the rest of the room. The room was very clean and neat.

"Whose room is this?" She asked quietly, fearing the answer. He barely heard her.

"Mine, but you can stay in here until you have healed some." That was the answer she feared.

"I can't take your room..." She started saying with a slight panic in her voice.

'Still the tiny baby bunny after all this time.'

"Don't be silly." Kaelan interrupted sternly. "It's the logical room for you to be in and you would have been in here from the beginning if I had thought of it." He stated gruffly as he gently placed her on the bed and pulled the covers over her.

Kaelan's bed and mattress were custom made to be longer than normal so as to accommodate his 193cm tall frame. As a result she just looked so tiny in it.

'I'll have to make sure the sheets are dark coloured so her pale skin doesn't blend with them. That way, I can find her amongst the covers... God! What a silly thought' However, that silly thought had him fighting not to smile at the ridiculousness of it.

For all the times she could be oblivious to the numerous things happening around her, the contrasts between his voice and actions didn't escape her. Yet, for some reason, his gentleness didn't surprise her in the least. Also, unsurprisingly, it endeared him to her even more so. This, of course, just added to her dilemma in regards to him.

"Umm... I don't mean to be a pain..."

He couldn't help rising his eyebrows at that and she frowned at him in return.

"...but can I have some more pillows behind me to prop me up please? You see, I don't sleep too well on my back and it's not like I can roll on to either side at the moment." She asked softly.

'How can someone who reacts to everything like the tiny shy baby bunny be able to deliver a kill shot thrice and still be that shy and nervous? I guess that's the sixty-four million dollar question and I don't have the answer. But, oh yeah, definitely a pain. Cute or not.' Without a word Kaelan placed pillows behind her until she said she was comfortable.

He stepped back and said, "Get some rest. I'll be back shortly with some food." Then he turned on his heel and left the room, leaving the bedroom door open.

At that point she was glad he had left. She needed the break from the confusion, nervousness and embarrassment he caused within her. She needed that time to get her heart and pulse back to their regular speed and location. It seemed nothing had changed for her in regards to him.

'Two years since I last saw him and he still has the same effect on me. I am so lost.' She leant back into the pillows to close her eyes.

She must have dozed off briefly because she remembered dreaming about Danny, Abel and Brandi. Of the last time she'd seen them. Tears flowed down her face at the loss of three dear friends. She grabbed one of the other pillows from beside her and buried her face in it to help muffle her crying.

However, it wasn't much help as the smell of Kaelan was all

over it and that just made her cry harder. She felt silly for being so conflicted about how she felt about the men who had been, and were still, in her life: her husband, Kaelan, Danny and Kaelan again.

'I loved my husband but he's dead. I'm attracted to Kaelan but he left and Danny walked into my life. I became attracted to Danny and it could have led to love over time if I allowed it, but I was too shy and had let it progress so slowly that a snail was moving faster. Then he was killed and Kaelan instantly waltzes back into my life. Only I discover I'm still attracted to him but it looks like he still isn't attracted to me. I just don't know what to do about it.'

She just buried her face further into the pillow and let herself cry. She was starting to ease up on the crying when…

A few minutes later, after informing the other two men she was finally awake, he entered the bedroom and paused suddenly when he saw her with a pillow pressed firmly to her face. With his heart in his throat and three quick long strides he was beside her.

While he knew she couldn't suffocate herself that way, he didn't know if she knew or not. After all the effort he went through in saving her life, he wasn't going to let her end it now. Quickly placing the tray of food on the bedside table, he yanked the pillow away from her face.

"What are you trying to do?!" Kaelan demanded, standing over her.

She looked at him as fresh tears rolled down her face, "What does it look like?!" She demanded back, pointing at the pillow. Between the tears on her face and the teary wetness on the pillows it was fairly obvious. To her anyway.

Frowning, he mentally sighed as he had thought she was trying to suffocate herself, and threw the now tear stained pillow to the other side of her as she wiped her tears away. He shifted slightly on his feet. 'Damned crying females' he thought then said, "I brought you some food. Eat it while it's fresh."

"Fine." She mumbled and stared out the window.

Kaelan paused then spun around and walked out the room. This time closing the door. 'This woman is going to be the death of me! I'm sure of it!'

Chapter 13

A couple of hours later Mick came into the room to collect her dishes.

"Thank you Mick." She said with a smile; albeit a sad watery one.

"You're welcome." He grunted and started to leave; seemed like things between them hadn't improved.

"Mick?"

He paused and looked at her.

"Can I ask a favour of you please?"

"What is it?" He asked in the same tone as if she was asking for more than a favour.

She ploughed ahead anyway. "Can you go to my place of business and let them know that I'm injured and won't be back for my clients until further notice please? I don't know how many days I've missed out on and my clients can't be too happy about it. Especially with no notice on my table." She finished, staring at her hands.

"Sure, Hon. Give me the address." Mick said quietly.

She stared up at him in surprise. It was the nicest he had ever spoken to her. She smiled a watery smile and wrote the address down on a sticky that she'd found in a drawer in the bedside table beside her. She'd gotten bored and snooped earlier. "Thank you Mick." She smiled at him.

"The... event... happened two days ago." Mick said gently as he pocketed the sticky then left with her dishes.

'Two days ago! I have been out for two days!'

She went back to staring out the window, trying to think of nothing. But 'nothing' didn't want to stay in her mind. The 'event', as Mick politely put it, churned through her head and wouldn't leave her alone as the thoughts and images chased each other round and round in circles.

Kaelan decided to try busying himself between cleaning house, shooting at the gun range at the back of his yard, working out in the gym and swimming. Anything so he didn't think about her. By the time evening came, he gave up and went inside. This time he busied himself with dinner. He served up some for Sarah and stared at it. He hadn't been able to get her out of his mind at all and he really didn't want to face her again just yet.

Sighing, he turned to Toby. "Take it to her would you?"

Before Toby could collect the tray Kaelan stormed back outside. He leant against the back of the gun range, facing the bushland at the back of his property, gently banging the back of his head against it in frustration.

'I don't understand why this particular woman is getting to me. I've been with other women, and knew more about them during those times, over the years and none, none of them affected me the way she's affecting me. Hell! Honestly, I have never truly felt for any woman before. Sure I can be shallow at times. Then there's been the sexual need that jerking off hasn't satisfied, but who hasn't been like that?'

He stared into the bushland but still his thoughts wouldn't leave the subject alone. He just ended up rehashing everything he'd ever thought about her and the subject in general, as well as what Ed had said to him back in February. Still, he didn't see a solution.

'They were only to meet the needs of my body. Nothing more. If it was a simple case of bedding her and moving on everything would be fine. But, for the life of me, she's different. She isn't the kind of woman to sate a body's needs then just walk away and never come back.' That final thought surprised him and Kaelan didn't understand why he would think that way but knew it was the truth.

'In the short time I've known her I've wanted to strangle her and praise her. I've wanted to leave her for the wolves but wanted to wrap her up and protect her. I've wanted to tell her she's being ridiculous yet wanted to make her smile. I've never wanted a woman in my life but I can't stop thinking about her. I've never been this conflicted over any woman before. Not only that, but I still don't know what to do about any of it. It's giving me a headache.' He sighed.

Deep down he knew some of his thoughts were superficial but he was trying to be honest with himself and that was just confusing him even further. Nothing was helping. With her in the house there was no relief. All of it was just chasing itself round and round in his head.

She must have fallen asleep somewhere along the line,

because the next thing she knew was Toby entering the room with her evening meal.

"Thanks Toby."

"You okay?" he asked with concern in his eyes.

"Yeah, as well as can be expected."

"You been crying long?"

Sarah touched her cheeks and they were indeed wet. "I must have been crying in my sleep." She said softly.

Toby knelt on the floor by the bed and took her hand. "It's okay to cry you know."

"I know. I just seem to be doing a lot of it."

"It's to be expected, with all you've been through."

"And what about you? Danny is a loss to you and Mick as well."

"I know. We have you now." She must have looked as confused as she felt because Toby then said, "Danny told us, Mick and I, that if anything happened to him then we were to look after you no matter what. So, you are stuck with us now." Toby had a gentle smile on his face.

"Toby, people aren't possessions to be passed from one person to another." She couldn't stop the tears from spilling down her cheeks.

Toby gently hugged her and stood up to leave.

"Where's Kaelan?" Sarah asked timidly.

"He's around here somewhere. His Jeep's still here." With that, Toby walked out.

Not looking at the food waiting for her, she stared out the window again. 'Now it's looking darker, early evening I guess.' She couldn't really see anything out of the windows because of the lace curtains that hung across them. All she could see was a faint light and some vague shapes of plant life, maybe trees.

Kaelan had been so wrapped up in his thoughts he hadn't noticed it was raining again. Not hard, but enough to dampen his hair sufficiently to send the occasional cold trickle down his back. The sun had fully set as well, letting him know winter hadn't long passed.

With another sigh, he pushed away from the wall and went back into the house. He ate his now cold dinner, too lazy to heat it up, had a shower, put on pyjama pants then went to bed. However, he wasn't tired enough to fall asleep straight away.

*

Once again she'd had a forty winks session as she woke up to a dark room. Totally dark. There were no lights of any form in the room, other than a little alarm clock with glowing hands, and no light coming in from outside. In a bit of a panic she swung her arm out to turn on the bedside lamp when her hand knocked something over and it crashed about rather loudly in the silence of the darkness.

Jerking to alertness after just starting to doze off, he heard what sounded like something falling over. Two thoughts ran through his mind... They found her or she was getting out of bed again.

'If she's out of bed, I'm going to throttle her' He thought as he tripped out of the sheets and burst into her room across the hallway from his, after picking himself up off the floor.

'Damn the woman! She has me being clumsy and tripping over myself.'

With a frown, he opened the door and flicked the light switch on, then just stood there for a moment. She was fumbling for the lamp switch when the door burst opened and the bedroom light flared into life.

"I-I'm s-s-sorry, I-I'm sorry." She stammered, her right hand covering her eyes from the sudden brightness.

He could hear the fear lightly tainting her voice.

"Are you alright?" A quick glance around suggested no one was in the room and the window looked fine. Little did he realise at that point, or even when he first met her, how often he would be asking her those words.

To Sarah, his tone was stern just like it had been ever since she'd woken up after having been shot. She squinted at him through her hand.

"No. Yes... I guess." Her voice dwindled into silence. She kept her hand over her eyes and concentrated on breathing so she wouldn't cry because she could feel the tears building. She didn't want to cry any more but knew it would be a losing battle. If not now then definitely later.

'Why the hell do I have to be so damned emotional?!' She wondered critically for the umpteenth time.

"So, which is it?" He moved closer to the bed and noted she'd knocked her drink over, that was the sound he'd heard, and she hadn't touched her dinner either. He paused and she didn't say anything so he sat down beside her. She then felt his hand on hers as he gently pulled her hand away from her face.

However, she wouldn't look up at him.

"Look at me Sarah." His voice gentle and it surprised her as she had never heard that tone from him before.

Still, she didn't move her head. Sarah could see he was wearing long pyjama pants, but no shirt. His chest was smooth except for a few scars and she wanted to touch it. Then his hand came into view. He touched her chin to lift her head as a large fat tear fell and landed with a softly audible splat on his hand. He ignored it and continued to gently force her to look at him. His touch sent tingles through her.

As he gently held her chin, he couldn't help noticing once again how nice her skin felt to the touch. He chastised himself then went back to the subject at hand. Pun not intended.

"Are you alright?" Kaelan gently asked again.

She blushed at her silliness – both the way she felt about him and her reaction to the darkness, but she couldn't help the way she felt about either.

"Yeah, I... I just hate total darkness. I can't see... I just hate it." she whispered.

"Why didn't you just say so?" Mentally sighing, he was relieved it was nothing worse.

"Because it's a childish fear." She responded glumly.

He could read the embarrassment in her face but didn't think it was a childish fear. There are things in the dark to be very afraid of and people such as herself have a right to be afraid.

"I'll be right back." He collected the untouched meal and left the room. At least it was something he could do for her without her carrying on so much. Placing the dishes in the kitchen he then went to one of the drawers to grab a little night light that just plugs into a power point/board. Then he grabbed a cloth to clean the mess on the bed side table.

Noting the mess made her notice the need to go to the bathroom. She slowly swung her feet over the edge only to discover her feet just touched the floor in the tiptoe position. The bed was rather high up off the floor. But then, so was he.

She had just finished when Kaelan came back into the room. He watched her as she slowly made her way back to the bed. She tried not to hunch over on herself but it hurt too much to stand up straight and walk at the same time.

Standing there, he watched her painful progress to the bed. 'She may act like a tiny baby bunny but she is a determined tiny baby bunny.' He kept the frown on his face while watching her, but honestly, he was amazed at her strength of will. 'Or is it stubbornness? Hard to tell with her.' He thought.

He walked towards her as she sat on the edge of the bed panting from the effort. When she re-positioned herself to get back in, Kaelan crouched down to help her swing her legs up onto the bed. She swatted his hands away.

"I'm injured Kaelan, not crippled." She said gently to take the sting out of her slap as he had started to frown at her; yet again.

So he stopped frowning, sat back on his heels and watched her as she hooked her left ankle under her right and used her left to swing both up onto the bed. It still hurt, and she couldn't keep the grimace off her face, but she completed the manoeuvre.

Kaelan didn't say a word, just stood up with a slight smile and proceeded to clean up the mess she'd made.

'I've done something to amuse him it would seem. Damn, he's so confusing.'

While she frustrated the hell out of him, moments like that equally surprised and pleased him. Then he frowned because he didn't understand how she could make him feel that way, or why she should matter to him at all.

'God! I hate all this. All the thinking, confusion and uncertainty she's causing within me. I've never been this way before. Ever.'

After two trips back and forth, he bent down and placed the night light in the power board under the bed and peered at it briefly with satisfaction as it glowed. Standing up he then gazed at her.

"Would you like something to eat?"

"Yes please." She said hesitantly because she was surprised to be offered more since she hadn't eaten the lot he'd just taken away.

Kaelan walked out. About ten minutes later he walked back in with a glass of juice and a sandwich.

"Thank you." Looking at the clock she noted it was about 2:00am. "I didn't mean to wake you." She had that rabbit tone in her voice again.

"I'm a light sleeper any way." He gave a slight shrug, but it was true even if he hadn't really been asleep at the time.

The movement made the muscles in his chest move and she never thought such a simple action could appear so damned sexy, but it did. With a mental sigh, 'Change the subject before those treacherous hormones became too active.'

"What do you do for a living?" She dared to ask and looked at him as she ate.

"What do you think I do for a living?" He asked keeping his voice neutral.

Seeing her looking a little wide eyed at him, her question took him by surprise and a dread started growing within him as he knew he had to answer her truthfully. Regardless of the consequences he wouldn't lie to her. However, he was expecting the worst when she found out.

While it was true he hadn't been looking, he hadn't yet found a woman willing to accept him with the job he does. Some of the women whom he had bedded in the past thought time with him was fun. However, even though he wasn't interested in a full time relationship, neither were they in the end.

A look of annoyance flashed briefly across her face. 'I hate it when people answer a simple question with another question.' Instead of saying so, she blushed and answered.

"From the first time I saw you I thought military or ex-military."

Kaelan stared at her with surprise. Nevertheless… 'Seems she is perceptive after all. Now, by how much I wonder?' So, he answered her. "Ex-military. What else?"

His reaction made her realise she'd been right in her suspicions.

"When I thought that as your career, I also thought maybe sniper and if not military any more, then perhaps assassin, hit man, maybe bounty hunter." She blurted out in a rush. She was so nervous in answering him then she felt silly for what she'd just said; revealing her silly thoughts, but she had never thought of him as anything else and wasn't going to lie to him regardless.

He was surprised by how his body reacted, tightened in response to the soft breathy rush of her voice. However, he couldn't stop his eyebrows from rising in amazement at her words. 'She is one very perceptive bunny. No wonder she seemed frightened of me when we first met.' He thought, then…

"You thought that about me when you first saw me?"

"Yes."

"Why?"

"It was the way you walked, held yourself. The way you spoke, an economy of words. Just a bunch of little things really."

"And none of it worried you?" He wanted to make sure. She was certainly full of surprises.

She shook her head as she took a bite of her sandwich.

'Then… Why was she frightened of me on the paintball range? She just keeps confusing the hell out of me.' He frowned with confusion but just wanted to make doubly sure.

"You really don't have a problem with someone in that line of work?"

"No. Should I?" Despite the blushing, she asked him calmly with a hint of genuine innocent confusion. It seemed her responses astonished him. She'd never thought about such things before but maybe her acceptance wasn't normal. 'What a shame someone's career condemns them in the eyes of others.'

He couldn't believe she was so calm about it. 'Is it a case with a gun in her hand she's a professional? Then without the gun she's an innocent and it isn't an act on her part? It's not a common scenario but not unheard of and not one I'd personally come across before. However, her reactions just now just don't mesh with that scenario.' He just didn't know what to think about it. The time didn't seem right to ask yet.

"The average normal person would be horrified at the

thought of someone being a sniper, assassin, hit man, etc." He wanted to make sure. He needed to make sure of how she felt about his chosen career.

"Yes well, their loss. I do believe there is a call for that sort of work whether people like it or not, and a lot of them just don't realise that it's needed outside of the obvious. Besides, while I may act the average normal person, I'm anything but when it comes to how I perceive things and I hate being too clichéd." She blushed. "So, now I ask again… what do you do for a living?" She gazed at him intently, giving him complete eye contact.

If Kaelan hadn't been sitting already he would have fallen. Her calmness and responses stunned him so much that he willingly told her the truth.

"I'm all of the above you mentioned. I hunt rogue humans, therians, vamps and anything that may come up as a job."

"I take it you enjoy it."

"Immensely." He grinned. He couldn't help it; it was just so much fun.

To her his grin was a big boyish grin. It made him look even more stunning and very attractive. 'He definitely should smile some more.' "Always good when someone enjoys their work." She said instead.

She smiled and his insides tightened again. "Do you?"

"Enjoy being a nail tech?" She asked, surprised he would think to ask her.

"Yes."

"Yes I do. Not as exciting as what you do, but I'm not exactly physically able to successfully go… hunting." She stated plainly.

"Maybe not the way I do it, but you seemed pretty good at ambushing." 'And she was. Maybe she would make a good sniper. It would be interesting to find out.' He thought. He watched as her eyes widened in surprised horror and he didn't understand why.

While that seemed like one hell of a compliment coming from Kaelan, she knew she had to ruin that perception immediately. "Oh no... That was nothing but luck. No training at all. Those two games with you were the fourth and fifth time I had ever played paintball and the second and third time I got any successful hits, which were just luck anyway. I know my limits and I know I'm not good. It was just a spot of fun at the time." She was babbling. She knew it and couldn't stop as she didn't want him to get the wrong idea about her skills.

'Why would she be scared? I just don't understand this woman. Just when I thought we were getting somewhere and she still plays innocent. She's been the only person to have successfully 'killed' me. Even on the job no one has come that close. Why can't she just be honest about it?! I'd thought if I admitted to what I was then she would as well.'

Kaelan just looked at her. No expression on his face as if a light bulb had been switched off. He stood up, took her now empty glass and plate.

"Get some rest Sarah." Disappointed in her unwillingness to be truthful with him he walked out, turning the light off.

His reaction confused her. It was almost as if he didn't believe her, as if she was lying to him and that hurt. 'I would never lie to him. Especially about that.'

She almost started to reach for the lamp again when she

noticed a soft bluish-white glow coming from under the bed. A smile softly touched her lips. Kaelan had placed a little night light in the power board under the bed without her noticing. It was very nice of him and it just intensified her attraction to him.

She settled herself to try getting some more sleep.

Chapter 14

Sarah would say she tossed and turned as per usual, but stuck on the flat of her back she just woke up a lot and tried to shift position slightly to make herself more comfortable. She started to shove the covers aside when Toby entered the room.

"What do you think you are doing?" He demanded with a frown.

"Don't you guys ever knock?" She frowned back at him. He had the grace to look embarrassed. "Now shoo and leave me alone for a bit and knock next time. And tell the others that too." She roused at him as she made shooing motions with her right hand.

He left.

Kaelan was in the kitchen enjoying his first coffee of the day when Toby came back out with the breakfast tray in hand.

"Still asleep or doesn't want it?" He asked the man, barely containing his annoyance. 'She needs to eat to keep up her strength so she'll heal and get better, but she won't if she keeps refusing to do so.'

"Neither. She just told me to go away for a bit because I didn't knock before walking in. She said to tell you both to knock before entering from now on." Toby finished, scratching his head.

'The poor guy, hit by Sarah logic/behaviour. I know exactly

how he feels.' Kaelan thought with an amused mental shake.

"I'll talk to her." Kaelan said as he put his cup down then pushed away from the cabinets. He knocked on the bedroom door and entered without pausing.

Watching Toby leave, she was beginning to think she was in a hospital instead of a bedroom in a house with the way everyone just kept entering without asking. Sighing, she sat on the edge of the bed working up the nerve to put up with the pain of walking. She was starting to stand up when there was a knock on the door.

"Go aw…" She started saying then the door opened so changed her words to, "Get out." before she even saw who it was. Unfortunately she lost her balance when trying to sit back down and let out a very audible hiss of pain that brought tears to her eyes.

"I thought I told you to stay in bed." The stern voice of Kaelan stated but was concerned about her having hurt herself like that.

"And you put me in here so I was closer to the bathroom." She grumped in a voice thick with tears. "Besides I need a shower."

"Then I'll help you." Then thought better of it as his body reacted to the unbidden thoughts which followed. But then…

"Oh no. Just because you've seen all of me before while I was unconscious doesn't mean you get to now." She said rather quickly. She was embarrassed enough as it was that he'd already seen her that first time.

"You're being childish, Sarah." While he experienced a small sense of relief at her objections he frowned at her reactions. It seemed she wasn't interested in him that way and that knowledge disappointed him more than it should have.

A frown creased his lovely face yet again. 'Why must he sound like he's always angry with me?'

"No. I'm pathetically being a typical woman who doesn't want some man who isn't her lover to see her naked and helpless now that she's conscious." She blurted out then could feel herself turn bright red. 'Why does he have to make a big deal about it? Or, more to the point, trivialise it as if he's nothing more than a professional carer with no interest in me.'

However, he got the impression there was more to it. While her reactions still confused him, it also meant there was still a chance for him. Then he felt more confusion at his own reactions since he was still maintaining not wanting a woman in his life.

"I'll get you a chair to sit on." Kaelan said calmly trying not to smile as he walked back out of the room.

Most of the time lately she irritated the hell out of him, but then moments like that and he wanted to hold her. That thought wiped the smile from his face. He sighed, grabbed a white plastic garden chair and headed back to the bedroom.

She sat where she was until he came back. Kaelan placed the chair in the ample sized shower cubicle for her, then stood there and, even though the distance from the bed to the bathroom behind it wasn't that great, watched her slow progress into the bathroom. She paused beside him and he looked down at her.

"I'm sorry I'm a pain in all things generally. I can't promise I'll do better because I probably won't." She murmured softly then paused. "I've been sweating during the night so would you be kind enough to open the windows for me. Also, I need something else to wear please." She glanced at him briefly, but for the most part she just stared at their feet. Both of which were bare. 'Such nice looking feet he has.'

"Go have your shower, Sarah." He said quietly then walked away.

She slid the bathroom door closed and had her shower as quickly as possible trying not to think. Typically for her, she failed with a few tears escaping and just tried to hurry through her shower. That desire to rush proved to be difficult with every twinge of pain as she bathed.

Once she had the door closed, he sighed then opened the windows, stripped the bed and remade it. After that, he grabbed a fresh tank top and boxer briefs as he listened to her having her shower. Then, he went for the first aid kit and sat at the foot of the bed to wait for her to come out. He concentrated on doing those things because he didn't want to think about how she was getting deeper under his skin, how each little thing endeared her to him even as they frustrated the hell out of him.

'God! I will be so pleased when that hit against those two men have been issued and she can go back to her own home!' He sighed as he stared up at the ceiling and hoped he could survive this trial.

Wrapped in a towel, she hobbled out of the bathroom only to pause beside the bedside table. She noted everything he had done and saw him sitting at the foot of the bed with a first aid kit beside him. She also saw another pair of men's boxer briefs and a tank top. She was about to ask him to leave so she could change as he gazed at her. Her mouth opened but no sound came out.

"Come over here and I'll help you. You can't do it yourself, you know it." Then thought, 'I swear, sometimes it's like dealing with a child.'

Sarah sighed and did as she was told because she knew he was right no matter how much she wanted to argue with him. She stood in front of him, between him and the head of the bed. Hanging onto him – which he felt no matter how hard he tried to ignore it – with the towel still wrapped around her, Kaelan fought hard to keep from smiling as she only lifted each foot a small way as he slipped the boxer briefs up to her knees.

In an embarrassed rush she pulled them up the rest of the way, while he sat back on his heels looking somewhat amused at her reactions. Then he helped her thread her arms then the rest of her upper body into the tank top. She only pulled the towel away once she was appropriately covered. In the end he couldn't keep his amusement from showing and she flushed brighter.

"Now just stand there. The bullet that entered your thigh went out the other side, so it's easier to look at it while you stand. You were lucky it missed the bone and the bullet wasn't the kind which shatters on impact. They were amateurs." Kaelan informed as he shook his head while taking off the thigh bandage and dressing. After inspecting it to make sure it was okay he then re-dressed and bandaged it up again.

"How is it?" She asked tentatively.

"Looks good." He muttered distractedly. Then he got her to sit on the bed and he slipped the left side of the tank top down so he could tend to that injury. His face is so close to hers that if she turned to face him she thought she would be kissing him. Suffice to say she couldn't make herself turn towards him, but she did allow herself to enjoy the woodsy outdoor scent of him.

"This one is looking good as well."

For once, his calmness pleased her. She hadn't realised it at the time, but she felt a knot of stress release itself from head to toe and let out a little sigh of relief.

Guessing she was somewhat anxious about her injuries, he supposed he couldn't blame her really. Other than the surgical scars on each ankle, her thigh and shoulder were the only non-surgical scars she seemed to have.

Realising she had never experienced anything like it before, it would be natural that her stress levels were going to be higher than usual and he should have realised that. But then, he still thought she had had some training. It seemed like she was better than even he had realised since she had no other scars.

With a struggle and a mental sigh of frustration, he pushed those thoughts away and lightly touched her arm. "You're okay Sarah." He said kindly.

She just nodded as he helped her into bed. The relief had made her feel weak so she let him. With her heart pounding hard and fast, a fine trembling started up within her and she had to clench her hands into fists so it wouldn't be noticeable. Once she was on the bed she placed her right arm over her eyes.

However, Kaelan had noticed her shaking as he brought the covers up over her. Then she heard him leave the room without another word but he wasn't gone long. When he came back…

"Here, take these. They're just every day pain killers and they'll help ease your pain." He handed them and a glass of water to her.

"Thanks." She said sounding subdued even to herself. She wouldn't look at Kaelan.

With nothing to keep him beside her he left.

He prepared her some fresh toast and a cup of tea and asked Mick to take it to her. Mick looked at him as if Kaelan was going to bite his head off but did as asked. Then Kaelan made himself another coffee and some toast and wondered what in the hell he was going to do about her.

A few minutes later Mick arrived with a cup of tea and some toast.

"Thank you Mick." She smiled at him. It had become habit to smile at him ever since he first made it clear that he didn't really like her. However, she'd made the effort for Danny's sake, not that Danny knew. Or, at least, she didn't think he knew. The point is, she tried to get along with Mick because at first she thought they would be a part of each other's lives because of Danny. Now, it's because Danny told them to look after her.

"You're welcome. Have you been giving Kaelan a hard time?" Mick asked, frowning at her.

"Not since before my shower. Why?" She said softly.

"Not sure. He doesn't seem real happy at the moment."

"He doesn't confide in me so I don't know what's wrong with him." She said as she looked at her hands. Then she looked at Mick. "Are you doing anything important?"

"No, why?"

"If it's okay with you, I would like some company. I might fall asleep but it would be nice to talk to someone till then." She rubbed the bridge of her nose in embarrassment. Whether they're friends or lovers, male or female, she couldn't hide her shyness and embarrassment no matter how hard she tried.

"Sure, I'll stay." For a long silent moment Mick stared at her and she could feel the weight of that look. "I owe you an apology, Sarah."

"What for?" The surprise plain in her voice.

"For thinking the worst about you from when we first met. I haven't given you a fair chance and for that I am sorry."

"I don't know what to say, Mick, other than apology accepted." Sarah smiled at him. "But why do you feel that you haven't given me a chance?" She had to ask, it was a puzzling comment to her.

"I'd thought you were like all the other women who'd tried to hang around him. That you only wanted the prestige of having been with a vamp or that you were a gold digger and just in it to see what you could get from him. I was wrong and I apologise." In saying all that, it was positively a speech from Mick.

She took his hand, "It's okay, you have nothing to apologise for. You were only being protective of him and that's a good thing. As I said, I accept your apology. Friends?" She looked him in the eyes.

Mick smiled and it was a lovely smile. "Friends."

They chatted about anything that came to mind while she had her breakfast.

Chapter 15

Obviously she'd dozed off again, because when she awoke Mick and her dishes were gone. For the past day or so she'd been trying real hard not to think. Not to dwell on what had happened that night. Of course, she hadn't really succeeded. Sarah threw the covers off and went to the bathroom. When she came out, she started rifling through Kaelan's wardrobe.

Thoughts of her chased themselves around in his mind leaving him knotted up inside and still he didn't know what to do. It was almost lunch time when he decided to go talk to her. Kaelan opened the bedroom door then remembered he should have knocked first. However, he forgot all about it and why he was there in the first place when he saw her snooping through his wardrobe.

She found what she was looking for and was just grabbing it when a voice spoke.

"What the bloody hell do you think you are doing?!" Kaelan demanded in a slow and quiet tone. 'Damn it! What is it with her not following simple instructions?' However, with what followed next, he started to regret going mad at her.

Hearing his voice, he didn't sound happy, Sarah spun around

in surprise and fright because there was no knock and hadn't heard the door open. Hurting her injuries with the sudden movement, she lost her balance and hit the partially carpeted floor hard. His robe fluttering down over her. Pain blossomed everywhere and started throbbing, along with her pulse racing hard and fast.

Four to five long strides and Kaelan was beside her, towering over her. 'He's very tall when I'm standing, I only come up to his chest. Lying flat on my back on the floor, he's positively gigantic.' Tears streamed across her temples into her hair line from the pain of the sudden movement and the fall combined.

He stared down at her and her freely flowing tears, but he was so damned angry. Angry she wouldn't stay in bed like she was supposed to, angry she'd frightened the hell out of him when she fell and angry at himself for letting himself care about her in the first place. Unfortunately, the anger came out loud and clear when he spoke to her.

"Damn it Sarah. I don't tell you to stay in bed just to hear my own voice."

"You didn't knock. I didn't hear you come in so you scared the daylights out of me." She cried between the sobs.

Kaelan wanted to hit her, he wanted to cradle her, he so wanted to throttle her. Instead, he scooped her into his arms and carried her back to the bed. His strength amazed her – while it wouldn't even occur to him until much, much later – as he'd just lifted her as a dead weight up off the floor. She still had his robe clutched in her hands. He placed her on the bed and tried to take the robe from her.

"You don't need the robe Sarah. Please give it to me." It was only because he had said please that she'd let go of the robe. He draped it over the foot of the bed.

Kaelan came back and sat beside her, gently checking her injuries and the back of her head.

"You're lucky. Nothing's bleeding." He sighed. "What were you trying to do Sarah?" He asked with a frown as he pulled the covers up to her chest, straightening them out then sat back down next to her. His hand was so close to hers he didn't have to reach at all to touch it but he didn't move.

'If I do I'm still likely to throttle her instead of offering comfort.'

"I wanted to sit in the lounge room or some other part of the house instead of the bedroom. I'm bored and lonely and barely see anyone unless it's a meal time or you coming to check on me, then you leave again." She sobbed at him. She was trying to calm down but the pain was rather intense. "If I wanted to be alone I would go back to my tiny apartment. Besides, I wanted to talk to the three of you and since you're all out there I thought I would join you."

Heaven help him, she started crying again. It never occurred to him she would feel lonely with no one sitting with her. Most of the times he had peeked in on her she'd been asleep. Then he realised she just said something about wanting to talk to the three of them.

"What's so important that you couldn't have asked one of us to get the other two so you could talk to us in here?" He felt a little ashamed at not thinking she would feel lonely but he quickly suppressed it as he concentrated on the subject at hand.

"Well, since I wanted a change of scenery as well as to talk to all of you, it would have defeated the purpose by having you all in here now wouldn't it?" She said between the hiccupping breaths.

Annoyingly, and surprisingly, her words made sense for a change and he decided to concede to her request.

"Alright, I'll set you up in the lounge room. Is that okay?"

'Are all women this exasperating? I've never spent as much time with them as I have with Sarah so I wouldn't have a clue.' While his thoughts muttered at him, he only just managed to not roll his eyes.

"Yes thank you." She said meekly as she attempted to dry her eyes for the umpteenth time. She hated crying but she could never prevent it from happening.

After helping her to stand, he assisted her into the robe and something in his chest tightened. She looked so damned cute right at that moment. With her so tiny, his robe was exceptionally long on her as the hem puddled around her feet on the floor. Her hair, freshly washed, was loose and trailing down her back in gentle waves where the hair had dried scrunched up under her.

She glanced down at the hem pooled on the floor and giggled at the silliness of it. The giggle escaped before she could stop it and his heart pounded a little harder just then. Then he was saved by a thought of common sense... or so he had thought. Realising she was going to trip over it if she tried to walk now, he scooped her up into his arms. Then she let out a squeak of surprise and her hand landing on his chest to steady herself. She could feel his heart beating against her hand strong and steady.

He just stood there holding her as she lifted her head to look him in the eyes. She couldn't read the look on his face. He had a frown and a slight smile, but there was something else as well and that was the part she didn't understand.

Holding her in his arms, he could feel her heart beating faster. When their eyes met, he was hit with so many conflicting emotions he was amazed he wasn't knocked to the floor. Run for the hills, never let her go, kill her and be free of her, wrap her up and keep her safe, slap her for her lack of sensibilities, kiss her and tell her everything will be fine.

However – how he managed it he'll never know, he just stood there and looked at her with a frown and a small smile. He tried but he couldn't completely hide what he was feeling. She had him so out of his depth he felt like he was drowning and didn't know what to do. He tore his eyes from her with some effort and headed towards the lounge room.

"Mick, Toby, can you set up the lounge for Sarah." 'At least they do what they're told.' Kaelan asked then thought to himself.

To Sarah, however, it sounded more like an order. Mick and Toby did it anyway. Once all done Kaelan set her down, then sat on the coffee table and turned his attention to her.

"What do you want to talk to us about, Sarah?"

Kaelan's question grabbed Toby's and Mick's attention and they looked at her as well. While, suddenly, she looked like she was afraid. Of what he had no idea.

'Gee… no pressure here.' She thought nervously.

"I…" Sarah cleared her throat and started again. "I want the three of you to help me get fit, to lose this weight. Basically, to organise an exercise and diet regime for every day of the week. I would also like you, Kaelan, to teach me armed and whatever unarmed training you think I can do with my… disabilities."

'Oh, now there is one hell of an attention grabber. This I wasn't expecting, but it is going to be interesting.' Kaelan waited because he knew she would explain even though he thought he was beginning to work it out for himself.

"So, an hour a day and we have you exercising." Toby said.

"No. Not just an hour a day but from when I awake to when I go to sleep, with meal and rest breaks in between." She stated as she watched their reactions.

Mick and Toby glanced at each other in disbelief, then at her. Kaelan, however, just kept looking at her. His intensity was starting to make her subconscious about herself but that wasn't that difficult.

Placing his elbows on his knees Kaelan leant towards her slightly. "Do you realise what you are saying?" Excitement started to grow within him but he had to make sure she understood the consequences of what she was asking. The exercises alone were going to have her in agony.

"Yes. Fourteen hours a day the three of you will have me do whatever you decide upon. I wake up, have a suitable breakfast, small meals throughout the day to keep up the energy and whatever else I need. At the end of the fourteen hours one of you will massage me to help ease the muscles because I know they're going to be extremely sore. Also, from the moment I wake up, and every four or so hours then on, you'll be feeding me pain killers because I'm going to need them as well. It's not just my ankles that are going to hurt."

So much trust in those words, it amazed him. With that little speech it was obvious she had been thinking about it seriously.

She knew what she was letting herself in for.

"Why?" He had to ask. While suspecting she wanted revenge, he wanted to hear her say it, just to be sure. He wanted no mistakes in this at all.

That was a question she was expecting, and, strangely, she thought he already knew why.

"First answer this…" She said, looking at Kaelan, despite being nervous.

For the first time ever, she looked him directly in the eyes and kept her eyes locked on his instead of her usual glancing away. He could stare down almost anyone, but if she wasn't so shy then he didn't think he could have stared her down; at least, not every time. Having her eyes locked with his like that almost knocked the breath out of him.

"You monitor all hits that are ordered don't you?"

"Yes." Kaelan answered, saying the word slowly, waiting.

"So you will know when they have a hit taken out on them, won't you?"

"Who?" Both Toby and Mick asked.

"Yes." Kaelan said again at the same time as Toby and Mick spoke. He was having trouble containing his excitement.

Kaelan noted she ignored them, her eyes never wavering from his.

"I want in on the hit."

'Yes! I was right!'

"What the hell are you talking about Sarah?" Toby demanded.

However, she ignored the other two men because the current part of the discussion had everything to do with Kaelan and nothing to do with them.

Her eyes stayed locked onto Kaelan's. The world was suddenly just Sarah and him, and for the first time he didn't see that tiny frightened baby bunny, and he was excited about it. Kaelan's eyes started to sparkle. She watched them.

"You sure this is what you want?" He asked as he watched her. His complete attention was uncomfortable but that sparkle in his eyes was unnerving and reminiscent of something else. If only she could remember.

"Yes." She responded determinedly.

"You truly understand what you are asking? Once you start down this road you can't change what it does to you. You can't go back." Kaelan would make sure a hundred times if he had to, to give her an out in case she didn't understand the ramifications, or had any doubts whatsoever.

"Yes I understand." While her response was sure, her voice came out almost a whisper.

He believed her.

Toby grabbed her arm, to get her attentions and it took more will power than Kaelan was willing to admit to not drop him to the floor.

"Sarah, what the ruddy hell are you talking about?!"

"Revenge." She'd snarled the word and it hung in the air like a low lying thunder cloud with the force of a raging storm.

To Kaelan the word just sat there, like a gun to the head.

'There! She said it! I was right!' Kaelan thought triumphantly. Her voice was so sure, strong and without hesitation. He was definitely finding it difficult to contain his excitement, but did so as he sat there and watched her, listened to her. Soon he would know the truth about her.

"No. It's wrong Sarah. You are not the law. You can't take the law into your own hands." Toby shook his head and took a step back distancing himself from the issue.

Mick was strangely quiet.

"You're right Toby. I am not the law. He is though." She said thumbing at Kaelan.

"What do you mean?" Toby frowned in confusion.

While Kaelan just never took his eyes away from her he could hear the frown in Toby's tone.

She looked at Kaelan and said, "If I understand this correctly; if a hit is called out on those two it will be a legal hunting because they will be classified as rogues and will, therefore, be treated the same way as rogue therians and vampires. This means that if you see it in time you get to be first to claim the hit, you'll have the law on your side when you go after them."

"Correct." Kaelan calmly confirmed then thought, 'Well, well. I knew she wasn't dumb, a little more than average maybe, but I hadn't expected this level of brightness. I figured she wouldn't know how it would work, but either she's still holding out on me or she'd managed to work it out somehow. I'm guessing the former.'

"If I go with you, even if it is for revenge, you can claim I'm an apprentice... of sorts... so I won't get into trouble." Again, she looked at Kaelan intensely as she said it.

'There. That look in her eyes, such force. A force to be reckoned with. This has to be the real Sarah, the one who was able to 'kill' me on the paintball range. She hides it well. Does she even know this about herself? Everything seems to suggest she doesn't realise it at all.' Kaelan struggled a little harder than he thought he would in containing his excitement as much as he had. 'Well, it appears she has really thought this out. This could be the perfect murder for her and I don't have a problem with it at all since I want them dead anyway.'

"Correct." Kaelan said again.

"I don't care how you look at it, Sarah. It's wrong, very wrong." She never expected Toby to be the one to object.

'Damn it, but he just might succeed in talking her out of it. Maybe.' Kaelan thought as he concentrated on keeping still.

Sarah swung her head around to face him and winced with pain the action caused. Kaelan had never seen her express such anger before. Wasn't sure if she could.

"They killed Danny for no real reason. He had never done anything against humans since they came out in the open. Not even before then. They killed him just because he was a vampire. You and Mick lost Danny. I lost Danny, Abel and Brandi. Do you really think those two are going to stop with just our friends?

"I may not have the guts to go hunting them by myself, but if Kaelan gets to claim the hit before anyone else then I'm going with him and I want to be as fit as I can possibly be. So fourteen hours a day, with meal and rest breaks, seven days a week for you three to get me into condition. You have until the hit has been ordered. Will you help me?" She looked at Toby.

'But then again, maybe not.' Kaelan couldn't look at Toby or Mick. He only had eyes for this other side of Sarah, even though he had just been reminded all of it would be for revenge over the final death of her vamp lover. However, the leaden feeling in his gut was overshadowed sufficiently by the excitement of the whole situation.

There was a pause of such silence, only cicadas and the occasional magpie could be heard. Then...

She could see Toby's conflict, then his resignation. "Yes I'll help you." However, he didn't look happy with his decision.

She looked at Mick. He nodded.

She turned her attention back to Kaelan who hadn't taken his eyes from her since he sat down on the coffee table. Since he had a snowball's chance in hell at keeping the anticipation and excitement from his face, he didn't try to.

"When do we start?" Was his only response with his eyes sparkling with what looked like anticipation. To her, he certainly sounded enthusiastic.

"When you say I'm ready to begin." She said quietly. She was suddenly tired. "Between now and then, the three of you can work out what you're going to do to me." She slumped back against the pillows as Kaelan nodded. She finally remembered what his sparkling eyes reminded her of.

'It was the same look for the same reason he took an interest in me in the first place the day he saw me hobble out of the paintball range.'

Despite his eagerness, Kaelan was concerned about her when she slumped back with such exhaustion. He decided she could rest just as well on the lounge as she could in the bedroom. So, he just nodded. Despite her reasons, he was excited as it would be the closest he would come to see how good she truly was.

Achingly, it also reminded her of his true interest in her. The only reason why she was in his house in the first place. Even though she had hoped otherwise. She was on the verge of ears again but bit down on the inside of her lip to prevent them from falling.

'So much for hope!'

Chapter 16

It was to be another month before the men would start her torture programme. However, it gave the three of them plenty of time to work out what they were going to put Sarah through as well as organising her high protein/low carbohydrates diet. She would, however, be starting the diet immediately.

During breakfast, Kaelan took serious note of the physique of the two men. Toby was a typical muscle/body guard/bouncer looking guy. So he really didn't have a clue as to what needed to be done other than building up the muscles in his upper body. Kaelan didn't want Sarah to go to that extreme. While Mick did enough to keep himself fit, with what seemed like no real regime, so he didn't have any real idea either.

Therefore, Kaelan felt it was left to him to work out what exercises to give her. The bulk of it would be based around her losing weight, but at the same time they had to build up her strength without giving her obvious muscles. After working that part out, he then had to work out how many of each set she would need to do. Since she would be doing fourteen hours a day worth, he decided to start her with a small number and could look at building the numbers up as time went by.

He delegated Mick and Toby to coach her through the

exercises. They could swap between themselves with who coaches and who brings her food and pain killers throughout the day. The thing that concerned him the most was the amount of hours she wanted to do but having seen her stubbornness, Kaelan didn't think he had a chance of changing her mind.

'God! It's going to be murder on her.' He mentally cringed and decided to think of ways to help ease her pain without it seeming like he was cutting back her chosen amount of hours.

As for himself? Well, weapons training wasn't hard, but he would also teach her to clean and care for the gun.

'Hmm… small hands… I think a… Walther PPK or… maybe the Sig Sauer P232 would be the way to go for her. Now, the hard part is working out what in the way of unarmed combat can I teach her? For the first week or two, I think, I'll just teach her with the pistol.' He mused to himself.

He decided not to start the unarmed training until after the first week. If he decided to do it at all.

'Assuming we get more than one week's worth of training.' Kaelan had one other problem to work out… How to do the job, or more to the point… how to set her up to do part of the job so she won't get killed. However, he had a month to sort all the details out before her regime could even get started. Hopefully.

From that point on, much to Kaelan's disgust, she spent more and more time out of bed and not on the lounge. She slowly hobbled about the house. With her refusal to stay in bed she ended back in her original room. For those couple of nights she'd spent in his room, he'd slept in hers and the smell of him was all over the pillows. She hugged one of them and cried herself to sleep because she wanted to hold him instead of the pillow and couldn't.

While for Kaelan, when he laid down that night he was enveloped by her scent. He guessed he managed to stay there for about five minutes before getting up and changing the sheets. With her scent all around him, he just couldn't get to sleep. It set his mind and body to thinking other things. Things he didn't want to think about. A cold shower after re-making the bed and he was finally able to get some sleep.

During the day, while she hobbled around the house, looking at everything, Kaelan made sure he was wherever she wasn't. Thankfully, she didn't go downstairs into the yard at all. He would have tied her to the bed if she had. With her slow movements and constant resting, it gave him the chance to clean each room while she wasn't in it.

He basically did anything and everything around the house so his thoughts wouldn't come back to her. General cleaning – the house had been shut up for two years and had still collected a lot of dust, and general maintenance and fix-it jobs; the weather wasn't gentle on his old home. When she was asleep, the three men worked on her exercise programme.

During the following month she slowly, and painfully, discovered that Kaelan's house was an old style single storey Queenslander, the kind she liked best. It stood about a metre off the ground for air flow, and flooding if it should occur, and had verandahs on all four sides. The front door was in the middle of the front of the house which opened up into a hallway that ran the length of the house till it met the kitchen/dining area at the back of the house.

When one first walks through the door there is a bedroom on

either side of the hallway. Hers on the left and Kaelan's on the right. Continuing down the hallway, towards the kitchen and there was another bedroom on the right – Toby's room – with the bathroom on the left, while between her room and the bathroom was Mick's room. All four bedrooms were spacious, all with free standing wardrobes and chests of drawers. The master bedroom – Kaelan's room – had the modern addition of an en suite, but his room was still sufficiently spacious.

There was also a sitting room and a lounge room. The lounge room was surrounded by Toby's room in front of it, Mick's room and part of the bathroom on the left of it, verandah on the right and dining room and sitting room behind it. However, it had a fireplace, a real wood burning fireplace. Not an original feature, but the addition was in a style that suited the setting.

The kitchen/dinning were one large area at the back of the house. It was huge as it ranged from the left side of the house to three quarters towards the right side. The last quarter was where the sitting room was. While downstairs was the laundry near the kitchen end of the house.

All walls in the public areas were done in a peachy cream colour with trims and ceilings done in white. Bedrooms seemed to vary in wall colour. Her originally assigned room was lavender, while Kaelan's was a creamy lemon – more cream than lemon. She hadn't seen the rooms Toby and Mick were in so she couldn't describe them. The floors throughout the house were polished timber with a few rugs here and there.

Sarah rested frequently during her wanderings as it hurt to walk for too long. Even when she'd damaged her ankles, once she was allowed to move about, she didn't stay still. Now wasn't any different. She just didn't go down the stairs into the yard. Not yet.

Meanwhile, Kaelan seemed to be staying out of her way while she walked about and she didn't know or understand why.

~*~

Two weeks before starting her training, Detective Harris phoned Kaelan. He asked if he could give the home number to Daniel's solicitor so the man could talk to Sarah. Kaelan gave his permission.

The next day Kaelan handed the phone to her.

She discovered it was a Mr Robertson, who introduced himself as Danny's solicitor. He wanted to talk to her about Danny's will. She thought she would have broken down and cried but she didn't.

Danny had left all of his books to her. She thought that had been nice of him. Just a shame they'd all been destroyed in the fire. Or so she had thought. The solicitor then said they had found some books in Danny's safe, which had survived the fire, as well as a couple more that had been placed into safe-keeping elsewhere. Those particular details weren't revealed to her at that point in time.

Mr Robertson told her she should be receiving them soon by courier and would have to sign for them.

"So, I will need your address so we can send them to you."

"My address to send them to?" At first, she didn't know what to say. She practically jumped in fright when Kaelan placed a hand on her arm and handed her a piece of paper. Looking at it she discovered it was his address. She looked at him in askance.

When she gazed at him like that, he wondered why she had to look so cute. Ignoring the thought, he nodded instead and sat back in the kitchen.

Turning back to the phone call, she cited Kaelan's address, said farewell and hung up. She was stunned and didn't know how to feel. After recovering, she then hid in her room for the rest of the day.

Sitting in the kitchen, just by hearing her side of the conversation, he discovered it was in regards to the blood-sucker's will and something about books. Apart from the issue with a need for an address and deciding to let her use his, she didn't talk to anyone about what was said other than she would be receiving a package sometime soon. It surprised him that she didn't cry. However, she spent the rest of the day quiet and in hiding.

Later she herself would be amazed that no tears fell at all. 'A first time for something I guess.'

*

With her injuries improving, it was about a week before her exercise program would start that she continued her wanderings and went out onto the verandahs. Mick and Toby were running errands and getting food, and Kaelan was... somewhere she wasn't as per usual. Meanwhile, Kaelan was grateful for the break from them as he had never had this many people in his house since he was a kid.

Gazing around the property, Sarah started at the front of the house and noted once again how it was set a distance from the road. The front yard was very low maintenance, as in just grass with a few trees here and there. She walked down the left side verandah and saw the yard was the same as the front, just grass. Two more houses from a medium density living suburb could have fitted between Kaelan's house and the nearest neighbour. She wandered back to the front and headed towards the right side verandah. It was the same as the left side but looked like three or four houses distance to the nearest neighbour.

Then she received a visit from a different solicitor. His arrival had been preceded by a phone call, yet again, by a Detective Harris. The next day the solicitor turned up. After pleasantries and refreshments offerings...

"I'm George Manning. How are you Ms Brackenway?" He asked as he sat in the lounge chair opposite her.

Mr Manning was taller than Sarah but shorter than Kaelan. He was also broader than Kaelan but not overweight. He had tanned skin as if he spent a lot of time out of doors and light brown hair that seemed to be somewhat sun bleached. His brown eyes barely settled on one spot for long.

"I'm doing better thank you and it's Mrs not Ms, but call me Sarah please." She corrected politely.

"My apologies and Sarah it is."

Kaelan came back with refreshments only to sit in a third seat so she was sort of in the middle of the two of them, forming something like a triangle. After a round of thank you's...

"Why are you here Mr Manning?" She asked but didn't think she'd kept the nervousness from her voice.

"George please. I'm here because you have been listed as

executor to the will of Mr and Mrs Abel and Brandi Jackson."

"Their will? Executor?" She repeated in a stunned tone. She couldn't seem to think straight as her mind went numb and her heart started feeling like it was in a vice grip.

"Yes. They have named you as executor of their will." George Manning stated calmly.

Expressions fleeted across her face so quickly if he hadn't been watching her Kaelan wouldn't have seen them.

Meanwhile she felt anything but calm as her mind flashed upon the last moments she'd seen them. She knew what an executor does, but...

"I can't... I mean... I'm still in recovery and trying to deal with their loss. I mean... I was there but I survived... Can you please take over that duty for me? I..." breathlessly she babbled and she knew it but couldn't stop herself from doing so. To make matters worse tears started trickling down her face as she stared at her hands, refusing to look at either Manning or Kaelan.

"I see. I had no idea. I can take on that roll if you like." Mr Manning said slowly.

Even though it was unspoken she understood he would do so at a cost. She just nodded.

"In that case I will set it up and call you with date and time the will is to be read." Mr Manning stated as he stood up. "But before I leave, do you know the contents of the will?" He asked lightly.

After shaking her head in the negative and a whispered no, she struggled to her feet they shook hands and he left. She'd followed them down the hallway only to enter her room. Surprisingly and annoyingly the tears stopped falling once she lay on the bed.

Kaelan suspected she gave in to her tears once in her room. After showing Manning out, he listened at her door wishing there was something he could do for her but heard no noise at all. But then she was able to cry silently. Something he had never heard from a woman before.

With a sigh Kaelan walked away and found something else to occupy his mind.

The next day Kaelan was on his bed with the laptop. He was monitoring what jobs were available even though he knew he wouldn't really take them at that point in time unless it was the ones who'd tried to kill her. Since he was on protective duty he knew he had the time.

While Sarah felt restless, she went out onto the veranda via the back door then continued walking anti-clockwise to circle around the house. Thoughts of the two major events in her life tumbling in her mind like clothes in a clothes dryer. The before and after the accident that took her husband away from her and the hit that took three of her friends away from her.

Their faces started haunting her with her husband's face joining the other three and they wouldn't leave her alone. With a tightness in her chest making it difficult to breathe easily, she wasn't paying attention to where she was going because she was trying to think of something else. As a result, she walked into one of the metal patio chairs. She clipped her left ankle and whacked the knee of the same leg on it, which caused her to put all weight on her right leg that sent pain through the injured thigh.

"Shee-oot!" She cursed softly as the tears started.

Hearing the exclamation, Kaelan realised it had to be Sarah.

She sat heavily in the offending chair and just gave over to the tears. It started with all the pain, but continued due to the four faces not leaving her alone. Between them and flashbacks she just couldn't stop crying. In fact, it just became worse. She placed her arms on the table and her head on her arms and cried softly. A few long moments later…

Kaelan wandered out the french doors of his room to the right side verandah and saw Sarah, hunched over with arms on the table and her head on her arms. It looked like she was crying.

"Sarah?"

She jumped in fright at Kaelan's soft call. She hadn't heard him come towards her. She wiped her tears away, trying not to cry by holding her breath, as she looked at him squatting beside her, his hand on the arm of the chair she was in.

"What's wrong?" He asked gently. While he couldn't' see any reason for her to be crying, by now he knew she never cried just for the sake of it.

For some reason, him asking that question right then had her crying again and she threw her arms around him. Normally, because of her confusion about him, she wouldn't have done such a thing. However, just at that point, she needed some comfort. Embarrassment or not, whether he wanted it or not, Kaelan got to be the one whose shoulder she cried on.

His heart started beating harder at the feel of her pressed so firmly against him. He couldn't help noticing the softness of her breasts squished wonderfully against his chest. With a mental groan, he dragged his mind back to the issue of her tears. While her crying wasn't uncommon, this particular crying seemed to be different. It wasn't the tears of her injuries hurting.

He wasn't sure what to do and just crouched there doing nothing at first. Then Kaelan slowly, stiffly and gingerly wrapped his arms around her and held her as she cried. It wasn't until his arms were around her that she finally realised why she couldn't stop crying. Sarah was finally in mourning.

While she had cried a number of times over her husband's death and classified it as mourning, she hadn't really allowed herself to truly mourn his passing. She had treated it as 'something that happens and life goes on'. When Abel, Brandi and Danny had died, she treated their deaths the same way while she dealt with her injuries. However, finally, all four together; triggered by Abel and Brandi's will? Some part of her couldn't handle it, and now she couldn't stop crying.

His chest tightened and he wanted nothing more than to comfort her and tell her it was okay, whatever it was, but told himself he shouldn't so he didn't. After a few more moments, Kaelan decided to shove the logical part of himself to the side and started to stand up.

At first, she wasn't going to let go and he stilled in that moment. Then she did let go because what was the use of holding onto someone for comfort when they didn't want to be there. So, she covered her face with her hands with her elbows on her knees instead.

Whatever was causing her to cry like that seemed to be too much for her to bear. So, Kaelan did the only thing he could think of. With a tenderness he had never shown anyone in his adult life, he gathered her into his arms and she pressed her face against his chest and kept crying. Once inside, he placed her on her bed and she rolled onto her right side away from him as he pulled the covers over her.

Next, he lay beside her and held her as she cried until she fell asleep. He didn't say anything, he just held her gently against him and was glad of the covers between them. He silently berated his body's reaction because all he wanted to do at that point was comfort her.

Eventually, she stopped crying and her breathing slowly calmed but he knew she was still awake. Still he didn't say anything. He just continued to hold her, offering silent comfort. Then, a few minutes after her breathing had settled into a sleeping rhythm, he gently got up and left.

Kaelan worked out in the gym to try not to think but it was just the same thoughts as before, except now Sarah had a place in his heart as well as his thoughts. Heading back upstairs after the workout hadn't helped, he came across Toby and Mick in the kitchen so the three of them talked about her exercise and diet regime. It was at that moment Kaelan worked out a way to ease her exercise programme into something more manageable: breaks between each set.

They had dinner, Sarah still slept, then he went to bed only to toss and turn most of the night as thoughts of her wouldn't let him be. He had never spent so much time just doing nothing or having his thoughts occupied by any one person.

Chapter 17

Sarah awoke feeling horrid so she had a shower, got dressed into a singlet, t-shirt and track pants and went into the kitchen to make herself a cup of tea. No one else seemed to be around and didn't know if they were even awake or not. While waiting for the urn to boil after topping it up, she went into the sitting room to look at the date and time on Kaelan's laptop.

'Huh... I'd slept the whole day and night away and it's now just after 6:00am.'

Back in the kitchen, she made her cup of tea and sat at the table to drink it. She had her back to the doorway of the hallway so she could stare out at the back yard. Of all the surrounding yard sections, the back yard was the best view.

At the far back was bushland with its Australian native plants and animal life. In front of it, coming towards the house, was a huge four space lock-up garage on the far left, with another large lock-up shed beside it and on the far right was a custom shooting range.

Coming closer to the house, and roughly in the middle was a large pool. That pool was her favourite part of the scenery. She had told the guys that they had to include the pool in the exercise regime. Between the house and the pool, but off to the right was another, smaller, building but she couldn't see what was inside it.

Sometime after one in the morning Kaelan had finally fallen asleep. It was now 0630 hours and he couldn't get back to sleep so he decided to make himself a coffee before everyone else got up. Hopefully enjoy a bit of hassle free time before she started wandering around and invading his mind and senses yet again.

However, when he entered the dining section, she was already awake, sitting at the table looking out at the backyard. While he could have snuck back to his room, Kaelan decided to make the best of the situation instead and tried to be nice. He walked up to her and placed his hand on her shoulder. With what the two of them had been through together so far he felt that little piece of familiarity was allowable. He was about to say good morning when…

A hand gently touched her on the shoulder, scaring the daylights out of her and caused her to spill her hot tea over her hands.

'Damn! I didn't see the cup of tea in her hand.' Kaelan rushed into the kitchen to grab a cloth and some ice for her hands and another cloth to clean up the tea.

"Ffff—ar out space cookies! Shee-oot!" Even in pain she refused to swear. A habit her husband had gotten her into, or out of depending on how one looked at it. Out of the corner of her eye she saw Kaelan.

"Damn it Kaelan… Make some noise when you come near me. Keep scaring the daylights out of me and I'll eventually die of fright."

'For a large man he certainly knows how to move quietly.' Despite being mad at him for scaring her like that, she also found the whole thing funny and she started to chuckle.

He didn't blame her for being upset. He would have been under the same circumstances. When she started to chuckle, he didn't know why. He couldn't see anything amusing, but wasn't going to complain.

'Better her laughing than sulking. Although, her version of swearing does amuse the hell out of me. Where does she come up with them?'

Kaelan came back with a cloth and some ice. She held the ice on her hands while he cleaned up the mess. Thankfully, it was only over the table and not anywhere else on her.

"I seem to be asking this question of you a lot lately, but are you alright?"

Still chuckling, "Yes. Good morning Kaelan. I didn't mean the grouching to be my greeting to you."

"Morning, and I'm not referring to now. I'm talking about yesterday." Kaelan sat opposite her so she could look at him without having to turn. But also so he could watch her intently. She looked and sounded wonderful.

Sarah sighed as she gazed at her hands without really seeing them.

"I could say that I'm not normally like this, but I have never lied to you since we first met so I won't start now. Yes I am an emotional person, I can't help it. When my husband died, I did cry but I recently realised I hadn't mourned. With Brandi, Abel and Danny's murders, I hadn't mourned them either. For some reason yesterday, the four deaths all together just came to a head. I guess the dam just burst and I couldn't stop it. I'm sorry you got caught up in it, but I have no one close to me anymore. No one I can turn to." Whenever she says things like that she always start off strong, then her voice dwindles away to almost nothing, usually ending with her blushing profusely.

This time was no exception.

'She has never lied to me?! What she said about herself at the paintball range was true? Have I misjudged her again? I usually don't misjudge so badly, but she has whacked me so out of alignment since I first met her.' Since there wasn't anything he could do about it right at that moment he concentrated on what she'd just said.

"No family?" He couldn't believe she was alone outside of his house, other than for him and the other two men in it. Alone was something he could handle but not her. To him, she seemed like the type of person not meant to be alone.

She shook her head, still not looking at him. To her, he sounded a little surprised.

Kaelan opened his mouth to ask her something but the personal discussion between them came to an end when Toby, then Mick, walked into the kitchen. Bad timing as she was enjoying the private time between them despite his questions. She felt sort of flattered that he would think to ask since he was so private and closed off.

"Morning." Toby called out cheerfully all bright eyed and bushy tailed.

'Definitely a morning person.' Sarah thought.

"Morning." Mick mumbled, looking like he had a fight with the bed during the night.

'And definitely not a morning person, but then neither am I.' She mused sympathetically.

"Morning." Kaelan and Sarah said together. She ducked her head and smiled more.

Something seemed to amuse her. He loved seeing her smile. Her face lights up and her eyes sparkle, at that moment her expression, while soft, was also a little mischievous with whatever thoughts were amusing her.

She remembered as a kid used to calling out 'Jinx' when two people said the same thing at the same time. She had to bite her tongue a little to stop herself as she wasn't sure how Kaelan would take that childish bit of fun. Especially if she got to punch him if he spoke before being released from the jinx.

"What happened to your hands, Sarah?" Mick asked, looking down at her.

"I spilt my tea over my hands" She said as if it wasn't a big deal. 'Actually, it hurts a lot.' But the moment she spoke all traces of amusement disappeared.

"Ouch." Mick responded.

She glanced at Kaelan right then and saw him raise his eyebrows at her comment. 'Why didn't she just tell the truth about how it really happened?'

With a slight blush she just grabbed the soggy cloth, put it in the sink and started walking out of the kitchen. Her hands were really red, and hurting, and she just didn't want to be real social right then.

Mick and Toby changed places at the bench with the hot water urn on it, Mick making his coffee and Toby coming to the table.

"Toby, can you get the first aid kit please? Sarah, sit down."

Kaelan said as he got up and came around the table towards her.

She frowned at him, not to argue but because of the way he just ordered her about. However, she did as she was told.

Toby came back with the kit and Kaelan leant against the table beside her. He grabbed some cream, paddings and bandages and tended to her hands. 'It looks like she won't blister thank god.'

"Thanks." She said softly and started to leave. Then she turned around, "Kaelan, can you come with me please?"

'Oh no… it sounds like I'm in trouble and she's going to be difficult. I want to strangle her… I want to strangle her… Damn it! While I could get away with it, I can't do it.'

Maybe it was the please, or maybe it just suited him to do so, but he followed her. She headed to the front of the house. She was nervous as ever, but she had to say something.

He was beginning to see patterns in the way she acted in different situations. When it came to confrontations, she's shy and nervous.

She wondered at that point if she would have the courage to tell him how she felt about him. She stopped at the little gate that separated the verandah from the stairs then turned to face him.

"I don't know if I'm going to make much sense or be that coherent, but I'll try not to babble too much." Sarah started, even to her sounding rather subdued. "I'm not one of your soldiers, or men, and maybe you're not treating me the same way you treat them, but you're certainly not treating me in a… a… normal, for lack of a better word, way. It's like you don't want me here, yet you're the one who brought me here and not to a hospital.

"Not that I'm complaining, but how did you manage to be Johnny-on-the-spot that evening? Why didn't you take me to the hospital and leave me there so you wouldn't have to put up with me, that I wouldn't be a burden? Why haven't the police been to see me about my friends' deaths and me surviving?

"Ever since I first met you, I liked the idea that maybe we could become... friends, but if you don't then fine. Your choice, and if that's to be the case then I'll leave as I value... whatever it is we may be to each other and would prefer not to end up hating you. I..." 'Damn it! I chickened out.' She took a deep breath and let it back out as she stared at her feet.

Kaelan didn't interrupt because he felt she had more to say and really didn't want her to start crying again. However, some of her pauses sounded like she was going to say something else but changed her mind perhaps. Maybe it was just her nervousness. He didn't know.

"I have this problem of being female and emotional, and maybe I'm reading too much into the way you speak to me. But I am a female and not one of your guys..." Her voice faded as she tried to get her thoughts together. Instead, with shoulders slumping, she turned and started to walk away. "I'm going back home, Kaelan, and while I hope I never need rescuing again, see you around sometime maybe." She bit her lip hard so as not to cry as she felt the tears starting to well up already.

'Crap!' He sighed and ran his hand through his hair. His confusion about how he felt about her had obviously shown through. 'Seems she's more sensitive than I thought.'

Now, while it was true that she did walk away from him, her steps were small and slow as large and fast hurt too much. Therefore she hadn't really gotten that far when Kaelan came up behind her and put a gentle hand on her arm to stop her from going further.

"The two men who offed your friends and lover announced their intentions on a website with all names involved. Even though they're amateurs, they had monitored who Daniel hung around with. Meaning your name was on the list. They were stupid enough to say when they were going to do the hit, but I didn't see the site in time. I didn't take you to the hospital just in case they tried to kill you there. With me I knew you were safe.

"As for the police, I'm a registered bounty hunter with an official licence so I was able to convince them to keep you still being alive a secret to protect you. With statements from Toby, Mick and myself, the police were okay with letting me keep you hidden and safe." He paused, thought about the words to use then frowned with what he had to say next. 'Telling the truth without upsetting her is going to be tricky at best I think.'

"I don't hate you and I don't think you're a burden. A pain sometimes, yes and the most frustrating person at times whom I have ever met. I don't want you to leave Sarah. Not while they're still out there should they learn you are still alive." 'She doesn't need to know that they do know she's still alive.'

For a brief moment he thought he saw her eyes light up, however, if they had then the light died as quickly as it had flared.

'If I did see her eyes light up, why? Why would they? If they did, what had I said to make them light up then dull like that? Damn it, she's so confusing!'

When Kaelan said he didn't want her to leave, Sarah's heart skipped a beat then thudded to her feet with his final comment.

'Skipped a beat? Oh fudge. Attraction is one thing, but something more? That means I'll have to do a bit of soul searching.' She mentally sighed, 'one problem at a time.' Then she sighed out loud.

"Fine, I'll stay. Only because you asked so nicely." She said with a touch of sarcasm and walked away.

He let her go that time and sighed. Kaelan was going to have to think seriously about what he was going to do about her. He was beginning to believe Ed when he'd said 'hook, line and sinker'. He was doomed. He just didn't want to face it.

'Give me the choice of a stadium full of therians and vamps or one tiny disabled young woman and I'll take the stadium any time.'

'Fine!' She thought when he didn't stop her and hid in her room for the rest of the day. After finding a few books to read to keep her mind active, she didn't want to think about what her heart skipping a beat meant. She ignored lunch, much to her loudly complaining stomach, and concentrated just on reading so her thoughts would stay away from him.

Toby and Mick tried to see her or get her to come out, but she told them to go away. Late in the afternoon Kaelan tried as well, but received the same response. He leant his head on the door for a little bit before leaving her to her hiding. He just wished he knew what to do, but she made it so difficult and confusing to think it through.

At one stage, after she had said to leave her alone she saw the shadow of bare feet stay put for a few moments longer than usual. She suspected that it might have been Kaelan and she thought it strange that he actually obeyed – word used loosely – her. She skipped dinner as well and that caused her stomach to start rioting instead of just loudly complaining, but she ignored it some more.

Just a little after dark she heard a car leave. She didn't know which of the guys went out and, for once, she hoped it was Kaelan. Somewhere along the line she fell asleep with training starting the next day.

At dusk, Mick and Toby decided to go out. Kaelan was of the opinion they were getting cabin fever. He was as well, but for a totally different reason. So, he stayed. He didn't want her left alone.

Just before midnight he left some clothing on the foot of her bed. She'll need them for the next day. Just before walking out he stood there and watched her for a few moments. She looked so peaceful without the fine small lines of pain around her mouth, brow and eyes. But that peacefulness was only temporary.

Kaelan sighed and went to bed.

Chapter 18

Sarah jerked awake as her alarm went off at 4:30 in the morning. She groaned. It was the first day of the torturous exercise regime. While she wanted to do the exercises, and that she was the one who set the start time, she also knew that she was going to be in an extreme amount of pain for days on end and that was the part she wasn't looking forward to.

Looking at the end of the bed after sitting up, she found a grey cotton sports bra, darker grey cotton boxer briefs, a dark blue t-shirt and black track pants. She grabbed them, went to the bathroom to have a shower and dress then went to the kitchen for breakfast.

Already awake and in the kitchen, Kaelan heard Sarah's alarm go off. Roughly twenty-five minutes later she walked out in the dark blue t-shirt and black track pants he'd left for her.

'Good, it looks like everything fits her fine. But damn! Despite them being tracks and t-shirt she looks great in them.'

"Morning." She seemed rather subdued. He guessed it was to be expected because he knew she was going to feel like the walking dead by that evening.

She wasn't looking forward to the coming pain but she was dreading dealing with Kaelan more. Things between them weren't improving. As a result she was becoming shyer around him so as not to set him off. Just once she would like to be normal and be able to tell him how she felt about him. But, she wasn't and she didn't.

The three men said morning back to her.

"Sarah, are you sure you want to do this much for the next fourteen hours?" Toby asked.

While he understood why Toby asked, Kaelan would have preferred it if the man had just shut up. Babying her wasn't going to get her anywhere. However, with what she said next, Kaelan realised he shouldn't have been concerned about it.

"Because of the pain I'm going to be in after the first set? Yeah I'm sure. That's why the pool and massage are to be included. I'm going to have trouble losing this weight and will need to work harder for longer to lose any decent amount of weight during that time. As I said, I'll end up crying and cursing, but I'll try to keep my wanting to throw it all in to a minimum." She said with as little inflection as possible.

Her mood wasn't just the up-coming exercise programme. It was also the fact she was making a fool of herself over Kaelan. Especially when it was obvious he didn't feel the same way about her. However, she couldn't help herself and that just made her feel worse about it all.

'Something's wrong. Something other than just the exercises that is.' It took effort on Kaelan's part not to frown. However, he didn't know what to do about the situation so he said nothing. Instead, they gave her breakfast and pain killers then started exercising her. He was sure she thought they were torturing her. He knew he felt that way.

Each individual exercise was a set of five which were repeated after each rest session. The three men had her doing the treadmill to build up her general stamina in walking and regaining some more flexibility in her ankles, or at least some strength in them. After that, various weight lifting to help her lose weight and along the way gain a bit of muscle tone. To help her with her arms and back they had her on the rowing machine; she didn't like that one much at all because it was just plain painful as far as she was concerned.

Out of all the exercises they had her doing she enjoyed the pool the most because her body weight was supported by the water. However, the men didn't have to work out a set of exercises for the pool because she already had them from when she had to do hydrotherapy after the accident that damaged her ankles. Kaelan just made sure she did rounds of ten for each exercise so she didn't overwork herself. Exercise within a pool could be just as exhausting and dehydrating as land-based exercises.

Once the first complete set was done, the men let her rest for ten minutes with food and pain killers – if it was time for some – then started the sets again. The cycle was repeated over and over until 1830 hours. However, about mid-afternoon, Kaelan took her to the shooting range and had her practicing for an hour before she resumed the rest of the exercises. Pistol training was also another form of rest for her even if she didn't see it that way.

Sarah was grateful when 6:30pm came. She was so sore and stiff and tired that she had trouble just hobbling back to the house after her last stint in the pool. Mick offered to carry her inside, but she stubbornly refused. It was painful just watching her go from the pool to the stairs, up them, then into the lounge room where the massage was to take place.

Although, she did let him lift and place her on the table that was set up for the massage. Once up there she rolled over onto her stomach and settled herself ready for a bit more pain. However, she fell asleep – passed out more likely – as soon as she was in position.

Mick looked at him questioningly and Kaelan told him to go ahead with the massage anyway.

"At least that way she won't feel any more pain until she wakes up again." Kaelan said as he and Mick stripped her to her underwear – her pool-wear was a pair of shorts and a t-shirt over her underwear.

Kaelan cooked dinner for the three of them as he didn't think she would wake up again until her alarm went off in the morning. However, he put some aside for her to eat throughout the coming day.

After Toby put her to bed, the three of them sat at the table and had dinner.

"I think this is too much for her. Sarah's just not physically up to this much workout so soon." Toby complained.

Kaelan paused in putting the fork in his mouth and focused on him. He knew it was the sort of look which warned others to 'beware what you do or I'll drop you'. It was a look he'd used on his teams at various times.

"This is her choice, for better or worse. Tell me, since you know her… Do you think you'll be able to dissuade her from the amount of hours she has set for herself?"

Toby shifted in his seat.

"No. No, I don't." His tone one of resignation.

"Then don't mention it again. There is nothing any of us can do to change her mind in this regard, so it is pointless complaining about it."

Toby glared angrily at him, but Kaelan didn't care. "You're not even trying to talk her out of it. You want her to go down this path. To become a killer."

Kaelan carefully lowered his fork and let himself go calm, empty. His men call it his killing look and he let it take him over.

"Be careful what you say. Sarah's friend or not, it might be the last thing you say. Yes it is true I have no problem with her going down that path, I would never force it upon her though. Sarah wants this. I have given her the chance to back out of it before it can change her but she has refused to veer away every time. So, if she won't turn away from it then I might as well teach her to the best of my abilities, and I am one of the best." He picked up his fork and was about to start eating again.

"Well, that's a bit conceited isn't it?" Toby stated obnoxiously.

Mick paused, eyes flickering from one to the other. He had sense, he stayed quiet and out of the... discussion.

Kaelan dropped his fork with a loud clatter as it hit the table and sat back. Then, with his hands flat on the table, he forced himself to sit there because if he stood up right at that moment Kaelan knew he would kill him. Worse... He wanted to. He counted to thirty before answering the man.

"No. I can show you a private and secure website which lists the top ten in my line of work within Australia and you will see my name near the top of that list. Now drop the subject and just eat."

Kaelan deliberately followed his own advice because the urge to kill him was so damn strong. 'God damn it! But between her and Toby, they're going to drive me around the bloody twisted bend!'

After dinner, he left the two men to do the dishes while he did a workout to relieve the tension – it didn't help much, had a shower then went to bed.

Chapter 19

Sarah jumped when her alarm went off. She moved to look at it and groaned in pain and dread.

'Yesterday wasn't a sleeping nightmare. It had been a waking nightmare.' She got up slowly and painfully.

'The last thing I remember was getting on the massage table, I think.' When she got to the kitchen, she was grateful for the pain killers that were beside her breakfast.

After watching her drag her aching body into the kitchen, Kaelan decided to add a massage at the beginning of the day as well as at the end and, she had to admit, she was grateful for it. She began the routine again.

Come 6:30pm, she was asleep on the massage table again, and once again they put her to bed.

That became the daily routine and it was torture to watch her like that. All he could do was make things as easy for her as possible. Not much but better than nothing at all. If Kaelan could spare her any of it then he would, but no matter how much she cried and cursed and carried on, she didn't give up.

While he felt like the biggest heel for letting her go through with her torturous programme, he was amazed and pleased, till it felt like his heart would burst, with her determination.

However, she did receive a small break for the first three days of the second week after another call from solicitor George Manning letting her know when she had to attend the reading of the will on the next Wednesday at 10:00am.

"We'll stop your exercises on Monday and Tuesday so you'll be able to attend the reading without any problems like exhaustion." Kaelan informed her in a tone that said there would be no arguing.

She hadn't planned on arguing with him. She just nodded, finished eating then resumed training.

*

For the past week Sarah cried and cursed as she said she would. She fell asleep as soon as she lay down on the impromptu massage table and woke up every morning in bed stiff and in pain. With all that, she was tired. Extremely tired and she found it difficult to stay awake. Then, half way through the second week, there was the reading of the will after two days rest – not that the rest made any difference...

Kaelan had insisted on coming with her. If he hadn't then she would have asked him regardless of how she felt about him and how he treated her. He gave her plain black trousers, white blouse, black jacket and matching shoes to wear to the reading, since she didn't have any of her own at his place. She hadn't worn enclosed shoes since the accident and found them strange to wear and a little uncomfortable around the toes.

They sat in the office with the rest of Abel and Brandi's friends – some she'd never met before, and wondered why she even needed to be there while Mr Manning read the will.

'Oh, I know I'm the executor but with him reading it I don't understand why I have to be here.' Until he read the final part of the will...

"And lastly to Sarah who showed the same love for it as we did, we leave you our house and property because we know you will keep our drive, our dream, alive." Then Mr Manning sat back.

Sarah didn't know what to say. She'd discovered at the beginning of the will that Brandi and Abel had no surviving family and already knew they had no children. But to be left with their home was something she had never dreamed of since she was the newest of their friends. She sat there stunned for a minute or two before she nodded.

"Thank you." She managed to croak out. "I... I have to... to go. Call me later if anything else needs to be done, finalised." She babbled quickly as she stood then rushed out of the office.

It was the fastest Kaelan had seen her move.

"Sarah?!" Both he and Manning called out after her at the same time. For the second time she had Kaelan stumbling over his own feet in his rush to get to her.

"Excuse me." Kaelan muttered as he hurried after her. She hadn't stopped and the lift she was in closed as he reached it. He had to watch it descend while he waited for the next one to arrive. Silently he cursed at having to wait for the next elevator.

Not stopping when someone called her name, she didn't stop until she found herself trying to open the door of the locked Jeep. She quickly let go when a shadow fell across her then the Jeep unlocked and she quickly climbed in. Once in she grabbed the GPS and started programming it while Kaelan sat in the driver's seat. She could feel him watching her but she wouldn't look at him. She couldn't. She didn't want to see him frowning at her, showing his disapproval yet again.

Sitting there watching her, he waited because he couldn't do anything else but give her the time she needed. Finally, she pressed the button to tell the GPS to route its way to her destination. Then she placed it back in the centre of the dash facing it towards him.

"Please?" She pleaded so softly she wondered if he heard her. However, that whisper was full of the emotions she was barely holding on to.

"Of course Sarah." Kaelan said gently. He couldn't help frowning because he was worried about her and she still wouldn't look at him. Strangely, no tears fell.

She could hear the frown in his tone. Even though she liked the way he said her name, she was glad she hadn't look at him. She didn't think she could handle his disapproval at that point. Kaelan drove, following the instructions of the GPS after Sarah had stated it was best to go via the Gateway Motorway.

An hour and a half later they were turning onto the property after she'd guided Kaelan to it because the GPS couldn't get an exact location. Driving along an over-grown winding gravel driveway, they finally arrived in what seemed like a small parking area. Once parked, the pair of them just sat there and stared at the house. It was a two storey dark brown brick house with a chimney rising up from the roof.

"The first time I came here was the first time I'd met Brandi then, later that night, I met Danny. I had met Abel the week before at a café in Manly. He had invited me for the weekend."

She said softly as she remembered. Then another memory floated up.

"It was the same day I thought I saw your Jeep actually, but if it had been yours, you didn't stop and I then thought I was just imagining it." She said quietly then blushed with what she'd just revealed.

Kaelan remembered that day.

'How can I respond to that? If I confirm it was me she would want to know why I'd slowed but not stopped. How can I answer such a question?' So he didn't say anything. 'So her reaction had been because she'd thought it was me.' He held his breath wondering what she would say next.

Only she didn't say anything more about it. Since he didn't respond in any way, she guessed it had been her imagination after all. The whole situation just made her feel worse for the way she had reacted that day, and was still reacting and for having revealed herself like that.

Sarah quickly opened the door and slid out of the seat down to the ground. She walked around the side of the house to the back. With no one having been around since their death the place was starting to look overgrown. She continued past the pool, between the callistemons to the manicured boxed gardens at the rear.

After a brief glance around the area she then spun on her heels to leave when she bumped into the unexpected solidness that was Kaelan. His hands caught her to steady her and she liked the feel of his hands on her. While his body tightened when her hands landed on his waist to steady herself. Her touch was like fire even through his clothing.

However, happy memories mixed with their final moments and she needed to be out of there. Once under some semblance of control she stepped around him and rushed – well, rushing for her at least – out, back towards the Jeep. A hand gently but firmly gripped her arm and stopped her.

"Sarah?" Kaelan questioned. No matter how much he tried Kaelan couldn't keep the concern from sounding through. Even he could see she was practically drowning in emotions which he suspected resulted from her memories.

She didn't have to look at him to know he was frowning once again. At least this time, he didn't sound angry at her.

"I... I can't! I can't live here and I can't b-b-be here now." She managed to choke out. Tears threatened but didn't fall and she pulled herself out of his grip as she hastily made her way back to the Jeep. Thankfully she slept on the way back home.

Then, hiding in her room so she wouldn't have to deal with the three men around her, but especially Kaelan, she released her tight grip on her emotions. As it was, while a few tears did fall, they didn't last long. Staring up at the ceiling, she knew she was only delaying the inevitable of dealing with the gifts her friends had left her.

By the time she fell asleep, she had decided she would face them after those rogues had been dealt with. While it was still a delaying tactic, she realised she needed time to come to terms with each drama in her life right then.

The next day she spoke with George Manning and they finalised the details in regards to the house and the fees owed him. Remembering her decision from the previous night, she couldn't think about the house just yet so she ignored it for the time being.

Later that day she resumed her exercises. The weather didn't matter, she did them anyway. Besides, she was too tired to notice the weather. Kaelan would have preferred her to rest some more. Only, she wouldn't take his advice.

*

During her first two weeks, Kaelan watched and listened to her cry and curse, continue with the programme and fall asleep on the massage table. The only time the three men saw her awake was during breakfast and the fourteen hours of exercising. Even then, he only knew she was awake because of her complaints and tears.

On the first day he had picked up her hands and looked at them. They were so small compared to his. It also took him a moment or two to get his mind back on track instead of thinking about how nice her hands felt in his and of what her hands would feel like elsewhere, that flashed through his mind.

Then, with more effort than it should have been, he thought about the various hand guns he had available. Since he knew her hands were small, he had ordered smaller ones as the pistols he did have were too large for her to hold comfortably. Finally, he decided the Sig Sauer P232 would be best for her tiny hands.

He placed the P232 in front of her, grip end towards her with the grip base facing to her right. "Pick it up and look at it."

She picked the pistol up with her right hand. Her index finger laying along the side of the trigger guard – not on the trigger as most amateurs and wanna-be's would do. The rest of her fingers wrapped around the grip with the skin between the thumb and index finger pressed under the hammer guard, and the thumb wrapped around the grip to meet with the rest of her fingers. Her left hand went to the grip base to act as support for the gun and right hand – it was called the tea cup grip.

She found it was a comfortable gun for her small hands. He was training her to be able to shoot properly both left and right handed, and be fast enough; along with proper gun care and responsibility. So, having a gun that fitted her hands nicely meant she would be more willing to learn.

Kaelan was pleased with the way she'd picked the pistol up and held it. Step one was complete without him having to teach her anything. He nodded his approval.

After that, he showed her how to pop the magazine out, loaded it with ammunition, and put it back in. Then he removed the magazine and the seven bullets, told her to fill the mag and load it back into the gun. While she did so, he set up the target. When she had finished he told her to fire at will. After she emptied the mag, he scrolled the target back toward them.

'Not bad.' He thought to himself, rather impressed.

All seven hit the target and all seven were in the target borders with a couple hitting the outer edges of centre. Next step was to improve her targeting and then speed.

*

She was on the last day of her second week and was practicing shooting with Kaelan. It was late afternoon and he had her practicing her aim and speed with both her left and right hands. She'd just emptied the mag into the target.

"Your aim is improving. Just need you to shoot a little faster." Kaelan stated calmly.

She simply nodded. She barely had the energy to nod let alone actually speak.

He frowned. She appeared... more... tired than she usually did lately.

"Try again." He instructed, having decided to watch her out of the corner of his eye and not the target.

She reloaded the gun, fumbling slightly then she aimed and noted her hands were shaking. She fired the latest seven shots as quickly as she could, but even he could see it wasn't as fast as she was capable of.

When the target finished scrolling back toward them, she could see that four of the seven had hit the target and none of them were even half way near the centre. She lifted her hands, with the gun still in them, off the table only to set them back down almost immediately. They were shaking so badly.

Placing his hand on hers, he could feel them trembling even at rest.

"We're finished for the day." Kaelan stated, taking the gun out of her hands. "Go back to the house and tell Mick I said you are to have the massage now."

"Okay." She managed to whisper.

She didn't have the energy to argue with him about not having finished the afternoon sets of exercising. She was just too exhausted to even think about doing them let alone actually doing them. Slowly Sarah hopped off the stool and almost fell to the ground, so she stood there a moment or two before starting towards the house.

To Kaelan, the fact that she hadn't argued with him despite the day not being over, was a sign of how exhausted she was. Frowning to himself, he started cleaning her gun as she took her time to get off the stool and head to the house. He continued to clean the gun. He didn't watch her and, a few minutes later, he realised he should have known better.

He heard the sound of a body hitting the ground. Thinking she stumbled and just needed help in standing up he took his time in turning around. When he saw her lying there in a crumpled heap Kaelan rushed to her, immediate concern and guilt stabbing through him.

'Fuck, but I hope Toby keeps his mouth shut as I really don't need him on my back again about the whole situation.' Checking her over, he allowed himself slight relief.

'Damn it but she is so bloody stubborn! She's let herself continue until she's collapsed in exhaustion.'

Picking her up, he headed towards the house and was met by Toby and Mick as they ran out of the house, both obviously concerned. Kaelan gently passed her to Mick. He was glad to see that the young man really did care for her compared to last month when the three of them waited for her to wake up.

"Give her a massage then put her to bed. I think she can have the next two days off to recuperate. Toby, can you grab her walking stick please. I want to put these guns away. After Sarah's in bed, the two of you can take time off as well. Go out, but come back sober because she will want to continue."

"I didn't think you'd be too concerned about this." Toby

accused Kaelan as he jerked his hand in Sarah's direction.

Kaelan looked at him and counted slowly. Really slowly.

"I don't like seeing her like this. Unless I am willing to tie her up, and gag her, I can not stop her. Are you willing to do that to her to get her to ease off?"

Toby sighed and shook his head.

"Fine. Get the fuck off my back about it then. She's tiny but her determination is not. End of subject!" Having noted the man's expression becoming irate, Kaelan turned his back on Toby and finished cleaning the guns and putting them away. He didn't give a shit about what the man thought right then.

By the time Kaelan had finished, they had her in bed and were getting ready to go out. He had a shower then flopped on the lounge until they left. Once the two men were gone he grabbed his laptop then sat on the floor outside her room and waited for her to awaken. The only time he moved was for food and necessities.

*

For some reason she awoke and she couldn't work out why. Gazing around the room she finally looked at the clock and saw it was 07:00pm. She sat up suddenly then groaned in pain.

Almost instantly there was a knock on her door.

"Come in." Her voice thick with exhaustion and pain and sounded more like a moan.

He entered and gazed intently at her. Her eyes were dark and she looked so tired.

'Why is it that when something happens to me, he's always on the spot?'

"How are you feeling?"

'If I knew I could get my way in the matter I'd make her take a week off instead of just the two days. However, knowing she'll more than likely argue about it, I won't bother making the suggestion.'

"How come I'm still in bed? How did I get here? What happened to me? The last thing I remember is being at the gun range." She blurted out then blushed profusely and stared at her hands. It was like a dam bursting.

Kaelan's lips twitched in amusement. "You collapsed in exhaustion on the way back to the house yesterday so I had you put to bed. I decided that you needed the rest so I let you sleep."

"Yesterday? Oh." She said meekly, followed by her stomach growling, voicing its displeasure at being starved for so long. Her fading blush grew stronger again.

Kaelan laughed. He couldn't help it, it was just too funny.

Right at that moment she couldn't remember if she'd heard, or seen, him laugh before and it was a wonderful laugh. His face lit up and she loved it, and she blushed even harder, which she didn't think was possible. Thankfully, hopefully, he would misinterpret the reason for the blush.

'Such a cute little bunny.'

"Come on, come have something to eat." Kaelan said with a smile then walked out.

Sarah got up – grateful he hadn't guessed the real reason for her blushing, put a dressing gown on and made her way to the kitchen. Peering around, there were no Mick and Toby.

"Where are the guys?" She asked as she sat at the table, trying to place her walking stick somewhere where it wouldn't slide and clatter to the ground loudly as it had a tendency to do. Frequently.

"They went out for the evening. You will be resting up tomorrow as well." Kaelan just watched her, waiting for her to be stubborn about it.

"Okay." Came a gentle soft reply.

"What? No argument?"

She gazed at him meekly and shook her head. Whether she liked it or not, even she realised she needed to rest or the collapse would be a repeat performance the next day.

Kaelan raised his eyebrows. He couldn't help but be surprised. 'Maybe she realised the need for her to rest... maybe.' He thought then continued with dinner.

She let him finish making their dinner in peace and said thank you when he served it to her. It was chicken and bacon carbonara with fettuccine and parmesan cheese liberally sprinkled on top.

"Mmmm... this is good." Was all she said. She didn't bother to try to make idle chatter as she'd already worked out that he didn't talk much. So she was surprised when he spoke.

"What happened to your family?" For the first time ever, Kaelan had the need to talk. He decided to get to know her better. He wanted to get to know her better.

She almost choked trying to clear her mouth to answer him.

"They're either dead or disowned me." She simply stated with a dismissive shrug. "And your family?"

'What? I can't believe it. Yes she's a pain but nothing so bad as to deserve disowning. I have to find out why.' Ignoring her question, "Disowned you? Why?"

It surprised her that he actually sounded incredulous, as if the thought of them disowning her was an impossible concept to grasp.

'Of all the questions to ask!' The fork sat sort of limply in her hand as she stared at it.

"Whether the general population like it or not social classes are alive and well. In the social order of things my family are classified as low class even though they don't think so. When I became old enough to understand such things I decided I wanted better, something more, for myself. However, lacking in social education as I was, I didn't really know how to go about it.

"The first thing I did was to leave home as soon as my schooling was finished and I was old enough. In doing so, I basically cut the family ties and refused to answer to my elders within the family whenever they ordered me to do whatever they told me to do. It wasn't done deliberately, I was just trying to find out how to better myself and they took offence to it. They frowned upon me for it and pretty much started treating me like I was some mega criminal. As in any minor mistake suddenly became a punishable offence. That was the beginning of them disowning me.

"A couple of years later I met the man who would become my husband. He showed me that what I was after wasn't just for the rich and showed me how to achieve it. He helped me improve my use of the English language and how to dress properly, better, however one wants to put it. You see, the way I looked and spoke back then was a product of my family's upbringing. That completed the disowning process. Because, in their opinion, I had apparently decided to place myself higher than my elders, they shunned me." She said quietly without looking at him. She had tried to keep the spiel unemotional, as if it was happening to someone else. She wasn't sure if she succeeded or not.

"So you married your husband." He stated thinking it was a typical act of defiance. However, he couldn't believe what he was hearing. To him she sounded like someone a family would – should – be proud of, but her words told another story altogether.

"My marriage to him was part of the final straw as far as my family were concerned. Like yourself, he was well educated – better educated than they were, and they judged him as being up himself. I married him because I loved him."

Kaelan didn't know why but her comment about his education surprised him. He hadn't realised she had noticed. He didn't even know how she'd worked it out.

"How did he die?" He didn't know how to feel. She seemed one of the lucky ones to have found love even if it had been for a brief moment then taken away from her.

She quietly took a calming breath.

"We were on our motorbike, him riding and me pillion. We had right of way when a car turned in front of us. We didn't stand a chance of missing it. I flew over the top to the other side of the intersection and he slammed into the car snapping his neck, dying instantly, among other injuries." Sarah recited matter-of-factly. He listened to her tell it like it was someone else's story.

"It must have been horrific for you." He stated quietly. While he had been through similar or worse in his line of work, he had a difficult time thinking of her suffering so badly.

"Actually, I don't remember anything about it. I saw the car directly in front of us and knew what was about to happen and closed my eyes. The next thing I knew I was on my back on the other side of the intersection with the wind knocked out of me, screaming in my helmet. I got the impression that I had been screaming for a while and what I heard was the tail end of that scream.

"Eventually, they worked out I was still conscious throughout the whole ordeal, however, it seems my mind blanked out everything after I saw the car until after I landed on the road. I was told by the police what had happened in between those two points, and they had received the information from witnesses of the accident. That's also how I had damaged my ankles."

There was a hint of sadness in her voice but he thought that was for the loss of her husband, not for the loss of memory. Between her ankles, lack of memory, her family and losing her husband, it surprised him she didn't feel jaded at life in general.

"Is that why you fell in love with Daniel? Because a vamp is harder to kill?" Kaelan's voice wasn't as gentle as before, or as neutral.

He tried not to be too judgemental of her choices, but the best he could do was go for neutral. 'I just can't imagine loving one of the monsters and am disappointed she can.' There was another thought running around in there but he decided to ignore it. He didn't want to deal with that one. Not yet. If ever.

'Is he jealous or disgusted that I could be attracted to the undead? Since he's a hunter I guess I can understand his disgust over my choice. But if he's jealous then that would suggest he has feelings for me. Wouldn't it? Then why does he always seem annoyed with me?'

"What makes you think I was in love with him?" She asked carefully, sounding confused for some reason.

"Are you saying that you weren't?"

"Just answer my question and I will then answer yours." Now she was a little annoyed. 'Why does he have to answer a question with a question? He did that weeks ago so I'm not going to let him get away with it this time.'

"I asked mine first." Kaelan couldn't help the twitch of amusement at the childish fun his comment caused him to remember.

"You're evading the question Kaelan. Just answer it please." She persisted. It was comments like those which surprised him by letting him know how determined she could be when she usually speaks so timidly.

"Their website said you and he were lovers."

"Ah, I see. No, we weren't lovers."

"You weren't?" While it was a question, he made it sound more of a statement. He had to make sure as something in his chest tightened.

"No we weren't. I knew how he felt about me, he never hid it. However, there were reasons why I never took it further." She answered softly.

"Oh? What reasons?" She couldn't tell if he was actually curious or just gathering information just by the tone of his voice.

"I was too shy to allow it to go beyond friendship despite that

I could see he was attracted to me. He willingly let the relationship progress at my pace."

"The other reasons?"

After a pause, "While I don't mind answering your questions, I am not going to expand on that one." She finished timidly. Despite being given the perfect opportunity, once again she'd chickened out.

"Your choice, Sarah." Kaelan stated non-committedly, despite being curious as to what the other reason/s may have been.

'I guess he was just gathering information.' And that saddened her. She sat there staring at the remains of her dinner. Even though she did want to finish it, she had a hard time making herself to resume eating it.

"So, you didn't love him?" He said again. He asked again, just to be sure.

"I was attracted to him and he had a nice personality. While it's true that we weren't actively lovers, there was the possibility that we may have become lovers over time."

Kaelan frowned at her wording then asked another question. "Did you let him feed from you and did you ingest his blood?"

Once again his tone was flat and somehow she knew he wasn't happy. Sarah gazed up at him with her own neutral expression and equally neutral tone.

"That's a rather personal question, but since you asked I won't lie to you or evade the question this once."

She paused while a glimmer of surprise flitted across his features.

"Yes I let him feed from me. Twice, but I didn't let it go any further and no I didn't ingest his blood."

His disappointment at the first part of her response was more than he thought it would be. 'At least she wasn't stupid enough to drink his blood.' He thought while keeping his face blank. He reined in the urge to call her an idiot and the want to go mad at her for it.

"Why would you do such a thing?"

She glared belligerently at him and stated, "I was curious." She paused and frowned.

He opened his mouth to criticise her reason but decided not to. It was her choice after all. Instead, he concentrated on her current reaction.

"What are you thinking, Sarah?"

"I... I was just thinking about my reaction to his death." She started, glancing briefly at Kaelan. Another look of surprise flitted briefly across his face. If she hadn't been looking at him right then she wouldn't have seen it.

"Go on." He urged despite his surprise.

She resumed staring at the fork in her hand, 'such a nice fork in its plainness. Thick for reasonable gripping and a nice weight to it so you know you are holding it.'

"Yes I do mourn his death, but I just realised that it is more as a very, very close friend rather than a lover I never said yes to." With a quick glance at him she hastily continued.

"I still stand by my earlier comment that we could have become lovers further down the track, but I wasn't truly in love with him at the time of his death." She said slowly as understanding gradually dawned for her. But she knew she sounded confused.

"So, that confuses you." Kaelan stated simply.

The tightness in his chest eased. He decided he might be able to live with the actions of her curiosity and felt relief at the fact she hadn't loved the blood sucker after all, but managed to keep his expression neutral. He didn't want to show anything which might scare her away. Nor did he want to admit right then, even to himself, what that relief truly meant.

She nodded because a part of the realisation did confuse her. "Why?"

"I don't understand why it took his death for me to realise that fact. Other than that, I really don't know why." Her voice was so low it was almost a whisper. But in reality she did know why, her shyness had her so knotted up she just couldn't admit it to him.

Kaelan gently took her hand in his and risked her seeing he cared despite not wanting to admit it to her or to himself. The action caused her to look at him. The butterflies were starting to wake up again.

While his expression was one of caring, in what way he cared for her she didn't know. She wanted to caress his hand but she couldn't make her thumb move. However, her fingers twitched from the effort and he had no idea how to interpret it.

"There is nothing wrong with the way you feel about anyone, including Daniel. Just try not to let it eat you from the inside out, Sarah."

She just nodded mutely at him as she barely returned his grip then he took his hand away, but the damage had been done. She knew it.

He suspected she was still confused. As it was, she barely returned any pressure even when he took his hand away.

Trouble was right then, despite her revelations, he wanted to do more than just hold her hand.

She had been so nervous and so shy she hadn't taken the risk of letting him know how she felt about him. Not only that but the butterflies were now awake and active, due to his touch, and they had no intentions of settling down any time soon. To top it off, she hadn't known how she was expected to react so she hadn't. Instead, they resumed eating.

After they finished dinner he collected their bowls, placed them in the sink. Then he went to the fridge and brought out an amazing looking dessert, topped with large amounts of strawberries and whipped cream, and set about serving it. When he handed her a bowl of it, she saw it was pavlova. He laughed at her and she gazed up at him.

"What?" She asked softly looking confused.

"I take it you love pavlova." Kaelan stated in amusement.

She blushed and that made him chuckle some more. "Very much so. Thank you." She smiled at him and started eating it. "Did you make this?" She asked.

"Yes, and I cooked dinner as well." He responded slowly, cautiously. Some women found it hard to believe a man could cook as well as, if not better than, they did.

"Wonderful. Oh yeah, you're definitely a keeper..."

Her eyes widened as she realised what she'd just said, dropped her spoon when she turned so red he was expecting a comical thermometer top-popping reaction. Instead she swayed and clutched at the table to prevent herself from falling.

That much of a blood rush and she would have been having one hell of a dizzy spell. Unlike the last dizzy spell he saw her have she wouldn't look at him. She just stared at her dessert instead.

She stared at a strawberry in her dessert because she so couldn't look at him right then. 'I can not believe I just said that out loud! To him personally at that!'

"I'm glad you like my cooking." He didn't even bother keeping the amusement out of his voice this time round. Although, her comment and reaction had him wondering.

'Was that an unfortunate choice of words? Or an accidental blurting out about how she feels? I have no way of knowing. She's so damned emotional it's hard to tell what the cause of her feelings truly are.'

Still blushing, but the dizziness started to subside she said sheepishly "Yeah I do." 'What must he be thinking?' She didn't want to think about it, while silently she chided herself. 'He hasn't shown any interest in me what-so-ever so why am I behaving so foolishly?' She mentally sighed as she resumed eating the dessert.

When she'd finished she stood up and started to take her bowl to the sink. She had decided to do the dishes for a change. 'I haven't done any housework since the night I was shot and it might be best if I finally chipped in for a change.' She didn't get far when Kaelan took the bowl out of her hand.

"Go relax on the lounge if you don't want to go to bed yet. There are magazines on the coffee table if you're interested." His voice was gentle and yet again it surprised her that it could be.

She opened her mouth to complain, 'silly me', she thought as he made a shooing motion.

"Go."

So, with a blush, she left and sat in the lounge room grabbing one of the magazines to read.

By the time he had completed the dishes and joined her, she was asleep on the lounge. He gazed down at her, so peaceful.

'Would it be right to hold curiosity against her? Even if I believe it to be foolish and idiotic?' He softly sighed. 'I know I have done the odd foolish and idiotic things that could get me into trouble. And yet… with what little she knows about me, she's willing to be friends with me. She's stated she has no problems with what I do. Can I do the same for her?' He sighed again, knowing the answer wasn't immediately forthcoming.

A moment or two later he gently picked her up, holding her close to him, and headed to her room. While he had carried her a number of times already, it was the first time she was relaxed against his chest and it surprised him how well she fitted there. How right it seemed.

However, the movement was enough to wake her.

She must have been more tired than she thought, because the next thing she knew she awoke in Kaelan's arms.

"Uh…" She sounded as she leant against his chest, his heartbeat so steady and strong and soothing.

"You fell asleep so I'm putting you in your bed." He said quietly and she settled against him and his heartbeat again as he carried her.

She was asleep once more before he had entered her room. He tucked her in then went to bed himself. Kaelan ended up lying there staring at the ceiling wondering for the umpteenth time what to do about her while he ignored his body's opinion on the subject.

'Why the hell am I so damned confused about her?' He sighed in frustration, rolled over then eventually fell asleep.

Sarah woke up sufficiently to roll over and reposition the body pillow so it would still support the higher most ankle. She opened her eyes. She didn't remember getting into bed.

'Well... yeah, I remember Kaelan saying I'd fallen asleep and he was going to put me in my bed, but I don't remember him actually doing it. I obviously fell asleep again.' Needing to be up she did the necessities and crawled back into bed and fell back to sleep.

The next day was a quiet one as she slept the day away and he let her. It could only benefit her once she started exercising again. During the two times she was awake, he fed her then let her sleep some more. Later that evening, Toby and Mick came home and three men went to their beds shortly thereafter.

Chapter 20

The alarm went off and she jerked awake. 4:30am, she groaned and crawled out of bed to start her torture regime all over again.

Before they started the next round, Kaelan decided Sarah had to weigh herself. Typically, she argued about it by saying she hadn't lost enough to warrant the weighing session. He told her she either did it willingly or he would force her. Perversely he thought it would be interesting to wrestle with her but in her current condition it wouldn't be that much fun. He shook his head at such nonsense.

It was only because it was a threat he could definitely carry out that she agreed to the weighing at all. However, to make it easier on her, he also told her they needed to know so they could adjust the programme if need be. With great resignation, she stood on the scales. She knew what the results would be and had warned them, but he couldn't believe she had only lost three kilos.

"Damn Girl, most other people don't even do a quarter of what you're doing in half the time yet they lose more than you have." Mick griped. Kaelan agreed with him on that one, but quite obviously she knew what would happen. But still.

"I told you before we started that I wouldn't lose much weight, hence why I'm working harder." She stated bluntly.

"But why should it be so much harder for you?" Toby asked with a frown.

"Sorry, I can't answer that." She murmured without looking at them. In reality, while not embarrassing, the reason was a personal one and she had no intentions of revealing it to them, and especially to Kaelan.

'I've never seen anyone work so hard only to lose so little weight before. By the way she speaks, I'm of the belief she knows the reason why and it's obvious she's keeping that information to herself for some reason. It must be rather personal for her to do so and for that reason only I'm not going to press the matter further.' Kaelan thought to himself.

The following two weeks were like the previous two weeks except she was a little less sore than before. However, her daily intake of pain killers was still the same. An added bonus was that she wasn't falling asleep before the massaging started. She now fell asleep during.

'Hey, it's an improvement… a little.' She thought to herself.

Even her walking was improving as strength built up in her ankles. The only problem was, at the end of the second fortnight, she collapsed from exhaustion again. Kaelan made her have two days off again and sent Toby and Mick away for their break. They appreciated it as well.

During those two days, when she was awake, he prepared her filling and delicious meals of which she happily ate.

That became the routine for the next eight to ten weeks… Two weeks of non-stop torture, collapse into unconsciousness and then spend two days off, only to start all over again.

*

Christmas came and went. Kaelan declared her exercises were to be a half day only that day even though she had every intention of treating it like any other day. The three men set about preparing the food she had been smelling, as it roasted, the day before.

Now, the ham and chicken were to be served up as cold cuts along with freshly home baked (courtesy of Mick) bread rolls and fresh garden salads. Other than that, Christmas was a quiet affair. There were no gifts because none of them really knew each other - except Mick and Toby, and Sarah wasn't able to go shopping.

About the fourth week into the regime, Kaelan and Sarah had another private session.

For weeks something had been niggling Kaelan at the back of his mind. They were on her second 'weekend' off when he realised what it was: her comment about being alone in her tiny apartment. The way Sarah had said it told him she didn't like it; the small apartment and being alone.

Toby and Mick were gone for the weekend so it was just Sarah and Kaelan once again. Surprisingly, he was looking forward to the private time between them – even if she did sleep most of it away – as much as he looked forward to training her.

Kaelan decided to ask her if she wanted to live in his house instead of her apartment. While he loved the house – it's all he had left of his parents, it does spend most of its time empty. Since first meeting her, he hadn't wanted to stay in it because it meant they were so near each other. However, the past two months together made him think it would be nice to have the house open all the time.

The two of them were in the lounge room when he broached the subject with her.

"Are you happy in your apartment?" Kaelan's voice sounded cautious in its neutrality.

"Not really, it's not what I wanted." She responded just as cautiously.

'Was hers cautious because mine was or did she have another reason?' He gazed around the lounge room, "This house spends a lot of its time empty. Would you like to stay here?"

"You sure you want someone invading your space? I mean, there will be three of us." While still sounding cautious she seemed surprised by his question. 'Can't say I'm not disappointed to hear that, normally, he's rarely here.'

Blinking at her, she had surprised him with her question. It was like she'd sensed his want for solitude. It was the only reason he could think of for her response. He had never met a woman who had attuned herself to him... to his needs. Then he frowned at her words.

"Three of you?"

"Yeah. It seems with Danny's death I've inherited Mick and Toby. So, if I choose to stay, there will be the two of them as well and me."

He thought about her words. 'So, the vamp cared about her

that much. Come to think about it, she does seem to have this knack of getting herself into trouble. Whether it's just falling over or almost being killed… Yeah, I can see the need of them being with her. Especially if I'm not going to be around. It would be a load off my mind during those times.'

Having decided, Kaelan turned his full gaze upon her, and for the life of her she couldn't read him. But then, she never could unless he wanted her to.

"I wouldn't have asked otherwise. You just pay the rates, power, other amenities and general upkeep if you decide to stay."

She regarded him for a moment then stared past him as she thought about his offer.

'Can I do it? Yes I can. Will I do it? Two factors come into it for me: 1. Practicality… His house is one hundred per cent better than my pokey little apartment. His home has everything I want in a home. 2. Emotionally… I think I love him.'

With that revelation, that personal admission, her heart skipped a beat then thudded hard and fast. She then wondered if she could stay there since she was in love with him. Practicality… yes; emotionally she shoved it temporarily to the back recesses of her mind because she so wanted out of her apartment and his offer was the best option available to her.

Kaelan was surprised with himself to discover he wanted her to say yes. That it was her whom he wanted to stay there. That he was liking the thought of her being there whenever he came back to Brisbane, despite his need for solitude and quietness, surprised him. He sat there waiting for her answer, hoping she would say yes.

Maybe, with her living there, they could become more than the friends they were. That thought surprised him. Despite her talk to him before the exercise programme, he had never really actively thought of her as a friend before.

'I may have referred to her as such when talking to others but personally never considered her as a friend. Until now. While annoying at times, she's actually quite peaceful to be around.'

"Okay, I'll stay. I so want out of that apartment and this house is awesome." She said glancing quickly at him then looking away again.

"Is there anything in your apartment that isn't yours?" While he worked at keeping his exterior calm, he couldn't believe how pleased he was that she had said yes.

"Out of the furniture, only the bookcases are mine. Everything that isn't furniture is mine. Why?" She couldn't help but frown slightly at his question.

"I'll organise some men to pack your gear and move it here. You can use the sitting room for your bookcases and books if you want."

"Okay, thanks… Umm…"

'To listen to him talk, one would have thought he was just talking business. If he feels something for me, there isn't any indication.' She just hoped that she didn't show too much emotion herself but knew that was wishful thinking. However, it made it tough to ask the next part.

She glanced shyly at him then down at her hands again.

"Ask Sarah." He prompted her. 'Never have I met anyone as shy as she is.'

While to her, his voice held no inflection at all.

251

"Would it be okay if I added another small building in the yard please?" She asked. Even to her, her voice sounded shy and hesitant and she hated that.

'Hmmm... Not what I was expecting, but interesting.' He thought, then enquired, "What would it be for?"

"My nail bar. I would like to work from home instead of renting floor space, but I don't want to take up a room in the house here. I would like to keep the nail business separate from the house... If that would be okay?" She was afraid he would say no. It was his place after all but she wanted to work from home if she could. She was just so nervous.

Just like that, the scared tiny baby bunny was back.

"That's fine, Sarah. I don't have a problem with that." 'Hmmm... yeah, the idea of her being here no matter when I come back sounds really appealing to me.'

"Thank you." Was all she could manage through her relief and she smiled at him.

He didn't really smile but with a slow blink he'd accepted her 'thank you'. When she smiled, while still shy, her face lit up and went from cute to lovely and he was glad he 'okayed' her request. They lapsed into silence then Kaelan grabbed one of his magazines. After a minute or two, she found something to read as well.

Sarah then realised that living in his house was going to be tough on her, because of how she felt about him and knowing he more than likely didn't feel the same way about her.

'If he does, then he's hiding it extremely well.' She mentally sighed. 'But I don't think he does. I hope I'm not making a mistake with my decision because I have a niggling feeling that

I'm setting myself up for a fall of some kind and that fall will be extremely painful.'

*

Half way through January, on the third set of days off for Sarah, Kaelan decided to take Toby and Mick with him when he went shopping. He decided to buy what she needed to set up her nail bar. The pre-fab building, which looked like an overgrown modern cubby house for adults, was going to be delivered within the week. The rest of the stuff he bought her, the three men hid all of it in the garage until it was needed. He even chose a theme for the décor inside and out and hoped she would like it.

Kaelan decided to set it up on the right side of the house, so he and the guys marked it all out, with a little car park as well. Once the permit was granted, they would start it while Sarah was training. He put out a call to some of 'his' friends who were qualified to do the plumbing, concrete laying and electrics.

While some owed him a favour or two, he knew he could get away with paying them off with beer and a barbecue. Despite being a loner, every now and then he would have a barbecue for his friends where they could relax without worrying about women and children being around.

As the men collected the groceries and headed towards the house they could hear singing but no music. At first Kaelan thought someone was there in the house with Sarah so he rushed up the stairs with Toby and Mick close on his heels. They dumped the shopping on the kitchen floor and headed into the lounge room. Kaelan stopped suddenly at the sight before him.

Still dressed in track pants and t-shirt, Sarah was sitting alone on the coffee table in front of the stereo system with her back to the kitchen and, therefore, the three men. She had on a set of headphones, which was why the guys couldn't hear any music. She had just finished singing one song when she started another. Suffice to say, Kaelan was stunned. He hadn't known she could sing and she was good. The three men just stood there watching her with their mouths open in surprise.

'It seems like I'm not the only one not to know.'

At the end of her sixth week, on the first of her relax days, all three guys were out and Sarah had the house to herself for a change. After breakfast she went into the lounge room, plugged headphones into the stereo then placed five cds into the stereo system, put on the headphones, sat on the nearby coffee table so she could bop while sitting then pressed play. Home alone, she could sing to the music without fear of the others hearing her.

Four cds later she was half way through Belinda Carlisle's *'Heaven is a Place on Earth'* when she turned slightly as she sang...

...Ooh Baby, do you know what that's worth? Ooh heaven is a place on earth. They say in heaven love comes first. We'll make heaven a place on earth...

...and she caught movement out of the corner of her eye. She let out a little scream and fell off the coffee table in fright. The trouble with having headphones on was she hadn't heard anyone come home or enter the house. That, and getting tangled up in the cord when she fell off the coffee table.

Kaelan was practically doubled over in laughter. He couldn't help it. Her reaction was just so hilarious. While Mick was the first to reach and helped her stand up after she ripped the headphones off.

"Fuuudge! How long have you three been standing there?!" She demanded, heart pounding away. "Don't sneak up on me like that!" She was bright red from both the fright and the anger, and Kaelan couldn't stop grinning.

"Didn't know you can sing, Girl" Mick said laughing, helping her to stand.

Sarah hit him in the arm, "Don't laugh at me. I know I can't sing. I thought I was home alone."

"Can't sing? I'll listen to your singing any day." Toby commented with a big grin as he too moved closer towards her.

She just blushed, arms crossed over her breasts – to stop them from bouncing which Kaelan had noticed numerous times before since she wore no bra while not exercising – as she started to hobble out of the room. Her arms crossed like that made her hobbling gait worse.

She glanced up through her lashes at Kaelan as she got closer. He knew he probably should have tried not to smile but he didn't. She blushed harder, both in embarrassment and in heart-stopping pleasure at seeing him smile, and pushed past him; nudging him out of the way.

'Poor baby bunny.' He chuckled.

She fled as fast as she could to her room and stayed there till dinner. That evening, no one said anything but, through her lashes, she caught glances and smirks aimed at her.

*

They were at the end of the eighth week and it felt good not to be so overly tired any more.

'Oh, I'm still tired but not to the point that I'll fall asleep if I stop moving.' She looked forward to the weekends the most. It was just Kaelan and her and she was enjoying them.

The day before, Kaelan and Sarah took turns reading various articles from the magazines each of them were reading. Sometimes they would read over the top of each other to try and drown the other out and ended up laughing.

He'd started it when it was her turn to read but was too impatient to wait. So, she got back at him by doing the same thing back at him and the scene just degraded from there. It had been a surprise to see that 'fun' side of him as he had a tendency to hide it.

'I hope to see more of this side of him and often.'

While they laughed, Kaelan thought it was good to see her happy. It surprised him to find himself enjoying such silliness with her.

Now being the second day off and only hours before Toby and Mick came home, she wanted to do something where the two of them could sit quietly together. She was in the lounge room looking at Kaelan's music and movies collection when she heard footsteps behind her.

Turning, she saw him standing nearby, watching her.

"Got anything planned?" She asked softly. She still didn't know how he would react to them watching a movie together. 'Over two months together and I still don't know that much about him. Nor have we watched a movie together.'

"Actually, yeah." He said, watching her and waiting.

"Oh, okay." And she turned back to look at his collection to hide her disappointment, but he still heard it in her voice. As far as she was concerned, she couldn't seem to catch a break.

He came up behind her, not close enough to invade her space, and said quietly so as not to frighten her. "I would like to hear you sing again."

She turned around so quickly she had to fight to keep her balance. Kaelan's hand grabbed her outstretched one to stop her from falling. "Sing?" She croaked out.

Whether it was his closeness, unexpectedly hearing him speak or his request that frightened her he didn't know. "Please." He asked gently.

Heat washed up her face and she knew she was blushing. 'He said please so nicely that it would be mean of me to refuse.'

She slowly withdrew her hand and gave a small nod as she went back to browsing his cds. She chose a home-made mixed selection album. The first one was Fat Boy Slim's *'Right Here Right Now'* and told Kaelan that there was nothing to sing in this one. Privately, it would help her not be so nervous.

She blushed again and he smiled to encourage her. His smile was genuine and showed something she interpreted as caring. She wanted, she hoped, to be the reason of that smile but she wasn't so sure she was.

Sitting on one end of the coffee table she was side on to him.

That way he could see her but she wasn't facing him where she would have to look at him. She found the situation embarrassing enough as it was.

Watching her, he noted she really did find it embarrassing and he just found it so endearing.

The next song was Fergal Sharkey's *'A Good Heart'*, and she sang that one. The music was loud enough to hear but not loud enough to drown her out.

'Damn, but she's good. I had thought maybe it was a fluke, but it's not.' Her voice matched itself to the vocals of the song. He didn't understand why she didn't do it professionally.

It was a shame her ankles didn't work properly any more. By the way she was bopping while seated on the coffee table, he was of the opinion that she would have been good at dancing as well. Then Fergal Sharkey's *'You Little Thief'* started and she really got into that one. He could see she loved the song in the way she moved and sang.

The fourth song was an instrumental and she asked him for some juice. A moment or so later he came back and handed it to her.

"Thank you. Don't blame me for the songs, these are your cds after all." She was afraid of what he would say. She said daringly but still shy.

"Good thing I like them then isn't it?" He said with a smirk. She just screwed her nose at him and he laughed at her. She blushed at being laughed at and at being so bold. Kaelan grew up with those songs so he knew them well even if he hadn't heard them in years.

It was good to see her so relaxed even if she was nervous

about singing. During their private times, each time she was shy and it always took a bit of time before she wasn't. But when she wasn't, he thought it was great to be around her.

Then the instrumental finished and a bunch of Bonnie Tyler songs played... *'Have You Ever Seen the Rain', 'Holding Out for a Hero'* – that one had her slightly emotional.

'Of all the ones to be singing to him. I guess I do see him as a bit of a hero.' She had put so much feeling into that one he suspected it may have been a little true to her heart.

Trouble was the next song was worse for her because it summed up how she felt about him – *'Total Eclipse of the Heart'*. Sarah couldn't look at him once the music started. The chorus was the hard part...

And I need you now tonight, And I need you more than ever, And if you'll only hold me tight, We'll be holding on forever, And we'll only be making it right, Cause we'll never be wrong together, We can take it to the end of the line, Your love is like a shadow on me all of the time (all of the time), I don't know what to do and I'm always in the dark, We're living in a powder keg and giving off sparks, I really need you tonight, Forever's gonna start tonight, Forever's gonna start tonight.

When the instrumental section played, she walked to the open door that led to the verandah and hung onto the door frame. She couldn't breathe properly and as a result she missed the cue to continue singing. But she just couldn't continue.

'I know now, without a doubt that I love him and I feel so foolish because he hasn't shown me anything in return to justify my loving him. To top it off I've been singing these songs to him like he understands and that it matters to him.'

He had noticed how she wouldn't look at him once the music started. How the latest song in particular was from the heart. More so than any other she had already sung. So much emotion as if it was her telling someone about herself instead of it just being a song. When the instrumental kicked in, he watched as she went towards the verandah doors and leant against the door frame.

When she missed her cue to continue singing, Kaelan realised the song, or something else, was truly affecting her. More than he had originally thought.

Her mind was like a tree in a storm, not knowing which way the wind would toss it. It was taking all her effort not to cry because of her foolishness over him. She had fallen hard for him and she didn't know what to do about it. She had never had to chase after a guy before.

As a result of her thoughts, she hadn't heard him come up behind her until he moved to stand in front of her.

Sarah stared up at him all wide eyed and breathy, that heart wrenching frightened baby bunny look, as their eyes locked. It seemed like she was trying not to cry and his chest constricted as if someone had kicked him hard.

Without thought, Kaelan raised his hand to touch her on the cheek. Her mouth opened slightly and her tongue darted out quickly to moisten her bottom lip and it was almost as if she wasn't breathing. Now was the perfect time to kiss her. Now he would find out one way or the other.

His hand was just a breath away from touching her. But, just before he could touch her they heard the voices of Toby and Mick.

'Shee-oot!! They're back early.' She exclaimed privately in dismay.

'Crappy timing!' Kaelan dropped his hand and glanced in their direction.

Sarah took that moment to duck out to the verandah and walked away as fast as she could. He had dropped his hand when they came home, so there would be no chance of finding out what would have happened. Not for the rest of the day, if ever. She still didn't know if he truly cared or not. From what she'd heard from Mick, he never left the house unless it was to go shopping.

'Maybe I'm convenient. I just don't know.'

He stared after her retreating form. He could have easily caught up to her but he let her go because it was no longer the right time.

'Did she feel the same way? It appeared like she did, but why did she walk away?' He clenched his hand in confusion and frustration. 'Was it the guys had scared her away from revealing how she feels? Or had I misread?'

Kaelan walked to the railing of the verandah and gripped it hard.

'I guess I'll have to wait till the next time we're alone to find out. Two long weeks to wait.' He sighed.

*

Nine weeks into the exercise programme a small box and a

letter arrived. After signing for them she read the letter...

Dear Mrs Brackenway,

Please find enclosed the following titles:

- Dracula by Bram Stoker – First Edition

- Five (5) volumes of Sherlock Holmes by Arthur Conan Doyle – All Second Editions

- The Complete Works of William Shakespeare in Two (2) volumes – Both Second Editions

These were all that had survived the fire. Should more be found they will be forwarded to you.

Yours sincerely,

Mr Niles Robertson

Solicitor

After reading the letter, she asked Toby to place the box in the sitting room with the rest of her stuff Kaelan had transferred from her apartment. Then, she promptly ignored it as she wasn't ready to deal with it yet.

*

However, the chance to discover how she felt about him two weeks later never came. As was his habit, Kaelan checked the laptop to see what hits were active then got up to get dressed. Entering the hallway, he saw her disappear into the bathroom.

Three months after being shot – she had to look at it that way or she would cry over the deaths of her friends – she discovered she'd lost about a third of her unwanted weight. The New Year was off to an okay start. The second month was not far in starting and she even felt better physically.

'Good, she's up.' He made his way down the hallway and leant on the wall opposite the bathroom, waiting for her to come out.

Soon Toby and Mick would be gone for two days. She smiled as she opened the door to leave the bathroom. Kaelan, dressed in semi faded blue jeans, a grey polo shirt (that clung around the chest but a little loose around the waist) with white and black piping and hiking boots – very yummy – was waiting for her as she came out of the bathroom.

As she gazed up at his face her smile faltered at his serious expression. He almost hated to have to wipe it away, because disappear it would with what he had to tell her.

"The hit has been ordered." He said as he watched her reactions while still leaning against the opposite wall.

Her eyes dropped briefly along with her heart and she took a deep breath, then she looked back up at him and nodded. 'So much for our personal time together.' For some reason Sarah had a feeling things between them would be coming to an end. She couldn't explain it, it was what she felt. Her smile was indeed gone.

"How do you feel about this?" He had to make sure. If she still had doubts then he would leave her behind and do all of it for her.

"Honestly? Nervous, but I still want to go through with it."

"Good. Get dressed, then come with me and we'll pack what we will need." It pleased him she spoke honestly. While he could see how she felt, he did prefer her to tell him. To voice it out loud so she couldn't hide from how she felt.

"Okay." She left to get dressed.

Kaelan went out into the kitchen to tell Toby and Mick what was going on.

Sarah dressed into a cream coloured lace pantie-like g-string...

'I didn't choose them but they are lovely.'

...a pair of powder blue, light cotton dress pants and a lace cream coloured bra. Over that she wore a camisole and sheer chiffon blouse with matching chantilly lace bell sleeves.

She applied a little make-up and tied her hair back from the temples, letting the rest hang free. Then she slipped on a pair of powder blue – slightly darker than the pants – one and a half inch heeled court shoes. The blouse sat outside the pants due to the style of the bottom hem being a drop/rounded cut.

Kaelan had given her the outfit last week and told her she would be wearing it for the hit. She didn't argue with him, besides the outfit looked good and fitted nicely. She checked herself in the mirror.

'Hmmm... with the small matching silver and lighter powder blue shoulder bag and the jaguar walking stick I have to say that I look reasonable for a change. I think the weight loss has helped some in that department.'

Then, she walked out into the kitchen. 'Kaelan has never seen me dressed up before. At least, not without blood all over me.'

He had to force himself to breathe. She was beautiful. He

couldn't have planned the outfit better if he had tried. She was definitely breathtaking.

Toby and Mick just stared and went wow, and Kaelan's expression flickered so quickly that, if she hadn't been looking at him, she would have missed it. Not that she could interpret the flicker anyway. He didn't trust his voice. All he could do was nod his approval...

'I guess that's all of a response I'm going to get from him in regards to the outfit he had bought me'

...and walk out the back door, and with a sigh she followed him. She followed him.

They went out the back to the small...

'When I say small I mean it is smaller than the garage, it's still large when looking at it from the outside'

...lock-up shed beside the garage, he unlocked it and they went inside. She had been in there almost every day since starting the exercise regime. It was Kaelan's weapons safe, though for its size, vault was a more appropriate name.

When one inspected it from the outside it appeared to be a matching extension of the garage. It was as wide as the garage but not quite as tall and not quite half the length. It had an outer door that swung outwards to reveal a second, almost bank vault looking door that swung inwards. Then they were inside and it was smaller on the inside as it had a two foot thick reinforced concrete inner shell.

The sight of all those weapons was always breathtaking, no matter what one's opinion regarding weapons were. Sarah wouldn't, or couldn't, use a lot of what he had in there, but it was impressive all the same. The vault was full of handguns of all kinds, large and small; rifles of varying sizes and length; some things that looked like guns but didn't seem to fall into either category as far as she could see.

'But then, I'm not the expert'.

There were also numerous knives and other bladed things and so many different grenades and other explosives that she didn't even know where to begin. Ammunition of all kinds imaginable, plus a few of his own making, were too numerous to count. If Kaelan wanted to be a dealer, he could have been with what was in that vault alone.

However, he wasn't, it was his personal collection. She also knew that a good portion of that collection was illegal.

When he had packed the bag with all that he wanted to take with them he turned to her.

"No questions?" He sounded like she was going to question everything he did.

Shaking her head, "You know what you are doing, I'll just do what you tell me to do." Her voice came out quiet.

"You don't have a problem with that?" He asked since she just about argued everything else with him.

"Have I ever acted as though I had a problem with what you've told me to do? And before you answer that, think hard about the importance of each subject in relation to the question." She added the last quickly.

She could see he had started to say yes to her having problems with him telling her what to do.

For once, she had him. He paused then nodded.

"You're right. Where it mattered the most, you followed

orders. Let's go." Kaelan grabbed the bag then walked out. He waited for her so he could secure the vault and walked to the Jeep where Toby and Mick waited for the two of them.

The two men weren't going with them.

Mick, Toby and Sarah said bye to each other even though she would only be gone for a day at the most. When Kaelan closed the rear door she got into the passenger side. She was settled in place by the time he started the engine.

"You sure you don't have any questions?" He asked as they left his property.

"Positive. Just tell me what I'm to do when we are almost there and I'll either do well or be dead." She said quietly as she stared out the windscreen to watch the passing scenery. She saw his head turn towards her for a moment before turning back to the road. She had to admit she did have reasonably good peripheral vision so she didn't have to really look at him to see him move.

"You seem to be taking that concept rather well."

"Would it help any if I carried on like a pork chop and got on your nerves about it?" She asked quietly

Kaelan chuckled, "Pork chop... That's funny, and no it wouldn't help." 'Where does she come up with these sayings of hers? Her forms of swearing and name calling are rather amusing.'

"Something m... I was called years ago whenever I'd done silly things. Since it's of no help, here I'll sit quietly." While she still loved her husband, she didn't think it would be good to keep mentioning him. She hoped Kaelan wouldn't comment about it. Thankfully, he didn't.

Kaelan frowned slightly at what she'd almost said. He was

sure it was her husband she was about to refer to, but he didn't really like the fact she felt she couldn't mention him.

'He almost sounds like he and I would have gotten along fine.' He kept his mouth shut because he didn't want her more upset than she already seemed about that particular subject.

Out of the corner of his eye he saw her slide down slightly in her seat and continued to stare out the windscreen. After a while she sat back up and pressed the lever that made the back of the seat go backwards. She then let herself fall asleep.

He let her sleep. She may look physically better than three months ago but she was still working out hard, so she was still exhausted. Sleep would be good for her right now.

Chapter 21

Kaelan knew he should have had his mind on the upcoming job, but he kept thinking about her. He wanted to see what she was capable of, if she could kill a person. However, he wanted to keep her safe and untainted by that particular lifestyle.

'It was something I had chosen many years ago, but I'm good at what I do. I just don't know if I want her to become what I am. Maybe her being able to accept me for what I am is enough. I just don't know.'

"Nhuh..." She jerked awake, looking around but not really seeing anything.

"You alright?" He asked, frowning with concern.

She didn't answer. Her heart was pounding and she tried to focus on where she was. For some reason it was harder than it should have been.

"Sarah?!" He said sternly, trying to get her attention.

"Nightmare, Okay? A nightmare." She responded somewhat angrily in a shaky voice. She set the seat back upright as she looked out at the bland scenery while she worked at calming her breathing and heart rate down.

"About the job?" If it was he wouldn't let her do it.

"No." She said softly as she kept staring out at the passing landscape of greenish tinged yellow grasses and the occasional shrubs and trees with the Great Dividing Range getting nearer.

'I've only been asleep for about thirty to sixty minutes. It almost looks like we're heading to Toowoomba. I don't care where those guys are, I just want 'em dead.'

He didn't know if she saw something interesting out there or so she wouldn't have to look at him.

"You sure?" He had to be certain.

"Positive." She said still refusing to glance at him. While she stared out the window she thought about the horrid, yet weird, dream.

'For some weird reason Kaelan and I were back at the paintball range. Except it was night with a full moon and no one else but us were there. Nothing bad about that. It could have even been romantic except I had let him kill me with a real gun without putting up a fight of any kind. Just a nightmare, a hell of a nightmare.'

"Want to talk about it?" 'Must have been a hell of a nightmare then to affect her like this.'

"Please don't be offended but not really." She still wouldn't make eye contact with him.

'How can I tell him of such a dream? It's just a stupid dream, nothing more.'

He didn't press her. Nothing he could do to make her. They drove in silence for a while.

She was thankful he let the matter drop. Then, like flicking a switch, her thoughts changed subjects. She realised at that point that she had the best scenario for committing the perfect murder just by being with Kaelan. She thought he knew her reasons for being there and he seemed okay with it.

That led her to wonder if he willingly committed murder and hid it using his job as an excuse. She thought about how it made her feel about him and if it changed the way she thought about him. A few moments later she discovered she didn't have a problem with it at all, and that surprised her.

'Normal people don't do these sorts of things and normal people don't just accept them as being okay. Am I normal? I guess if he's getting rid of murderers instead of society supporting them in prison, then what does it matter how they're gotten rid of? Maybe that's an idealistic view of dealing with such things, but I'm not one for supporting criminals with my hard earned and paid taxes during their punishments.' She thought critically.

'Well! What does that really say about me? I really am a law-abiding person, but three friends have been murdered for no reason other than one of them being a vampire. Not only that, but I almost died – by what Kaelan had said months ago – so I'm not up to feeling charitable towards those two men right now.'

The brief glimpses he got of her face suggested something bothered her and that she was in deep thought about it. Whether it was the nightmare and/or something else, he couldn't tell. He watched her frown then her eyebrows rose slightly as if surprised about something then she reacted like she sighed. Since he was watching her, he knew she hadn't.

She was actually rather expressive in her silence and he didn't think she knew about it. After a while of just driving in silence he decided to give her the plan of attack.

"We will wait till dusk to take them out." Kaelan stated out of the blue.

"Okay."

"We'll park the Jeep a short distance from the property. You will make your way to the house and asked for their help. The Jeep won't start but you have plenty of fuel. I'll sneak around the back. You shoot the one who comes towards you and I'll take out the other. Intel says there's a woman as well. However, there's no other information about her except she isn't a vamp due to being seen outside during the day."

"Okay."

"No questions?" He raised his eyebrows at her. Her responses were accepting but quiet. To him she seemed subdued.

'If only I knew what was going on in her head, if she would just talk to me.'

"No. It seems fairly straight forward. After you've parked the Jeep a small way from the property, I'm to hobble up their driveway acting the damsel in distress which will lure at least one of them close to me. When he is, I shoot him. Then... What? I wait for you to meet up with me and, if necessary, shoot anyone else who comes towards me?"

"That's it." He responded. For someone who claimed she had never done that sort of thing before she certainly grasped the instructions quickly. She said she had never lied to him and yet he couldn't help wondering. He saw a service station with a cafeteria ahead so he turned into it.

"Hungry?"

"Yes I am." She said with a hint of surprise that she really was hungry considering the circumstances.

He smiled. "Since we've plenty of time we'll spend a bit of time here to relax."

"Do you really relax before a job?" She asked curiously, watching him as he parked the car.

"Depends on the job." He said as they reached the doors.

"And this one?" She questioned as they walked inside.

"Relaxed." and he sounded it. "You?"

"Nervous, but first time for anything makes me nervous." She said as she looked at her feet. She was embarrassed at revealing such a truth but she couldn't lie to him.

Once again he was surprised at how honest she'd been about it all so far. Most would have tried to portray false bravado, but not Sarah and he was pleased with her honesty.

Then they arrived at the counter so she looked at what was on offer. Turning away from the wall menu, she browsed over the cold drinks in the tall fridge off to one side. She chose a peach iced tea, walked back to Kaelan and ordered a chicken and bacon burger with cheese and lettuce but no sauce.

While not healthy, he allowed it since she had never complained about her diet while she had been in his house. Since Kaelan had the money, she left the drink with him and chose a table off by itself outside the cafeteria. She waited for him to arrive with their order.

"I'm surprised you chose a table out here." He commented as he set her drink and burger in front of her then sat down opposite her.

She just shrugged and couldn't stop the blush that crept over her face. Since he was looking at her at the time she knew he saw the blush.

"Sarah?" He asked and she knew he was asking 'why'.

"I thought you would appreciate this one more than any other table around here." She said meekly as her blushing grew hotter and, therefore, redder.

"I hadn't realised you had noticed." He was surprised. He hadn't thought he had been that obvious about his preferences.

"I'm not totally self-centred." She responded glumly. It saddened her that he could think so little of her.

"I never said you were. You are the least self-centred person I know." While she irked him at times he had never thought badly about her. Although, it was as if she was used to people thinking the worst about her.

"Thanks." She whispered. She then felt shame at herself for thinking so badly of him. They ate in silence for a while.

"What are you going to do when this is over?" Kaelan asked, looking at her intently.

"I'll go back to work and try to salvage what's left of my business and more than likely having to start all over again. You?" She asked daringly, but not expecting him to answer.

"I have a job up north after this one." He said.

"Oh, I see." Hoping she managed to sound neutral and not as saddened as she really was. The pair lapsed back into silence for many minutes.

'If I didn't know any better I'd say she sounds disappointed but I'm not sure.'

"Would you consider doing this particular line of work again?" He asked, surprising her, watching her intently.

She thought about it before answering.

"I don't know. I don't know if I'm cut out for this sort of work, will have to wait and see I guess. If I did, maybe only humans since I'm not exactly fast on my feet. I don't think I would stand a chance against therians and vamps." Sarah didn't look at him when she spoke.

"Fair comment." Was all he said. While being a fair assessment about herself, he thought it was an interesting answer. They lapsed back into silence.

They sat there, mostly in silence, until the bottom of the sun hit the top of the mountains. Then they left.

Chapter 22

They drove in silence and arrived outside the property a few minutes later. Kaelan did the stop-start thing as they slowly drove past. It gave the impression of car trouble while the pair looked at the property. A short distance past it, Kaelan stopped the Jeep, grabbed the bag from the back, opened it and handed her the P232.

Sarah automatically checked it by ejecting the magazine, looked at how much ammunition was in it then pushed the mag back in until it clicked. When she realised he was watching her, she blushed as she glanced at him.

"Don't be embarrassed. I'm pleased." He said with approval in his voice and expression.

She gave a slight smile and nodded.

Then he handed her an inner pants holster. Over the past few weeks he'd shown her how to apply it. It clipped onto the inside of her pants on the left side and she reached for the gun through the side pocket of the pants. The inner seam had been opened up to allow access.

Kaelan had her practicing to draw the gun out through the pocket with the track pants he had her wearing at the time. Like her track pants, he had her dress pants modified slightly so the inner pants holster could sit a little lower than normal for the pocket draw. The loose fit of her pants hid the holster perfectly.

With stealth in every move, Kaelan placed his bag on the road then got out; keeping low till he could crouch down. An amazing thing to watch in someone so tall. Yet he managed it quite well. Then he got her to get out on the driver's side and stand there so he could see how the outfit looked with the gun and holster in place.

Apparently her pants didn't sit quite right as he adjusted them slightly. Sarah tried to ignore the rising activity of her hormones at his touch then concentrated on withdrawing the gun and putting it back a few times until he was satisfied.

"Good." He said, looking up at her. "Let me get into the grass before you start up their driveway. Pop the bonnet if you have to."

Then he was gone.

Thankfully, the grass around the property was long enough he could crawl in amongst it without being seen. There was a slight breeze so his movements could be attributed to the breeze. Just as he entered the grass, he heard her pop the bonnet. He continued on his way so he could be in position before she could be half way up the driveway.

She did as he suggested and popped the bonnet and pretended to look at various parts of the engine, moving around. Then she looked back towards the house, closed the bonnet, took the keys out of the ignition, locked the car and then put them in her left pocket as previously arranged by Kaelan. She noticed her hands were shaking as she pocketed the keys. She was so nervous.

'Thank goodness for the walk to try to calm myself.'

Pushing the bag in front of him, he belly crawled as fast as he could towards the house. Then he skirted around the perimeter until he found what he was looking for. One guy was near the front. Kaelan decided to leave that one for Sarah. He found the other man at the back of the house. The van he saw that gut-wrenching day was there as well; not far from the lounging man. There was no obvious sign of the woman. From where he was Kaelan could see the beginnings of the driveway and could see Sarah hobbling slowly towards the house.

She then made her way back to the entrance to the property. She paused as she looked at the driveway in dismay.

'Freaking gravel.'

She hated walking on gravel ever since her ankles became damaged. She sighed and started walking. She spent more time watching where her feet were going, while trying to keep her balance on the moving stones, than looking ahead of her. In its own way, it helped her to calm down some. However, once she noticed a figure a short way in front of her she stopped looking down and hoped for the best in not losing her balance.

Quietly opening the bag, he withdrew a Remington Long Range Tactical Rifle, the 700 XCR; one of his favourites. He set himself up, settling the rifle against his shoulder and watched his target while waiting for Sarah's shots. He had decided not to teach her anything else other than to use the pistol and to draw from her pants pocket. By teaching only that it should become an unconscious action, something she could do blindfolded if need be.

His target was rather helpful as he sat in one spot just soaking up the last of the sun's rays. Kaelan alternated between watching him through the scope and scouring the surrounding area. It wouldn't do well for the teacher to be killed by not paying full attention to everything else around him.

"Hi." She called when she could actually discern some feature of him as she got a little closer. There was a flash of memory to suggest she vaguely recognise him but she couldn't make out details in the memory flash and therefore couldn't be sure.

He was taller than her and extremely fit, even if he was scruffy looking. One of the first things she noted was that his style seemed more American than Australian. She found it hard to explain, it wasn't just any one thing. He had straight brown hair as long as hers and tied back. He wasn't handsome, attractive or cute but there was something about him that did please the eye. With his lips – thinner than hers and a little less defined – set in a slight sneer, his medium blue eyes looked at her from the feet up and she decided right then that she didn't like him.

"My Jeep won't start and I know nothing about it to get it going and was wondering if I could use your phone or something?" She said as she hobbled a little closer, pausing every now and then. Basically playing up the ankle situation.

"You check the fuel?" He asked with a hint of condescension with his sneer as he stared at her up and down again. This time her skin crawled and it took a lot of effort to not shudder and keep her smile in place.

"Oh yeah. It's about the only thing I know for sure. Plenty of fuel. I have my keys here if you want to have a look." Sarah paused again and patted her left pocket, jingling the keys. She was still a few metres away from him.

She stood there, leaning heavily on the walking stick and made a show of flexing each ankle. He took two more steps towards her and that put him just outside of his arm's length. She put her hand into her pocket, jingled the keys as if she was grabbing them, but quickly drew the Sig without it catching on anything instead. 'Thank goodness for training.'

Sarah had the gun out and pointed at his heart before he realised what was happening. She quickly pulled the trigger twice, like she had trained to do before it could fully register in his brain what she was doing.

The look of surprise on his face was almost comical. Then she heard a loud crack of a shot going off.

While looking around, he heard two gun shots. She'd killed him.

The one sunning himself jumped up then dropped like a rock when Kaelan's shot hit him. Kaelan stood up, put the rifle back in the bag, withdrew his pistol and strode towards him while keeping an eye out for the woman who was supposed to be with them. Reaching the rogue, Kaelan put another bullet in the man's head just to be sure.

Sarah didn't feel anything. She didn't even cry. She just looked down at him and thought, 'For you guys... Brandi, Abel and Danny.' Then she heard a second, slightly different sounding, shot. Kaelan had killed the other.

She started to turn away when she heard a scream and saw a

figure rushing towards her from the house out of the corner of her eye.

A woman was suddenly leaping in the air at her. Impossibly high for a human. Then she saw the claws coming out of the woman's hands.

'Shee-oot! A fudging therian!' Her brain didn't allow her time to panic.

Sarah quickly raised her gun and fired four or five times at the therian, hitting her, but the woman didn't stop. One clawed hand swept down from Sarah's left shoulder to just above her belly button, to miss it then start again just below it and continuing down across her right thigh. She started screaming.

Never had she felt pain like that before. It was worse than being shot as far as she was concerned. The therian's other clawed hand grabbed at Sarah's right shoulder and dug in from behind. Somewhere during the woman's attack, she lost her gun. She was now on her back with the therian on her chest, still screaming in agony.

Then he heard a scream which started out human but didn't finish as human, then five more shots and another, definitely human, scream of immense pain. He thought his heart had stopped and would never breathe again. Then he bolted to the front of the house.

He rounded the corner and saw Sarah on the ground with a therian on top of her. With the scene before him, he knew there was two possible outcomes and decided to spare her as he would any of his men.

Watching them as he ran, he couldn't see the cream and blue

of her outfit, there was way too much blood. He had to stop to get a clear shot of the therian.

'Damn it! They're just too close, I might hit her.'

When he paused and exchanged the pistol for the rifle again, he decided to take the shot anyway. It was only one shot and it hit the therian in the shoulder, just missing Sarah in the process. The shot knocked the therian back a fraction but it was enough to halt the attack temporarily and allow him to get closer to finish the job.

Pausing long enough to swap the rifle for the shotgun, he ran until he was almost in touching distance and fired point blank into the therian's head and then another and another. There was nothing left of its head by the time he was finished. He followed it by blasting a hole where its heart was.

He hadn't thought to pack ammunition for killing a therian. He reserved the right to berate himself later. Now, he dealt only with the situation before him.

Dimly, she thought she heard running feet, then she heard a gunshot, then another and more until the creature was no longer on top of her. She stared up at the darkening sky when Kaelan slid into view. She blinked at him.

'She's still alive, thank goodness!'

"Sarah?" He called gently at first.

"Hi." She said softly as she watched him frown. She tried to lift her hand to him, but she couldn't really feel either of them.

Kaelan saw her hand twitch, so he gently lifted hers to his face. "Can you move?" He asked but thought he already knew the answer.

She thought she saw concern in his eyes and didn't know if she answered him or not.

"No pain" She whispered to him. She looked at him and gently smiled, but couldn't really see him any more as a different kind of darkness fell.

That wasn't good and he watched as her eyes started going glassy and she sighed as her eyes closed.

"SARAH!" He screamed at her then held her tightly against him with no response from her at all. Dimly, he felt relief that she had died and that he wouldn't have to kill her.

She heard her name faintly and everything floated away as the darkness swallowed her.

Chapter 23

After a few moments, it finally registered she still had a pulse. Kaelan double checked.

'Yes! She's still alive.' However, there was too much damage to try bandaging up. With the immensity of his relief, he forgot his self-promise and rushed to get her to the hospital.

Placing the gun bag on the other side of her, he lifted her in his arms, grabbing the bag as he stood. He ran to the Jeep, dropped the bag to the ground before carefully placing Sarah beside it so he could open the car. He gently slid her into her seat, strapping her in then chucked the gun bag into the back and got into the driver's seat.

He had to admit he was reckless when he took off. Once the car was turned around, he floored it, spinning the tires and fishtailing down the road, and sped to Ipswich hospital. It was the closest and, thankfully, it had the best therian attack trauma centre in the south east Queensland. He even ran red lights if it looked like he wouldn't endanger anyone else.

Storming into the E.R. with her in his arms, he was suddenly surrounded by medical personnel.

"What happened?!" A member of one medical team demanded as they took her away from him.

"Therian attack." He informed as they took Sarah away.

"Are you hurt?" A male from the second team asked him.

"Will she be okay?" Kaelan continued to stare in the direction she was taken.

"Sir, are you injured?" A female doctor asked as she attempted to check him over.

"She's lost a lot of blood, will she survive?" He brushed her off, not even glancing at her. He couldn't take his eyes from Sarah.

They kept asking him questions and trying to check him over, but Kaelan was only interested in what was happening to Sarah. He was becoming pissed off that they weren't answering his questions. While the medical team were becoming frustrated with him for the same reason. Then the police arrived, threatening to arrest him after they spoke with the lady doctor he had brushed off.

"The blood's not mine, it's hers." He sigh, showing his licences.

"Be that as it may Mister Ridgeleigh, let the nice doctor check you over anyway."

Grudgingly, Kaelan conceded and ended up spending the next three or so hours being checked over by the doctors and questioned by the police, giving them his statement. Citing the job number, he informed them of running red lights to get her to the hospital in time.

After taking his vehicle registration number they said they would check the system and deal with any tickets he may have incurred since it was an emergency while on the job.

Almost four and a half hours after he had arrived and having changed his clothes, they finally let him see her after they wheeled her out of recovery. He was exhausted, from the adrenalin rush and from what they told him of her condition.

"No doubt?" He asked quietly.

"None what-so-ever. Despite the surgery taking just over four hours, we're talking worst case scenario here. I'm sorry." The doctor stated. Kaelan wouldn't say gently. The doctor's bedside manner was practically non-existent, but then there was no easy way to say it. However, the news was devastating.

'I don't know how I'm going to do it but I have to be the one to tell her. It was my fault after all. If only I hadn't let my selfish desires get the better of me. If only.'

"Then I'll tell her." He sat in the chair beside her bed, closed his eyes and waited. The doctor left.

Despite his concern for her and his weariness, Kaelan opened his eyes and phoned in a clean-up crew to the property, letting them know of the shotgun and the P232 which had been left behind. Later, he would call to Toby asking him to bring some clothing for her to wear. It meant he had to tell Toby where they were, but that would be all Kaelan would tell him. In the mean time, he went back to waiting for her to regain consciousness.

Sarah opened her eyes.

Looking ahead of her she worked out that she was in a hospital. 'They just have that unified sterile look about them no matter which one it is.' She turned her head to the right and saw Kaelan slumped in a chair.

"Kaelan?" She croaked then coughed. His eyes snapped open when she spoke his name.

At the sound of her voice, he was instantly alert. Taking her hand, he stood beside her after she winced when she tried to move it.

"How long have I been here?"

"Nineteen and a half hours." His voice was neutral because he didn't know how to break the news to her.

However, he guessed he didn't have to tell her. He watched her take stock of how she felt and watched the realisation widen her eyes. He tightened his grip on her hand in comfort.

That in itself told her something was wrong. She started to move, expecting mega amounts of pain. Instead, she was stiff, sore and felt like the injuries were weeks old rather than hours old. She didn't know what she looked like but Kaelan's grip suddenly tightened slightly.

"No, nonononono…" She whispered, sounding devastated as tears welled. She looked up at Kaelan.

"Don't let them lock me away. Please!" She whispered pleadingly as the tears started falling.

"I won't. I promise." His voice sounded strained but that was the only hint that anything bothered him. 'No, I won't let them lock her away. Regardless of how I feel about the situation, she will still have her freedom.'

She just nodded and rolled towards him as she cried. She didn't reclaim her hand from him as she needed his touch right then. When she managed to calm down, she realised that Kaelan had sat back down so he was now closer to her level.

"How much longer before I can be discharged?"

"Twenty-four hours at the least, they told me."

"Then there is no doubt?"

"None." Kaelan looked and sounded devastated.

"I'm sorry Sarah I…"

'It's my fault. I should never have taken her with me. I shouldn't have given in to my curiosity about her abilities.' His thoughts were going around in circles as guilt wracked him.

She yanked his hand pulling him slightly closer. "It's not your fault. I'm the one who wanted to go with you…"

"I could have said no…" He interrupted.

"Wouldn't have stopped me." She interrupted back. "It's not your fault the intel wasn't complete. Blame them."

"I do!" and his voice was savage in its contained rage. 'And I do! Hell, do I ever! There will be more than just words exchanged about it that's for sure.'

She sat up, adjusting the bed into a sit-up position. She was about to throw off the covers when she realised she only had a hospital gown on. "I need clothes."

"I'd text Toby just before you woke up so he's on his way with some. He'll be here in another hour."

"Good! I'm walking out of here once I'm dressed." She sounded so determined regardless of the consequences.

"Sarah…" He sounded like he was about to go mad at her. 'Damn it! Still so blasted stubborn.' They were still holding hands when she gave his a gentle squeeze. 'The situation could be so damned intimate if it wasn't for the shitty reason we're here.'

"It's okay. I just want to go home." She stated softly.

Just then, the doctor walked in.

"Ah, you're awake… And I see you have been told the news."

"It wasn't hard to figure out once the time passed and pain levels were put together."

"Yes, well... quite right." He mumbled, looking uncomfortable.

"What species?"

"Surprisingly, Jaguar. We didn't know there were any in Australia."

Sarah just nodded. "When can I go?"

She took the information in stride like when she had been shot and once again she had impressed Kaelan.

"Now, don't be hasty here young lady. You have a responsibility to the safety of the general public. I..."

Kaelan was about to severely correct the doctor when she beat him to it.

"Stop! Don't you dare say it. That is just so wrong. A support system is needed, not locking away. If you must know, I volunteer at the Therian League and have friends there so I will have all the help I need to see me through this." It was Kaelan's turn to squeeze her hand. She'd started shaking when she spoke out against the doctor. She didn't do so well when in a confrontation. Even if she started it.

Despite the majority of therians not attacking humans since they had revealed themselves to the world over a decade ago, humans still lock the newly created away never to be seen again. She so didn't want that to happen to her. That's why the doctor's words upset her so much.

Kaelan gently squeezed her hand in comfort once she had started shaking as she told off the doctor. However, it was a surprise for Kaelan to hear she was a volunteer at the therian league. He never knew.

'I think it's time to start researching more about her. Keep an eye on her through my network of informants.'

"Well! In that case, you can go home when your friend arrives with your clothing." The doctor said huffily and started to leave without checking her injuries.

Right then, Kaelan really wanted to hit him for his attitude.

"Thank you Doctor. Is there anything else that has to be done before I leave?" She asked ever so politely.

Kaelan knew he wouldn't have.

The Doctor paused and looked at her. "No." Then he left.

Sarah leant against Kaelan and he sat on the bed beside her and wrapped his arms around her. She just clung to him while she waited for the fine trembling to stop.

'Why couldn't this closeness happened weeks ago? Now, it's a case I have to think very carefully about what's going to happen next.' He thought in frustration.

Thirty minutes later Toby arrived. Kaelan took her clothing from him and told Toby to head back home, that he, Kaelan, would take her home as they still had a while before the two of them could head home themselves. Toby didn't look happy but did as he was told. Kaelan handed Sarah her clothing and stayed where he was.

"Go outside please." She said softly.

"No. I'm keeping you in sight till we get home just so I know you won't get in to any more trouble." And he crossed his arms over his chest and didn't move.

She sighed. While she wanted to argue she knew it would be pointless to do so. "Then please turn around?"

He shook his head at her silliness then faced the other way for her. As she got dressed, she noticed that the piercings were gone. 'Becoming a therian I should have realised I would lose them.'

She sighed and Kaelan started to turn around, wondering what was wrong now.

"Argh… No you don't. I'm not done yet."

"I've seen it all before, Sarah." His voice sounded like it was both amused and annoyed at the same time.

"I don't care. I wasn't conscious then." She said as she put her top on.

"And less hassle then." Amusement seemed to have won out.

She flicked him with the gown.

"Toad." She said with amusement lightly tainting her voice.

He turned at her sudden intake of breath. 'Was she hurt?'

"What's wrong Sarah?" His voice thick with concern and he was instantly beside her.

"I'm sorry." She whispered, not looking at him. Calling him 'toad' had been automatic. It was something she'd called her husband whenever he'd teased her.

"For calling me a toad? Nothing to be upset over. Get dressed and let's get out of here." He said gently.

Sarah just nodded and finished pulling up the track pants. She slipped on a pair of shoes and they left, but he had the feeling he had missed something.

The Jeep smelled of blood; her blood and it was déjà vu but worse. After Kaelan went back inside he came out a few minutes later with a bucket and a few cleaning cloths. The two of them cleaned her seat and the steering wheel the best they could.

At least the interior was no longer covered in blood. He would have to get it professionally cleaned tomorrow. The silence was thick between them. Neither of them spoke as they cleaned.

The drive home was two hours long and happened in silence. She guessed they both were lost in their own thoughts as she stared out the window at the passing dark scenery.

'So, I'm now a were-jaguar. I'm one of the monsters that he hunts. If there had ever been a chance for us at all, it's now gone.'

With that realisation the tears welled up then trickled down her cheeks. She didn't cry long, but she was sure it wouldn't be long before the tears wouldn't stop.

Kaelan didn't know what to do. She had now become something he hunted for a living.

'Sure, I do the lawful hits, but there were a lot of unlawful hits available as well. I enjoy those just as much, if not more so. Can I love her now she has changed? Now she isn't human anymore? I need more than the drive home to seriously think about it.'

Kaelan shoved the thoughts aside to concentrate on driving. Or at least he tried to.

When they finally got home, Toby and Mick were waiting and fussed over her. She hugged them both then excused herself and shut herself away in her room. Neither Sarah nor Kaelan explained as to what had happened and why she was in hospital.

She left the light off and flopped down on the bed, but didn't sleep. Her mind wouldn't get off the round-about of how things would never be between Kaelan and her.

Within a couple of hours he too went to bed. However, he didn't sleep either. He laid there staring up at the ceiling even though he couldn't see it.

While he wanted to think seriously about their current situation, his mind avoided the subject. Instead he thought about his next job, having to leave and going to the BHA in the morning to confront the director.

'Depending on his attitude will depend on whether he'll still be alive when I've finished with him.' He thought angrily.

Many hours later, all lights were off and the three men were in bed, Sarah decided to grab something to eat. She didn't bother with any lights as she made herself a cup of tea and grabbed some plain wafer crackers to nibble on. She sat out on the verandah and watched bats and clouds flit through the night sky.

Almost 0300 hours, it was dark in the house and everyone else was in bed. With his shoes in one hand, Kaelan gathered his gear and headed to the front door. Not knowing when he would return he turned around to look back through the house, when he noticed the back door was open. He went to close it but saw her sitting on the steps, with a cup beside her, looking up at the sky. He quietly walked towards her.

She heard the soft sounds of bare feet padding towards her.

"You're going to leave aren't you?" She asked without turning around.

The bare feet paused then continued towards her. She felt the air currents move as he stood beside her then crouch down.

'She had heard me?'

"Yes." Kaelan simply said. 'How had she guessed my intentions?'

"When?" She whispered she couldn't look at him. She wanted to but he was leaving and she couldn't force herself to.

'If only she would look at me. I want to see what she's feeling. I need to see what she's feeling.'

"Now."

"I want you to promise me something." She said softly, still not looking at him.

"Ask."

'Yesterday I would have promised her the moon. Somehow, under the circumstances, I don't think she would want it anymore.'

"If a hit is ordered against me, I want you to be the one to take the job. You will kill me outright. Others would be tempted to prolong it, make it a torture. I don't want that. Promise me." Her voice stayed a whisper.

Of anything she could have asked him he wasn't expecting that, but he couldn't refuse her. He blamed himself after all. He wouldn't want anyone else attempting to kill her anyway.

"I promise." His chest tightened as he spoke those two words.

Despite the quietness of his words, his voice was neutral and revealed no hint of what he was feeling at a time she needed to know the most.

She just nodded. She couldn't speak. And still refused to look at him. She felt his hand move towards her, but stopped himself. The tears started flowing again. The dam was breaking and she couldn't stop it. Instead, she concentrated on steady breathing in the effort of delaying the inevitable.

He was torn in two and didn't know how to reconcile the two halves. He stood up. With a final glance down at her, Kaelan turned on his heels and left. There was nothing else for him to say. The promise was the best he could do right then. Something inside him broke and hurt immensely as he got in the Jeep and drove away refusing to look back. Never to look back.

A few minutes later, she heard the Jeep leave and the dam burst.

Just as the dawn started lightening the sky, Mick and Toby found Sarah prone on the verandah crying. Mick picked her up, carried her to her room and tucked her into bed. She rolled away from him and just cried.

She cried for her lost humanity. She cried hating the self-pity she was drowning herself in. She cried for a love she thought she would never experience. She cried because she would never see him again. She fell asleep crying.

The End

of part 1

Extras

Bio

Back in 1967 KC was born on the morning of a black Monday on the Sunshine Coast north of Brisbane, Queensland, Australia. KC is the first to admit that her life was nothing special. She has worked as mechanic, in a book shop and in an IT company. Her interest in computers led her to do volunteer teaching online within the graphics community. Her internet time also sparked her interest in puzzle based games, graphics and internet communities based around her pastimes. Eventually, her pastimes led to the first in her Unnaturals of Brisbane series. She is an avid reader and a cat lover.

Below are ways to follow KC. While she's slack with posting, she uses her facebook author page as her blog.

http://www.kcrileygyer.com/

https://www.facebook.com/KCRileyGyerAuthorPage

https://www.facebook.com/KCRileyGyer

https://www.amazon.com/author/kcrileygyer

https://www.goodreads.com/KCRileyGyer

Meeting the Characters

Oh my goodness. I can't believe it's the night of Meeting the Characters again. Hard to believe that this is the second one. Where did the time go? It only seems like yesterday that the first one was held.

That first event had gone so well that I had received emails asking when the next one was and if they could sign up to be part of the audience. That made me so happy that I had started contacting the next round of possible guests. The replies I'd received were all in the affirmatives.

However, I am no less nervous this time as I was last time. Thankfully, Skipper has helped me through this one as well. Setting my crutches aside, I set about organising the room for the event and setting up the refreshments. It was almost time for everyone to arrive.

Stopping in the middle of the room, I looked around. Info sheets for playing the part of the host? Check with no small thanks to my behind-the-scenes friend. Chair for host? Check. Seating for guests? Check. Chairs for audience? Check. Refreshments for everyone? Check. Small tables for host and guests to set their refreshments onto during the Q&A session? Check. Lighting?

I hobbled over to the light switches and played with the dimmers to set each control to the right brightness. Then I chuckled as I realised that everything I had just done was the same as last time. Right then, I decided it would become my routine if the event should be held again and again. A routine will reduce my nervousness somewhat. Hopefully.

Closing my eyes, I stood there and took a slow deep breath in, held it for a bit then slowly let it out. I also decided this part would be regular as well. Anything to help keep the nervousness at bay for a little bit longer.

Opening my eyes, I gazed around the room. What pleases me the most is not only the return of the guests from the first event, but also new guests arriving. I'm hoping tonight's event will be just as successful.

Being back in the same room as last time meant I didn't have to learn a new layout nor try to arrange the furniture to suit both the room and the purpose. However, I did have to add more seating since the two sofas couldn't seat all the guests. Breaking out of my internal musings, my time was up.

A knock on the door the audience would enter, sounded. Grabbing my crutches and the audience list, I opened the door. I was greeted with a smile from Jayne. I remembered her from the first event.

"Hello Jayne, welcome back." I smiled back as I ushered her in. As I did so, I noted more guests coming down the corridor.

"Hi KC, how are you this evening?" She greeted with a grin.

"I'm good, thank you, and you?"

"Thrilled to be here again, thank you for the chance to learn more." Jayne responded happily.

"Well, since it's your second time, you know the routine. In you go." I grinned.

One by one, I greeted them, placed a tick beside their name and pointed them towards the refreshments and their seats. Once all had arrived, had a beverage in hand and were sitting in their seats, I made my way up to the stage and stood by my chair.

"Welcome to an evening of Meeting the Characters. Tonight, we have an eclectic collection of guests, from unaltereds to therians, to military, to bounty hunters. All of them have crossed paths with one particular person. They have played games together, socialised together and been there for each other as situations arose. Please welcome, from Changes in Degrees... Sarah, Kaelan, Scott, Zac, Ed, Antonio, his wife Maria, Mick and Toby."

While the audience and I applauded, as I turned towards the curtain on my left, in walked our guests. They smiled and waved to the audience then gave me a hug before sitting down. With Antonio, Maria, Sarah, Kaelan and Ed on my right, Mick, Toby, Scott and Zac sat on my left. A moment later, with grins and thank yous' from our guests, the audience quietened down. Then I continued.

"For those of you who are unsure of what follows, you the readers have this opportunity to delve deeper into the lives and minds of the characters in the 'Unnaturals of Brisbane' series. Our guests have generously given up some of their time to be here tonight, so let's make it worth their while!

"Changes in Degrees is about Sarah and the path her life leads her. It's about the people she encounters along the way and the impact they have on her and her on them. Without further ado, it's question time from the audience." I stated and hands rose into the air.

A young woman I had never seen before had her hand up so I selected her.

"Hello all, I'm Mandy."

"Hi Mandy." Everyone greeted in unison as if rehearsed.

"To Sarah, do you enjoy being a nail technician? If so, what do you like about it, do you find it easy to talk to clients and do you have therian customers?" Mandy asked.

"I love doing people's nails. I love making them look beautiful. Every woman should have beautiful nails. As for talking to clients, sometimes it is easier to talk to them but I'm usually concentrating on what I'm doing that I'm listening to them more than anything else. Well, apart from not having been able to work for the last three and a half months, no I don't have any altereds as clients at all." Sarah answered with a shy smile.

Jayne was next so I pointed to her and she stood up.

"Hi, I'm Jayne."

"Hi Jayne." We chorused.

"My question is for Kaelan. Why do you dislike all therians, vampires etc. so much?" Jayne asked.

Kaelan looked at me and I smiled sweetly at him.

"Sorry Jayne, I've been instructed not to reveal anything that comes up in the next two stories. All of you are just going to have to wait a little longer for that one. I may be one of the best in my field, but KC can kill me faster than even I can react." He responded with a deep throaty laugh.

Some low chuckles sounded around the room as Jayne sat down. As hands rose in the air, I chose another.

"Hi all, I'm Ann."

"Hi Ann." Everyone greeted.

"I have a question for Sarah. Have you had any experience with guns before you met Kaelan?" Ann queried.

"Yes I had. My husband had been into guns and he signed me up to a gun club when I expressed an interest so, that's when I had first started learning. Kaelan just continued that training after I had been shot. The combination of my targeting and speed wasn't that great before then." Sarah answered. She kept her eyes on Ann the whole time, while Kaelan watched her and listened as if he never knew that about her.

I selected the next person.

"Hello, I'm Robert."

"Hi Robert."

"Question to Sarah. What is your favourite meal, you appear to me as a vegan?" Robert asked.

Sarah stared at him in disbelief and Kaelan burst out laughing and spoke first.

"You obviously don't remember the scene of her eating my chicken cabonara with fettuccini."

With a grin, Sarah slapped him on the arm.

"I am by no means a vegan of any kind. I love meat, dairy, eggs, etc. My favourite food is most meals with chicken in them. But, really, I love anything that tastes good."

After Robert sat down, I randomly chose another person.

"Hey Everyone, I'm Emma."

"Hi Emma."

"This Question is for everyone. Do you have any special

hobbies or interests?" Emma asked as she made eye contact with each of them.

Kaelan nudges Sarah. She glares at him.

"Why me first?"

Chuckles erupted around the room and she blushed.

"I enjoy reading...," Sarah started.

"And singing." Mick piped up. She poked her tongue out at him. Laughter sounded throughout the room.

"...and sewing...," She continued.

"And singing." Antonio stated.

Sarah's shoulders sagged in exasperation as she appeared to be trying not to smile but failing. At the same time, Maria slapped her husband on the arm while everyone else laughed again.

"Next." Sarah stated as she indicated to the others, obviously giving up on the question.

Again, we laughed.

"When I have down time I enjoy photography, working with wood and making stained glass items if I have the time." Kaelan stated.

"Tonio and I love cooking together. At night we love reading and movies." Maria supplied in her usual bubbly tone. Antonio laced his fingers with hers and smiled happily.

"Action movies are my thing in my down time." Ed stated. "Especially at the cinema."

"Surfin' and movies with my mates." Mick piped up.

"Working out at the gym, reading and crossword puzzles for me." Toby informed us.

"I love working on cars from the sixties and seventies, as in restoring them and beers with my mates." Zac responded.

All eyes turned to Scott, the last in the group.

"I do whatever I'm in the mood for at the time. Could be any of the above, except for surfing, singing and sewing. As for my cooking, it's basic at best." He grins mischievously.

His comment elicits a few laughs and I point to the next person.

"Sarah, since the accident, what do you miss doing most that you can no longer do?" Mandy asked.

It was almost comical to see the relief on Sarah's face.

"Oh that's easy. The ability to step on tip toes. I'm lost without it because I'm too damned short to reach up to things."

The room erupted into laughter and I chose the next person.

"Toby and Mick, how did the pair of you meet Danny?" Questioned Ann.

"You first, Toby." Mick said with a somewhat sad smile.

"Well, I was 18, clubbing and got mugged when Danny came to my rescue. I had been beaten pretty badly and he healed me with some of his blood. I was curious about him and that led to us chatting. I was also having a difficult time in getting a job so, after a while, he ended up offering me one. By that stage, we were becoming good friends." Toby then nodded to Mick.

"While for me, it was the other way round. I was hanging late at the beach one night when Danny was being attacked by someone. Not knowing what either of them were, I jumped in to save him. He was small compared to the other guy. Like Toby, Danny and I chatted, got to know each other and he offered me the same job. But man, I'm still annoyed over bustin' my favourite board over that other guy." Mick pouted.

We laugh and Toby punches him in the arm.

"Suck it up Dude. It was ages ago."

Still laughing, I indicated to Jayne.

"Antonio and Maria, how do you manage to fund the centre and how hard it is to get volunteers?" Jayne asked the two were-leopards.

Maria looked at her husband. He grinned at her.

"Well at this point in time, funding for the centre comes from the leader of the were-leopards, Jonathon Sutterton. He's also the chairperson of the Queensland Therian League." Antonio informed.

"As for volunteers, I guess we're no different from any other volunteer organisation. Sometimes we have more than we can utilise and at other times we're struggling to get enough volunteers. Take Sarah for example. She helped a fellow therian and that action introduced her into our circle of things then ended volunteering herself to help out." Maria answered.

I chose Ann next.

"My question is to Ed. Why do you think Kaelan is able to discuss his feelings with you when he obviously finds it difficult to express his emotions?" Ann asked.

"Well, there are some things I can't reveal yet. As Kael said, KC can kill us off faster than we can blink if we do." Ed laughed as he winked at me.

I couldn't help smiling at him. He has such a contagious smile.

"What I can say is, some of that is based around us being such long term friends. Sorry I can't go further into it. Soon though."

He finished with another laugh.

I nodded at Jayne

"My next question is for Scott and Zac. How long have the two of you known, worked, with Kaelan?" Jayne asked the pair.

With just a slight incline of his head, Zac indicated for Scott to speak for the pair of them.

"Zac and I met in the army when we joined at the same time up in Townsville in 2005. That put us in the same group. About a year or so later, we were transferred to Brisbane and ended up with Kaelan as second in command. The three of us worked well together that the pair of us naturally went with him when he left the army and joined the Bounty Hunter's Association. So, roughly twelve years by this point."

Both men aimed almost half smiles at Kaelan. He nodded at them in acknowledgement.

"Alrighty, just before we have one more question, I have something. Earlier in the week, I had received a question but they didn't leave their name, so here it is. For Kaelan, who would you say is the inspiration behind your character?" I read from a sheet of paper.

"No idea on that one. Maybe KC can answer that one better than me." Kaelan states with a laugh.

All eyes turned to me and my nervousness jumped up a few notches. By the few chuckles and Ed patting my hand, I guessed it was obvious.

"Well, Kaelan is based on two people. One is my longest time best friend, and no I'm not going to name names. And, the other is a fictional character I really enjoy. I combined the two and that was how Kaelan came about."

Looking at the audience, I selected Mandy once more.

"Sarah, do you feel stronger and ready to face the first change or are you scared of it, and have you been researching what to expect?" Mandy inquired.

"Well, it's only been a little over a day since the attack so I don't know if I feel stronger. I know I haven't had the chance to start researching yet but I will soon. As for being scared, yeah I am and it's only going to become more intense as the week passes." Sarah responded softly.

Then our time ran out.

"Sad to say, but we have to call an end to this enjoyable evening. You have been a wonderful audience. Please give a round of applause to Sonja, Kaelan, Scott, Zac, Maria, Antonio, Mick, Toby and Ed for sharing themselves with us."

As we applauded, we all stood. Our guests smiled and waved then each hugged me and left. One by one, the audience grabbed their belongings and said farewell to me then went home. They chatted merrily as they exited the room.

It was over. I was grateful that the second round of this event went as well as the first. If this keeps up then it will definitely be a regular thing. Glancing around, I noted there was no rubbish lying around. That pleased me since I was too exhausted to clean up.

"Come on KC, let's get you home. Another good event."

I smiled, happy but tired as I grabbed Skipper's hands. He flicked the lights off and closed the door as we left.

Excerpts

Turn the page for a sneak peak at
the next book by KC Riley-Gyer...

Objective: Crimson Empire
Now available

Chapter 1

Well, I'd set myself up for it yet again and shook my head at my own stupidity as I wondered when would I learn. What was that saying about me? 'Fool me once shame on you, fool me twice shame on me', and this *was* the second time.

This time round I'd been left standing on the crowded dance floor of the night club all alone. It wasn't the first time my co-workers – they're called co-workers because work mates don't treat their friends like that – had done such a thing to me. However, it was certainly going to be the last as far as I was concerned.

What a waste of a Friday night, and it was my own fault.

The first time was over a year ago when the nine of them had invited me out to dinner, to even out the numbers they'd said. I'd accepted in the effort of not being so shy and make friends. Back then, before that first outing, they hadn't been so nasty. Between them and I, it had been typical office staff interactions.

We sat in a pleasant café with restaurant-styled service, ate dinner, made useless small talk as they'd never asked any true questions. Whenever I did, they gave nonsense responses back. Once the food had been eaten they then started disappearing in twos and threes only to have left me with an expense of two hundred dollar plus, instead of fifteen to twenty, which would have been my share.

What they'd done to me kept them amused for the following

week or more. The second time, and definitely the last, they invited me out to the night club to go dancing with them. At lunch time, they cornered me in the staff room…

"We're all going to the new dance club on Newmarket Road tonight. We've been there before and it has great atmosphere, reasonable drinks, some food and music. Why don't you join us? We'll arrive at ten, dance for a few hours, and have a drink or two. It'll be fun." One co-worker said.

"Yeah, come on. The only expense is the entry fee and one round of drinks each if you have something to eat before coming out and then dancing the night away." Encouraged two others.

"Oh yeah, and don't forget the all the cuties looking for a good time." Piped up a fourth.

"Oh definitely can't forget those. Come on, say yes, you'll enjoy yourself." The rest urged.

Suffice to say I said sure. They had sounded genuine and sincere, that maybe they were truly interested in being friends. Stupid me!

The arrangement was that we would meet at the club. So, I went home and spent the early part of the evening having dinner then finding light-weight filmy clothing where the layers would look good. I didn't have anything in the way of clubbing clothes but I did have some wonderful velvet, gauzy and silky fabrics which were stylish and of colours that went well together.

In the end, I'd decided to go with black velvet tights and a blue with a black floral design long sleeved asymmetrical hem lined shimmery satin top. It was the best I could do, with a couple of other layers underneath on the top half of me. Being winter, I didn't want the top half of me getting too cold to and from the club.

The finishing touches were a vibrant red sheer scarf around my waist, black velvet ten centimetre heeled knee-high pirate boots and a touch of make-up. A quick glance in the mirror and I was done.

After catching a taxi, I arrived at the club at ten that night. Since I barely went anywhere, I had the money to splurge on a taxi to and from the night club. However, it was a good thing that I did because it was pouring rain when I walked out to the footpath. The street lights glittered off every wet surface possible and, while slow, the trip to the club was a light show in of itself.

In reality, I didn't mind the slow trip to the club. Staring out at the neon colours glittering off all the wet surfaces, I was nervous and apprehensive. Deep in my gut I had a feeling the night wouldn't end well. For the umpteenth time I mentally shook my head and willed myself to give them the benefit of doubt. It didn't ease the knot of tension in my stomach.

My co-workers were waiting for me just outside the front doors, like they'd said. Not long after that we'd paid our twenty dollar entry fee and were all dancing near the bar after I'd bought the first round of drinks. My first clue that I didn't pick up on.

Turn the page for a sneak peak at
the next book by KC Riley-Gyer...

Changes in Life

Sarah's story part 2

Now available

Chapter 1

It had been four hours since he had walked out of her life for the second time since she'd met him. Two days ago, when she woke up, she had thought the New Year was off to a good start. Today she didn't want to know about it. There were still almost eleven months left. She hoped it would improve as time went by, but doubted it would. Not now.

Having had next to no sleep during the past two days, since he had told her the hit was a go, she sat at his kitchen table, in his house and she was stuck there. He had all her stuff packed and moved to his house, and the apartment she used to rent was now occupied by someone else.

Deciding life must go on, she had dragged herself out of bed since she couldn't sleep. Sitting in her usual spot at the table she stared out the window looking at the bushland and the rain, which was a constant drizzle with everything looking grey. The weather suited her mood; miserable and bleak. With her hands wrapped around her cup of tea, she was building up the courage to pick up the phone to call Antonio. She had to do it. She had no choice.

There was less than two weeks to go till the next full moon and that didn't leave much time to learn things before the first change. She sighed, knowing she couldn't put it off any longer, stood up and headed into the kitchen. Rinsing her cup out, she then grabbed the phone and called Antonio.

"Hello, Antonio here." A chirpy Italian male voice answered.

"Hi Antonio. It's Sarah." She greeted hesitantly.

"SARAH! Shit Luv where the hell have you been...?"

"I..." She didn't get the chance to say anything more.

"...No one has heard from you in almost three months. We thought you died in that fire at Danny's place..."

"An..."

"...You are an inconsiderate cow. You know that don't you?" He interrupted with a comment only a friend could get away with.

"ANTONIO!" She shouted in exasperation.

"WHAT?!"

"I'm a therian and need your help." She responded quietly.

"Oh Luv, I'm sorry, but you had us worried you know." Antonio suddenly sounded upset instead of angry.

"I'm sorry. The past three and a half months haven't been the best for me either and it's a very, very long story. This is my address in Gumdale... Are you able to come over?"

"You sound horrid Luv. Sure, I can come over. What flavour are you?"

She sighed softly. "I'm okay, and jaguar."

"Well, shit. They're rare out of the Americas. I didn't even know there were any here at all. I'll do a bit of research and see what info within Australia I can find out for you Luv. Despite the fact that he's the head of the leopards, I'm going to bring Jonathon with me since he's also the chairman of the league. He might have some ideas as to how to help you since jaguars are similar to leopards. See you soon okay?"

"Okay, till then."

They hung up.

The day had just started and already she was tired; and not just from a lack of sleep. She just wanted to crawl into a hole and never come back out. However, she knew that would never happen. She sighed. The next chore for the day was to talk to Mick and Toby, but before that happened she needed another cuppa. So, she concentrated on making it instead of thinking about anything else.

She went back into the kitchen and grabbed her cup, placed a Twinings English Breakfast tea bag in it – she was too lazy to make up a pot of tea just then and opted for the easy way out. She walked over to the eight litre electric urn that was on 24/7 and three quarter filled her cup from it. After dunking the tea bag for the desired time, she removed it, scooped in three teaspoons of sugar...

'Hey... I'm a crabby ole cow and need all the sweetening I can get.' She thought to herself. It was a regular teasing comment she made about herself whenever someone mentioned her sugar intake.

Turn the page for a sneak peak at
the next book by KC Riley-Gyer...

Changes in Choices

Conclusion to Sarah's story

Coming soon
August 2015

Chapter 1

A week later, Sarah finally showed up back home for the first time since that night at the paintball range, and she was sure she looked like crap. She knew she felt like it. She hadn't really cared at the time because she had stayed away from people so no one saw her. If anyone was to ask her how she got home she wouldn't have been able to answer because she didn't know how she had managed it in the first place. However, she didn't get the chance to get off the scooter before a set of hands grabbed at her arms roughly, savagely pulling her off the scooter.

"Where the fuck have you been Sarah?! We've been so worried, we thought you were dead." Toby yelled at her, his face red with anger.

She just stood there as his grip bruised her arms, letting him stare at her helmeted head as it mimicked a bobble headed doll as he shook her. Mick gently placed a hand on Toby's arm. Toby frowned at him. Mick shook his head then Toby let her go with a slight shove so she staggered back a step then rocked on the spot. Standing there for just a moment she then reached up to take off her helmet. She didn't look at them and didn't make any move towards the house.

"Geez Sarah! What have you been doing?" Mick exclaimed softly.

Gazing at her from head to toe and back again, he noted her condition. While he knew her dress was dirty with the hem shredded in various spots and generally a mess, he wasn't expecting the sight of her face and hair. Her hair was matted and her face dirty with dark circles under her eyes like someone had used her as a punching bag, and she smelled like she had been rolling around in week old mud even though he could see that hadn't been the case. Without warning, he scooped her up into his arms and headed towards the house. The helmet dropped from her hand as he lifted her.

"Toby, grab her walking stick and helmet please."

After a few moments, "Sarah, where's your stick?" Toby demanded.

"Gone." She answered softly and tonelessly as her head rested on Mick's shoulder.

"What do you mean 'gone'?" Toby demanded angrily as Mick took her upstairs, but she didn't respond.

Mick sat Sarah at the kitchen table, made her a cup of tea and set it in front of her. She just stared at the table with her hands in her lap.

"Drink your tea Sarah." Mick encouraged.

Like a statue, she didn't even blink. Just sat there not moving, staring at nothing. Mick was becoming worried.

'Sure she has withdrawn a number of times before but never like this.'

"What's wrong with you Sarah?" Toby asked as he entered the kitchen. Even in her current state she could hear the frown in his voice.

"Nothing." She responded in the same tone of voice as before.

Toby threw up his hands in frustration.

"I give up. Fine, be that way. We don't hear from you for a week after Antonio told us about the hit Jonathon took out against you. He told us that you said you had organised such a situation with a friend to complete the hit if it should happen. Was it bloody Kaelan...?" He paused after snarling the other man's name, shook his head and made a sound of frustration before continuing,

"Fuck Sarah! With no thought about us being worried about you, you then just rock up like nothing is wrong and you don't think we deserve an explanation of any kind. There are times when you are a selfish bitch and this is one of them, Sarah."

"I'm sorry." While the response was automatic she did mean it However, her voice was still lifeless. She couldn't do what he wanted. Tears weren't even welling up like they normally would have.

Mick placed his hand on Toby's arm again, giving it a gentle tug. Seemed her peripheral vision was still working just fine as her brain registered what she saw. Mick pulled Toby to one side and spoke quietly to Toby, and she discovered that her hearing was working well also.

"Look at her. If I didn't know any better I would say she's in shock. She has never let herself look like that ever during the couple of years we've known her. She's just sitting there unmoving and hasn't even blinked. Something happened and it hasn't had a good effect on her."

Long moments of silence passed.

www.ingramcontent.com/pod-product-compliance
Lightning Source LLC
Chambersburg PA
CBHW060515180626
46817CB00002B/373